I0614163

Christmas at Solace Lake

Love at Solace Lake, Volume 4

Jana Richards

Published by Jana Richards, 2023.

CHRISTMAS AT SOLACE LAKE

First edition. October 18, 2023.

Copyright © 2023 Jana Richards.

ISBN: 978-0995279193

Written by Jana Richards.

Praise for Jana Richards

LIES AND SOLACE

"This is a slow burn and sensual story that will leave your heart warmed by the happy ever after." Kim Janine Lignon

SECRETS AND SOLACE

"Author Richards shows her gift for building suspense...This is one honey of a story." Kathryn Cottrell

TRUTH AND SOLACE

"This was my third journey with the Lindquist sisters and I loved every one." Linda Tonis

Get Your Free Gift!

GET **HOME TO SOLACE LAKE**, your free prequel to the Love at Solace Lake series when you sign up for news from Jana Richards about upcoming releases, sales, giveaways, and exclusive offers only for subscribers!

Christmas at Solace Lake

Chapter One

HERE HE WAS, IN THE last place he wanted to be.

Drew Barnes pulled his car into the crowded parking lot of Solace Lake Lodge. He found an empty spot, turned off the ignition and frowned up at the impressive log building. An extended stay at the lodge hadn't been in his plans, but his uncle was desperate for help. Family came first. Always.

Even if they didn't believe he was a fully functioning adult.

And even if they didn't trust him. Not that he blamed them. He didn't trust himself either. Not anymore.

Huffing out a breath, he left the warm confines of the car and headed for the lodge. The front porch was decorated for Halloween with numerous snaggle-toothed jack-o-lanterns, stuffed scarecrows, and witches on broomsticks. Scarlet, his uncle Cameron's wife, was likely responsible for the decorations, since she had a flair for such things.

The massive doors flew open. "There you are. What took you so long? I thought you'd be here an hour ago."

And so it starts. "There was an accident on 194 outside of Minneapolis. I had to take a detour."

Drew's uncle, Ethan Hainstock, ran an agitated hand through his dark hair. "Sorry. Didn't mean to jump on you. Come inside. It's cold out here."

Drew stepped into the lodge and closed the doors behind him. "How's Harper?"

"Antsy, but okay," Ethan said with a sigh. "She hates being stuck at home, but her doctor said she needs to rest and avoid stress until the twins are born."

Harper had gone into premature labor and Ethan called Drew in a panic, asking him to take over her duties at the lodge. "I'm glad Harper and the twins are okay."

"Yeah. Way too early for the babies to come. If anything happened to them or Harper..." Ethan looked away. When he turned back to Drew, his mouth was set in a determined line. "Come on. I'll show you around Harper's office."

Ethan led the way with long strides, obviously anxious to complete their business. They passed the front desk, currently manned by a middle-aged woman Drew didn't recognize. It wasn't surprising he didn't know her. Staff had likely changed in the three years since he'd been here. His face heated in embarrassment as he remembered the reason for his self-imposed exile.

They soon reached the office located just off the lodge's main lobby. Ethan closed the door behind them as soon as they entered. "My wife insists she's fine, but I'm not taking any chances. I finally convinced her we need to stay at our condo in Minneapolis till the babies come so we're close to the hospital. I don't want to be stuck out here in the middle of nowhere when she goes into labor again. We're leaving first thing tomorrow morning."

Drew's uncle had a point. The lodge was more than a two-hour drive from Minneapolis. The nearest hospital in Brainerd was about a half hour drive away, but at this time of year, a sudden Minnesota snowstorm could turn the short drive into a nightmare.

"Harper wanted me to go over a couple of things with you." Ethan pulled a notebook from a desk drawer and handed it to Drew. "She has all the passwords in here, along with the combination to the safe. Guard this with your life, and keep it with you at all times. I mean it, Drew. You need to take this seriously."

It was humiliating to know his uncle had so little confidence in him that he felt he had to remind him how to handle sensitive information. He tamped down the indignation that rose from the pit of his stomach and made his throat burn. He wanted to shout, to bang his fists on the desk and defend himself. For two years he'd been treated like a half-witted adolescent. But how could he demand respect when he'd behaved exactly like an adolescent the first time he'd been given adult responsibility?

He had no one to blame except himself. One careless moment had upended his career and destroyed the trust of his family.

He lifted his chin. "I take guarding the book very seriously."

Ethan nodded curtly. "Good. We have a duplicate copy with us, but I don't ever want to have to use it."

Drew thumbed through the book. Passwords and usernames for the accounting program, payroll system, bank accounts, the lodge's security system, and the local internet network. The names and contact information for the lodge's staff was written at the back of the book in Harper's neat handwriting.

"I hear you know how to operate the accounting system, for paying bills and stuff," Ethan said.

"I do. I've been using the same program for months at the Hainstock Foundation." The Hainstock Foundation had been set up by Drew's parents to manage the money Ethan won in the largest lottery win in Minnesota history a few years previously. The money had been both a blessing and a curse—for the whole family.

Ethan dismissively waved his hand. "Yeah, okay, good. Harper wrote some notes in the book about paying bills and other accounting things she does. If you have any questions, check her notes."

"I'll check Harper's notes, but I'm telling you I know what I'm doing. I've been doing it at the Foundation for months." Not to mention that he'd studied accounting at university and received his business degree with majors in accounting and finance.

Ethan gave a distracted nod and ran his hand through his hair again. At thirty-five, he was only eleven years older than Drew. But both Ethan and Cameron, his mother's other younger brother, had always treated him like a kid. Things only got worse after he lost his job, his first full-time job. The embarrassment and shame of that loss was still fresh, even after two years.

"Sorry," Ethan said. "Are we done here? I need to get back to Harper. I don't like leaving her alone."

Drew straightened. "We're done."

"If you have any questions, call me. I don't want you to bother Harper with anything."

It would be pointless to call Ethan since he knew nothing about accounting, and it pissed Drew off that his uncle automatically assumed he'd run into trouble and need to be bailed out. Drew bit his lip to keep from making a sarcastic reply. Ethan was understandably stressed about his family, and he needed to cut him some slack. "I won't bother Harper."

"Good." Ethan opened another desk drawer and pulled out a key chain holding a single key. "Here's an extra key for the house. You and Carrie have the run of the place while Harper and I are in the city."

His younger sister Carrie had been staying with Ethan and Harper and working at the lodge since early summer. He'd been amazed by how much he missed her. Drew accepted the key and put it in his pocket.

Ethan pushed his arms into his jacket, then stuck his hands into the pockets. "Damn it, where are my car keys?"

Drew plucked a set of keys from the desk. "These keys?"

"Yeah, thanks." Ethan shook his head. "Christ, I'm a mess."

"Totally, but I promise not to tell anyone." He handed the keys to Ethan. "Everything's going to work out. The lodge will carry on as usual, and Harper will put her feet up and rest for a while. She and the twins will be fine. When's the due date again?"

"Christmas day. Nine more weeks. The doctors say the longer the twins stay inside Harper, the better their chances to be born healthy. They can do a lot with preemies these days but..." Ethan shook his head.

The seriousness of the situation suddenly hit Drew. His uncle was fighting for the survival of his family. Drew would do whatever he could to make things easier for him.

He clapped Ethan on the back. "Go home and look after your family. Tell Harper I'll take care of things in her office. Not to brag, but I'm a brilliant accountant."

Ethan laughed and squeezed Drew's shoulder. "I'll make sure to tell her."

His family might tick him off from time to time, but when the chips were down, Drew could count on them. Just as they could count on him. He only wished they'd realize that.

DREW PORED OVER THE information in the accounting system, familiarizing himself with Harper's previous work and the day-to-day functioning of the lodge. As he suspected from the full parking lot, the restaurant was doing well. The lodge was doing well, too. In the last three years, between Memorial Day and Labor Day, the lodge had an impressive ninety-five to one hundred percent occupancy rate. The rest of the year wasn't as stellar, but occupancy had improved steadily in the three winters since the lodge's renovation and reopening. The number of events the lodge hosted, like weddings and anniversaries, had also increased every year.

The old fishing lodge had been in Harper's family for decades and her dream had been to bring it back to life. She and her sisters, Scarlet and Maggie, had inherited the crumbling lodge from their grandfather, and Harper couldn't bear to see it fall into ruin. Ethan's investment in the lodge had made Harper's dream come true, and in the process of renovating the lodge, they'd fallen in love.

A familiar melancholy settled over him. He wished Maggie could have fallen for him the same way, but he knew now it had never been in the cards.

The office door swung open, and Carrie burst inside. "Drew! I'm so glad to see you!"

Drew skirted the desk to give his sister a hug. "It's good to see you, too. It's been a while."

She pulled out of his embrace and tilted her head. "Only because you wouldn't come to lodge until there was a real emergency."

"Let's not get into that."

Carrie closed the office door. "You have to get over her, Drew. Maggie and Luke are married now, and they're very much in love."

Drew sat in the office chair once more, putting the desk between them. "That was a long time ago. I *am* over her."

Carrie's eyebrows rose skeptically. "I know you, Drew. You liked Maggie a lot more than you let on."

He didn't argue the point. He'd been crazy about Maggie Lindquist, now Carlsson, from the moment he first met her. But she never felt the same way. Maggie and Luke Carlsson had a history he couldn't hope to compete with. And aside from that, she was three years older and always considered him too young. The knowledge had stung.

He was lucky that Carrie was the only person in his family to realize how he'd truly felt about Maggie. "Seriously,

Carrie. I've moved on. I'd much rather talk about you. Do you enjoy working in the lodge's kitchen?"

"I love it! Working in a restaurant is what I'm meant to do. Maggie and Celeste have really shown me the ropes. They've even helped me develop some of my own recipes."

Her enthusiasm made Drew smile. Carrie had moved to the lodge shortly after her high school graduation at the end of June. She'd always loved cooking and baking but was undecided about going to culinary school to become a chef. Working in the lodge's kitchen gave her a chance to test drive her proposed occupation.

"So does that mean you're going to apply to culinary school?"

Carrie's smile disappeared. "I'm not sure yet."

Her answer confused him. "Why not? You just said that working in a restaurant is what you're meant to do. Why wouldn't you go to culinary school?"

"I don't have to go to a culinary school to work in a restaurant." Carrie set her chin at a stubborn angle, an expression he'd witnessed many times before. It told him his sister wouldn't easily change her mind. "I can learn on the job."

"That might be fine for working here, in our uncle and aunt's business, but if you want to work somewhere else, you're going to need to back up your experience with education and a diploma."

"Maybe I don't want to work anywhere else. Maybe I like it here."

Drew stared at her. A few months ago, she'd been researching culinary schools and had spoken about certification being essential. Her top contender had been the highly regarded culinary program at St. Paul College. "What's really going on here, Carrie? Why don't you want to go to school?"

She avoided his gaze. "I told you. I like it here. I want to stay."

"I'm sure Uncle Ethan will give you a job once you finish culinary school. The course at St. Paul's is only ten months, isn't it? It's not that much time."

Carrie's eyes flashed. "I told you, I don't want to leave, so get it through your thick skull!"

Drew stared at her, trying to figure out what had happened to his normally sensible little sister. Why was she so determined to stay at the lodge?

And then it hit him.

"You've met someone here at the lodge, haven't you? Is that why you don't want to leave?"

Carrie appeared uncomfortable. And guilty, like he'd caught her doing something wrong. It made no sense. At eighteen, she'd only had a couple of boyfriends, at least that he knew of. Though pretty and smart, she was introverted and shy. She was also a lot more mature than many of the boys her age.

He knew all about immature boys. He'd been one.

Carrie's gaze didn't quite meet his. "I *have* met someone."

"Okay, great. When do I get to meet him?"

She folded her arms across her chest. "Not anytime soon."

"What's the big deal? I've met your boyfriends before. Why can't I meet this guy? What makes this one any different?"

"Because he's special, and you're so judgmental! You won't give him a chance!"

Alarm bells went off in Drew's head. "Why do I need to give him a chance? What has he done?"

"Nothing! He's done nothing! He's a good person. He's smart and kind and funny. But I know you, and I know Mom and Dad, and you're all going to think there's something wrong with him. But you know what? He's perfect. I'm the one who's not good enough for him!"

To Drew's astonishment, Carrie burst into tears. Before he could get out an "I'm sorry," she threw open the office door and ran out.

What the hell?

Drew raced after her, afraid his baby sister was in way over her head.

USING A PIPING BAG with an open star tip, Celeste Bishop swirled the first pink buttercream rosette onto the chocolate layer cake she'd baked. She worked her way around the bottom of the cake, creating rosette after rosette. After years of experience, her hands were quick and sure, knowing the exact pressure and turn of the wrist necessary to craft the perfect rosette.

Once the bottom three rows were completed, she stepped back and rotated the turntable to examine her handiwork. Though she liked the pink, the cake needed some pizzazz. For the next three rows, she'd use an apricot-colored buttercream, and then finish the top in white. Satisfied with her choices, she put a stick of butter into the stand mixer and began beating it.

Celeste hummed as she worked. Baking and decorating cakes was one of her favorite things to do and working in the kitchen of the Solace Lake Lodge gave her ample opportunity to indulge her passion.

The kitchen door suddenly flew open. Carrie ran toward her, crying. Her tears shocked Celeste. She was usually such a happy, even-tempered girl. "What's wrong? What happened?"

Carrie gulped a shuddering breath. "Drew's here. He—"

Drew Barnes burst into the kitchen. Celeste hadn't seen Carrie's brother since Christmas three years ago, her first at the lodge, when he'd come here with his family. He looked different than he had back then. More polished, more mature.

And more handsome. But it was definitely him.

"Carrie, talk to me," he pleaded. "If you like this guy, it shouldn't make you so unhappy."

Carrie shook her head. "You won't understand."

"I have no idea if I'll understand. You won't tell me anything!"

Drew's raised voice only made Carrie turn away and hide her face against Celeste's shoulder.

"I think you should go," Celeste said, putting her arm around the younger woman. "Maybe later, when both of you have calmed down some, you can talk. But for now, please leave my kitchen."

He turned the full force of his intense scrutiny on her. Celeste lifted her chin and returned his stare, refusing to be intimidated. He was tall, probably over six feet, with broad shoulders, narrow hips and a lean build. With his dark brown hair and eyes, he resembled his uncles, yet there was something about him that was completely unique. Carrie had told her that her brother was six years older than she was, so that made him twenty-four. She did a quick calculation in her head. Nine years younger than her thirty-three.

Why the hell do I care how old Drew Barnes is?

His eyes softened and he tipped his chin in agreement. "Celeste's right. When you're ready, we'll talk. Whatever you need to tell me, I promise not to judge."

Carrie turned in Celeste's arms to look at him. She wiped tears from her cheek with her fingers. "Okay."

Drew attempted a smile. "Okay."

For a second, Drew's gaze connected with Celeste's, and she read the genuine worry in his eyes. He was a brother concerned for his younger sister. She tried to reassure him with a smile. "It's all right. I'll look after Carrie."

He nodded and, with one last troubled look at his sister, he left the kitchen.

Carrie stepped away and pulled a tissue from the box on the desk in the corner. "I'm sorry, Celeste. I didn't mean to put you in the middle of my squabble with Drew."

"I don't mind. Your brother doesn't scare me."

Carrie grinned through her tears. "He doesn't scare me, either. Not really."

"Good for you."

Since Carrie's arrival at the lodge in the summer, Celeste had taken her under her wing. Carrie soaked up information about food preparation and running a kitchen like a thirsty sponge. She was a hard worker and a willing one, too, which was all the more remarkable since her family owned the lodge. She could have coasted or lorded it over the rest of the staff. Instead, whenever they were short of wait staff in the restaurant, she stepped in to help. She'd even volunteered with the housekeeping staff a couple of times when someone called in sick. Celeste liked the girl and felt more like her big sister than a co-worker.

Carrie wiped her eyes and blew her nose. "Drew's not going to like the age difference between me and Ryan. Mom and Dad won't be happy about it either."

Celeste worried the age difference wasn't the only thing her family would be concerned about. But that wasn't what Carrie needed to hear right now. "Once they get to know Ryan and see what a remarkable person he is, they'll come around."

Carrie gave her a grateful smile. Celeste hoped she was telling her the truth.

Chapter Two

THE NUMBERS SWAM IN front of Drew's eyes as he stared at his computer monitor. Since his run-in with Carrie earlier in the afternoon, he'd buried himself in work. He'd found an invoice in Harper's 'to be paid' file that was incomplete. According to Harper's notes, every invoice needed to be accompanied by a purchase order and a packing slip to verify that the supplies had been legitimately ordered and received. Instead, this invoice for baking supplies—namely flour and sugar—had neither. He supposed the missing documents could simply be an oversight, but what seemed odd was that just before she left, Harper had paid another invoice from a different supplier for flour and sugar. That invoice, which had an accompanying purchase order and packing slip, was dated three days before this second, incomplete invoice. How much flour and sugar did they need?

According to the invoice in question, the lodge owed over three thousand dollars for these supplies. A substantial amount. Ethan had been very clear about not bothering Harper with questions. He supposed he could double-check with Maggie to make sure all the supplies were received. But the last thing he wanted was to question Maggie on his first day.

With a groan of frustration, he looked away and rubbed his eyes. He might as well take a break because he was getting zero accomplished.

He leaned back and stared out the office window. What had Carrie gotten herself into? He was genuinely afraid for his sister and more than a little worried about the tight hold this new boyfriend seemed to have on her. Had she already had sex with him? Drew would have expected Ethan to check him out, but with the difficulties in Harper's pregnancy, he'd likely been too distracted.

So, Drew would do it himself. At the first opportunity, he'd talk to this guy, whoever he was, and let him know Carrie's family would not sit by and let him use her.

As Drew's mind wandered, it landed on Celeste Bishop. He admired her defense of his sister but was annoyed she'd defended Carrie against *him*. Did that mean she approved of this so-far nameless boyfriend? He didn't know Celeste well, having only met her once three years ago, but she'd struck him then as level-headed and sensible.

And beautiful.

She was tall and slim, and even in her chef's whites he detected the pleasing curves that lay beneath. She had the most beautiful café au lait complexion and a perfect oval-shaped face. Her dark, expressive eyes had flashed at him in annoyance and warning. She wasn't going to let anyone ride rough-shod over Carrie.

Somehow, that reassured him.

Drew tried to remember what he knew about Celeste. She'd come from South Carolina to work at the lodge as Maggie's sous chef, accompanied by her little girl, if he remembered correctly. What had prompted her to move so far away from her home state? He knew she was unmarried. Had he heard something about her being widowed?

He wanted to know more. If Carrie ever spoke to him again, maybe she'd fill him in.

A knock sounded at the office door, and Drew sat up straighter. Maggie and her husband, Luke Carlsson, entered. Drew stood and walked around his desk as Maggie extended her hands to him.

"Drew, hello. Welcome to the lodge. I'm so happy you were able to come here and give us a hand while Harper is away."

He squeezed her hands briefly before letting go, his heart doing a little stutter-step at seeing her again. Maggie's hair had grown since he'd last seen her. Three years ago, she'd sported a short, pixie hairstyle. Today, her dark brown hair had grown to shoulder length. It suited her.

He schooled his features into a pleasant smile. "I'm glad I could help."

"Yes, we're glad, too." Maggie glanced at Luke before continuing. "I hope coming here isn't too awkward for you. I don't want anything to affect the working arrangement you have with me, and especially not with Luke."

Drew worked hard to keep his expression neutral. He admitted, at least to himself, that he was devastated when Maggie turned him down three years ago. He'd been totally enamored with her and believed he'd never feel the same way about another woman again. Today, he was embarrassed by the way he'd let Maggie's rejection keep him away from the lodge for so long.

But he was here now, and he had a job to do. He wouldn't let past feelings get in the way. "I can promise you my entire focus is on the efficient running of the lodge. I look forward to working with both of you while I'm here."

Luke extended his hand to shake Drew's. "So do we."

"Perfect." Maggie clasped her hands together, looking relieved. "Speaking of work, there's something we want to run by you, since you're the designated money guy at the moment."

"Oh yeah? What's that?" Drew motioned for them to sit as he returned to his chair.

"We're thinking about Christmas." Luke sat in one of the chairs in front of the desk and Maggie sat next to him. "We've been hosting a Christmas Open House the day before Christmas Eve for the last three years, and it's been tremendously successful. It's built a lot of goodwill in the community for us, but very little income. In fact, it usually costs us because we provide free treats and activities. So, we were thinking, why not create another event, a Christmas party with a dinner and dance that we can charge admission for? Hopefully, some attendees would book rooms and make a weekend of it."

"Makes sense. We have to give people a reason to drive out here to the lodge, especially in the winter. A Christmas dinner and dance sounds like a great idea. When are you proposing to have it?"

"We're thinking mid-December," Luke replied.

"That's what, maybe eight weeks from now? Does that give you enough time to pull everything together?"

"I believe so," Luke said. "I've already made some tentative arrangements, like securing a live band. Scarlet is onboard, and she's ready to start an advertising campaign to promote the event."

"Can you work up a budget so I have an idea of how much money we'd have to put out?" Drew asked.

"Way ahead of you." Luke pulled a sheet of paper from the folder he'd brought with him and handed it to Drew. "I'm pretty confident we can make a profit."

Drew looked over the figures. Luke had been very thorough. He'd come up with a ticket price based on the costs for putting on the event, then estimated how many people would have to attend to break even. Drew was impressed.

"Any profit is based solely on ticket sales," Luke pointed out. "It's impossible to estimate how many people would stay at the lodge overnight. There's likely to be some, but I wanted to make sure the event alone could pay for itself, or at least break even. I believe we've shown it can."

"What about food? I assume you've worked up a menu?" Drew asked.

"Yes, we have," Maggie said. "Can you show Drew my menu, Luke?"

Luke pulled another sheet of paper from his folder and handed it over. This one had a menu with appetizers, salads, three choices for the main course, assorted dessert selections and several wines. Based on these choices, she'd estimated a cost per plate.

"These are all foods that are readily available, and we know the price we can get them for," Maggie said. "We've included the cost of the extra kitchen and wait staff we'll need, but we'll keep the labor costs down by serving buffet style."

"Do you know for sure you'll be able to get extra staff to help?"

"I do. I've already been in touch with Miller's Golf Resort down the road. You know Ethan owns that resort, too, right?"

"Yes." Having worked at the Hainstock Foundation for the last year and a half, Drew was well acquainted with all his uncle's properties.

Luke continued. "I spoke to the manager at Miller's, and we'll ask some of their dining room staff to help us out for the evening. If things go as well as I hope, we can send attendees to Miller's if the lodge gets fully booked with overnight guests."

"It looks like a great meal. Did you discuss this with Ethan and Harper?" Drew asked.

"We talked about it briefly with Ethan," Maggie said. "But then Harper went into premature labor. I think they have enough on their plates right now."

"I agree, but I don't think we can move forward with an event as big as this without their okay. I'll talk to Ethan, send him your estimates, and see what he says."

Maggie frowned. "Ethan is pretty stressed right now. Maybe we should go forward on our own so they don't have to worry about it."

No way was he going out on a limb without Ethan's okay. If the whole thing fell apart and the lodge lost money, he'd get blamed for being impulsive and careless. He did his best to hide his anxiety. "It's up to us to take the stress of the lodge off their shoulders, but they need to see the plans and give us their approval. I'll make sure to let Ethan know that you and Luke have everything under control."

Maggie leaned forward in her chair, making Drew believe she wanted to argue the point. But Luke put a hand on her arm.

"That sounds great. We'll leave it with you." Luke got to his feet and extended his hand once more. "Thanks for hearing us out. I look forward to working with you."

"Me, too." As Drew shook his hand, he remembered the invoice. "Quick question, Maggie. Did you put in a large order for sugar and flour lately? I have an invoice without a matching purchase order."

"Yes. We're gearing up for Christmas baking, so I ordered extra supplies." She frowned. "It's odd there's no purchase order. I always make one up for restaurant supplies. Or at least I thought I did. Maybe I forgot this time."

"It probably got misplaced. I'll take another look for it." If he couldn't find the missing purchase order, he'd dig into the situation further. But he'd have to be quick about it. He didn't want to be condemned as irresponsible if a vendor wasn't paid on time.

As they moved toward the door, Maggie asked, "Are you staying at Ethan and Harper's house with Carrie?"

"I was going to, but Carrie and I had a little...disagreement. It might be best if I stay at the hotel, at least for tonight." Drew sat up straighter. "Do either of you know anything about the boy she's been seeing?"

Maggie and Luke exchanged a look that Drew couldn't decipher. Maggie turned to face him. "I think it would be best if you talk to Carrie about him."

"Maggie's right. You need to talk to your sister," Luke said. "All I'll say is that Carrie's friend is someone I admire and respect. Once you get to know him, I think you will, too."

"Thanks." Drew made himself smile. "As soon as Carrie's speaking to me again, I'll ask her about him."

Luke and Maggie said their goodbyes and left the office. Drew watched them through the open office door as they walked across the hotel lobby, hand in hand. When Luke brought Maggie's hand to his lips for a kiss and she smiled up at him in adoration, Drew knew for sure he'd never had a chance with her.

He'd known it for some time but seeing them together really brought it home. Time to put his fixation with Maggie Lindquist in the past, where it belonged.

He closed the office door and turned his attention to the here and now. Luke's remark about Carrie's boyfriend being someone he admired and respected struck him as odd. It didn't sound like Luke was describing any eighteen-year-old boy he knew.

CELESTE'S PHONE VIBRATED as she folded clothes still warm from the dryer. When she pulled the phone from the back pocket of her jeans, she saw her mother was calling.

"Hi, Mama. How are you today?" Celeste stifled a yawn that she hoped her mother didn't hear. It had been a long day.

"I'm fine, CeCe," her mother said. "Just missing you. When are you coming home for Christmas?"

It was never good when a conversation with her mother began with a question like that. The old familiar guilt pressed on her chest. Her mother was getting older and even though she had plenty of friends in Myrtle Beach and she was involved in activities at her church, she'd been asking Celeste when she was returning to South Carolina ever since she left.

"You know I work over the Christmas holidays, Mama. Hope and I will come for a visit after the New Year. We'll need a little sun by then."

"If you came home to live, you and Hope could have sun all year long," Nora Emerson countered.

"You know I can't do that, Mama. The reasons I left Myrtle Beach haven't changed."

Her mother made a dismissive sound. "That was three years ago, CeCe. Nobody cares what that chef says anymore."

Celeste closed her eyes on a sigh. Her mother had no idea how vindictive Chef Andrew could be. According to former co-workers in Myrtle Beach who would still speak to her, Andrew was as powerful as ever.

Though she missed her family, there was no going back.

"I'm afraid people *do* care what he says. Besides, I love my job here. Hope is happy and has made lots of friends at school."

"Yes, but I'm sure there's very few other black children in that school. Hope should be with children like her."

It was a conversation they'd had many times. Her mother wasn't wrong. And Celeste didn't want Hope to feel like an outsider, or different, because of the color of her skin. So far, Hope seemed to be fitting in at the school.

Celeste glanced over at the cookies she'd just finished decorating. In a couple of days, Hope would take them to school for her class Halloween party. With their faces and hands iced in chocolate brown, she hoped to show her daughter and her friends that scarecrows could be African-American, too. It might seem silly to some people to turn a cookie into a political statement, but as one of only a handful of black kids in the rural Minnesota school, Celeste felt it was important that Hope see herself represented in all kinds of ways. To show she belonged.

"Hope is truly happy, Mama. I wish you'd come and find out for yourself."

"We'll see."

That was her mother's standard answer whenever she asked her to visit the lodge. "I wish you'd come here for Christmas. It's beautiful in the winter with all the lights and decorations."

"And cold!" her mother said. "My poor old bones would freeze!"

"I'll make sure you have a warm parka if you come," Celeste said with a chuckle. "Boots, too. I'll pay your airfare and make all the arrangements. You won't have to do a thing."

Nora hesitated before speaking again. "I'll think about it."

Celeste bit back her impatience. Getting Nora Emmerson to do something she didn't want to do was nearly impossible. "Sounds good, Mama."

"I miss you and Hope, CeCe." The wistfulness in her mother's voice floated over the distance between them.

"I know. I miss you, too."

"I have to go now. I'll talk to you soon."

"Goodbye, Mama. I love you."

"I love you, too, baby girl."

Celeste ended the call and stuck her phone back in her pocket. She hoped her mother would come for Christmas, but she didn't think there was much chance. Celeste tamped down her disappointment. Having her mother visit would mean a lot to her, and she knew it would mean a lot to Hope, too.

Hope was the reason she'd come to Minnesota. If she was on her own, she might have stayed in Myrtle Beach and toughed it out. But Hope needed stability. By the time Maggie Lindquist hired her, Celeste was completely broke and living with her sister and her family. She was baking cakes for birthdays and other occasions out of her sister's kitchen, advertising her wares through her Instagram page, but she couldn't make a living from it. She'd taken a leap of faith and accepted the job at the lodge because she didn't want her child to live in poverty, dependent on family for her next meal. She wanted to show her daughter a strong, confident, independent woman, not one beaten down by life.

Much of her confidence had returned since working in the lodge's kitchen and because she was living rent-free in an apartment the lodge provided, she was able to repair her financial situation as well. But she still had far to go to gain true independence.

The answer was buying a car. And learning how to drive.

Right now, learning to drive was as insurmountable as flying to the moon.

"OF COURSE YOU KNOW Carrie, and I believe you've met Celeste," Luke said.

"Yes, we've met."

Drew smiled at Celeste and she smiled politely in return, while Carrie briefly dipped her head in a nod before looking away. He smothered an impatient sigh. Seemed his sister was still mad at him and still trying to avoid him. He hoped it wasn't going to be like this the whole time he was here.

Drew had spent the morning of his second day at the lodge with Luke, familiarizing himself with the layout of the lodge and members of the staff. They were about to leave after Luke introduced him to the rest of the kitchen staff, when the kitchen door opened and a blonde woman breezed in.

"Hi, everyone," she said.

"What are you doing here so early, Cheryl?" Luke asked. "Your shift doesn't start for another two hours."

"I know, but my car's in the garage and I had to catch a ride with Lorraine. I'll hang out in the restaurant with my book till my shift starts. Unless you need my help, Celeste?"

Celeste shook her head. "No, we're fine. Go have a cup of coffee."

"Cheryl, have you met Drew Barnes?" Luke asked. "He's taking over Harper's duties while she's away. Drew, this is Cheryl Johnson. She's one of our sous chefs."

Drew extended his hand. "Hi Cheryl. How long have you worked here?"

She gave his hand a firm shake. "About three years now. I started around the time the lodge reopened. You're Carrie's brother, right?"

"Right." He glanced toward his sister, but she continued to ignore him. "Nice meeting you."

"Nice to meet you, too," Cheryl said with a smile.

They left the kitchen and walked through the restaurant. Luke introduced him to a couple of servers, including the head server, Lorraine, who'd given Cheryl a ride today. Because they were busy, Luke kept the introductions brief.

"Come on," Luke said. "One more introduction and then we'll get to work."

Drew followed Luke to the front desk. "Drew, this is Melissa White. She's one of our newest hires."

"Good to meet you, Melissa." Drew extended his hand to her. He recognized her as the clerk who'd been behind the front desk yesterday. "How long have you been at the lodge?"

She gave him a bright smile as she shook his hand. "Please, call me Mel. All my friends do. I've been here about two months and I love it. Management and staff are so friendly."

"Yes, everyone's been very welcoming."

"How long will you be with us, Drew?" Mel asked.

"That depends on Harper and when the twins make an appearance."

She tucked a strand of silver-gray hair behind her ear. "Well, I hope you enjoy your time here."

"Thank you. I'm sure I will."

"We'll let you get back to work, Mel," Luke said. "Drew and I have some things to take care of, too."

"Enjoy your stay." Mel lifted her hand in a wave.

Drew smiled politely at the older woman. From the personnel records, he knew she was the same age as his mother, though with her gray hair and matronly figure, she looked much older. "Thank you. I'm sure I will."

When they reached the office, he pulled the key from his pocket and unlocked the door. Luke gave him a perplexed look. "You locked the door? We weren't far away."

"Maybe not, but I'm not taking any chances. There's a lot of confidential staff and financial information in here."

"Makes sense," Luke said.

Drew planned to keep the office door locked whenever he wasn't working there. Except he'd already messed up. Yesterday, when he sprinted after Carrie, he'd left the door wide open. He needed to be more careful.

"Our first order of business is creating the staff schedule for the upcoming three months," Luke said. "Harper usually does it, but she wasn't able to get to it before she had to leave."

"Can we copy a previous schedule?"

"Pretty much. The majority of shifts run in a predicable repeating schedule, like four days on, three days off, that kind of thing. We try to accommodate the kind of shift staff members prefer as much as possible. Most people prefer to stick to one type of shift, like all days or all nights."

Drew brought up the previous schedule and copied it. After making changes for any staff members who would be absent because of sickness or vacation, he turned his monitor so Luke could see. "I believe we've got all the shifts covered. What do you think? Does this work?"

Luke examined the screen. "I think it looks okay. Oh, wait." He pointed at a line. "Except here. Jeanette can't work evenings on the front desk anymore. Harper left me an email saying Jeanette's husband is about to start a new job working permanent evening shifts, so she has to be home with her kids."

"How do we fix it?"

"Maybe Mel would be willing to take over those evening shifts. I'll give her a call."

Luke picked up the office phone and hit the number for the front desk, setting the phone on speaker so Drew could hear. "Mel, it's Luke here. Do you have a moment to talk to Drew and me? We have something we need to run by you."

"Of course. What is it?"

"Are you aware of Jeanette's situation? She's not going to be able to work evening shifts—"

"Oh yes, she told me about her husband's new job. I was going to mention to you that I'd be willing to take over her evening shifts."

"That would be very helpful, Mel. Thank you."

"Actually, you'd be helping me out, too. I'd prefer to be at work." Drew heard her sigh. "The evenings can get pretty lonely at home on my own. In fact, why not put me on permanent evenings and overnights? It's easier for me to work those hours than it is for people like Jeanette who have kids."

"Are you sure?" Luke asked. "There's only one clerk on duty during those shifts."

"I can handle it. It's usually not as busy as a day shift."
She chuckled. "Besides, I've got all those years of experience,
remember?"

Luke laughed. "Yes, I remember. We'll make the changes
to the schedule and send you a copy."

"Thank you, Luke."

"No, thank *you*. You've helped us out immensely."

"My pleasure. Oh, I've got a call. Gotta run. Talk to you
later."

"Bye, Mel."

Luke disengaged the call. "Glad we got that worked out.
We're really lucky to have Mel here. She's got twenty-five
years of experience at the front desk of a hotel in
Minneapolis and was highly recommended. She actually
came out of retirement to work with us."

"What made her decide to do that?" Drew asked.

"She told me that when her husband died, she needed
a change. She doesn't have any children, so she decided she
wanted to live in a small town and get involved in the
community."

Drew could relate with wanting to make a fresh start.
"I'll switch Jeanette's shifts with Mel's. And if she prefers
to work overnight shifts, I can exchange her day shifts with
Dave Peterson's overnights. Do you think he'd be okay with
that?"

"I know he would. He told me he has trouble sleeping
during the day. I've been trying to get him off that shift for a
while now."

After Drew made all the changes, he turned the monitor
toward Luke once more. "What do you think?"

"Looks good. Now that we have all the kinks worked out, you can send it out."

Drew emailed the document to staff and then closed it. "Good thing you know the staff so well."

"Not as well as Harper. She's got her finger on the pulse of everything going on here. If you're going to replace her, you're going to need to get to know the staff."

"I don't plan on replacing her. I'm only here until Harper has her babies."

Luke's brows lifted. "Really? I got the impression from Ethan you were going to be here for at least the next six months."

"If I am, no one bothered to tell me." Drew couldn't help the note of irritation that slipped into his voice. Perhaps he was naïve in thinking his time at the lodge would end once Harper gave birth, but it rankled that Ethan automatically assumed he'd stick around, without even asking.

Luke held up his hands in surrender. "Sorry. I must have got it wrong."

Drew shook his head. "I'm sorry, too. I didn't mean to jump on you."

He was happy to help out, but he hadn't expected to work at the lodge long-term. From what he could tell, Harper's job consisted mainly of administrative tasks, like creating the staff schedule and bookkeeping. Neither were his favorite jobs. He'd made that discovery since working at the Hainstock Foundation and doing those very things. He'd wanted to learn more about the investment end of the business at Hainstock but instead, his parents had put him in the administrative role.

Because they didn't trust him with more important tasks.

He couldn't blame them. He had his dream job and lost it. His parents had given him the admin job when he couldn't find anything else.

Luke waved off his apology. "Don't worry about it. But I think you should talk to Ethan. If we're going to have to hire someone for Harper's position, we should figure that out sooner rather than later. Speaking of Ethan, have you had a chance to talk to him about the Christmas Ball?"

"Yeah, I called him last night. He said it sounds like a good idea, and he trusts you and Maggie. If you think a Christmas party will be a success, he said we should go for it."

"That's great news!" Luke jumped to his feet. "I'm going to tell Maggie we're a go. See you later."

"Bye. Thanks for showing me around this morning."

"You're welcome." Luke stopped in the doorway and turned. "Your family may not have told you, but I'm sure they appreciate you taking over this role on such short notice. And if they don't appreciate it, I'll make sure to tell them they should."

That made Drew grin. "Thanks for the vote of confidence."

Luke gave him a salute. "See you later."

"Later."

Drew leaned back in his chair. He'd been prepared to dislike Luke, but he was a stand-up guy. After looking up his personnel file in Harper's office and reading his resume, Drew knew the lodge was lucky to have him as the hotel and restaurant manager. He'd worked in that same position at two well-known hotels in the Napa Valley and was an expert on California wines.

Sometimes it was good to be wrong.

He hoped his concerns about Carrie's new boyfriend turned out to be wrong, too. He'd spent the night at the hotel in order to give her some space. He hoped they'd get a chance to talk today because he hated being on the outs with her. And he didn't want to spend the next few weeks in a hotel room.

He'd had way too much time to think last night. For some reason, between worries about Carrie, Celeste Bishop's face kept popping up in his head. He didn't know why, aside from it being a very pretty face.

The ringing of his cell phone brought him back to the present. Drew was startled to see Harper's name on his screen. "Hey. How are you, Harper?"

"I'm fine. Just bored." She gave a frustrated sigh. "I'm not really a daytime TV-watching kind of girl, and Ethan won't let me do much else."

"He's worried about you. You and those babies gave him quite a scare."

"I know. Ethan means well. He's trying to remove every possible shred of stress from my life but sitting around is only stressing me out. That's why I'm calling you."

Ethan would not be happy he was talking to Harper. "What can I do for you?"

"Can you keep me in the loop? I just want to know what's going on at the lodge. Ethan won't tell me anything."

"Ethan specifically told me not to bother you. You're supposed to put your feet up and relax. You've got to keep cooking those babies."

"You wouldn't be bothering me. I'm the one bothering *you*. There's a difference."

"I'm not sure Ethan would appreciate the distinction. I don't want to get on his bad side. I'm sorry, Harper, but I think I should go."

"Wait! Don't hang up! Ethan's told everyone not to bother me about work at the lodge." He heard the barely restrained tears in her voice. "But the lodge is my baby, too. I have to know that everything is all right."

"Maybe you should tell Ethan how you feel."

"I don't want to upset him any more than he already is."

Drew thought it ironic that neither of them wanted to worry the other, and yet that was exactly what was happening. "If Ethan finds out—"

"He won't. I'll only call you when he's away from the condo. I sent him out today to buy me ice cream from a specialty place across town. Please, Drew. Throw me a bone. I left in such a hurry, I didn't pay all the bills or even make up the staff schedule. And if people don't get paid—"

"Don't worry, Harper. I know what needs to be done. Luke and I just finished the schedule for the next three months. We've got everything under control."

She let out a breath. "Thank goodness! I appreciate everything you and Luke are doing. I should have trained someone to take over for me during my leave, but I thought I had time. I left things too long and then I didn't have any time at all."

"I understand." Three years ago, he thought he had all the time in the world to make Maggie think of him as boyfriend material, but he'd been wrong. "There is a new development at the lodge, but you have to pretend you don't know anything about it or Ethan will kill me."

He told her about the plans for the Christmas dinner and dance. "Maggie and Luke came up with the idea and worked up a great menu."

"That sounds exciting. You guys need to come up with a fun name for this event. Like Santa's Workshop Party or the Christmas Tree Hop." Drew heard her sigh. "I wish I could be there."

"You've got a bigger job to do right now, Harper."

"Yeah, I do. It's the biggest, most exciting, scariest job I've ever embarked on. Thank you, Drew. You've really eased my mind."

"Good. I'm glad."

"I've been talking online with other moms of twins, and it's becoming increasingly clear to me that my life is going to change drastically once the babies are born. I naively assumed I'd go back to work full-time soon after their birth. But talking to these other mothers, I don't think that's going to happen. How long do you think you'd be able to stay?"

Drew's heart sank. It looked like Luke had been right about his extended stay at the lodge. It wasn't what he wanted, but for the time being, Harper needed to be reassured that everything would be okay. "I promise I'll look after things here until you can look after them yourself, or other arrangements can be made."

"Thanks, Drew. That makes me feel a whole lot better. I should let you go so you can get those bills paid."

"I'm on it." He briefly considered asking her if she knew anything about the invoice that was missing a purchase order, but he rejected the idea. He didn't want to give her anything to worry about.

"I promise I'll make sure Ethan's away when I call you again. I'm going to be eating a lot of ice cream in the next few weeks."

Drew laughed. "Sounds like a sweet plan. Take care of yourself and those babies."

"I will. Bye, Drew. And thank you for putting your life on hold to help us out. It means the world to me."

"I'm glad to help. Bye, Harper."

Drew ended the call and set his phone on the desk. Now that he'd made his promise, he wouldn't go back on it. He'd do his part to keep the lodge running.

Perhaps he was looking at this all wrong. Maybe working here at the lodge, and doing a great job, would give him the opportunity to show his family he was someone they could count on. He was tired of being thought of as the family screw-up.

He tapped his fingers against the desk. It wasn't like he had anything pressing to do back in Minneapolis. Sure, he missed the city and his friends, but they'd still be there when he got back. The building supervisor at his condo complex was checking on his place. His mother told him they'd already found someone to fill his position at the Foundation while he was gone. He didn't need to hurry back.

He didn't have a girlfriend waiting for him, either. He'd dated a few girls in the last three years, but none of the relationships were serious, at least for him. They were all perfectly nice, attractive, intelligent girls. But none of them were Maggie.

Drew leaned back in his chair. He needed to get over her. Completely. For God's sake, she was married! It was ridiculous to pine over someone he could never be with.

He wondered if staying at the lodge for an extended period would make getting over Maggie easier or much, much more difficult.

Chapter Three

CARRIE GAVE A RED PEPPER a hearty whack with her cleaver. "Celeste, please come with me to talk to Drew. If you're there, maybe he won't yell at me."

Celeste stirred the pot of simmering tomato sauce she was preparing for a dinner spaghetti special. She didn't want to get in the middle of a family drama, but Carrie was insistent. "I'm sure Drew isn't going to yell at you."

"Maybe not, but I could really use moral support." Carrie finished dicing an onion and set it aside. "Please, Celeste. I need to tell Drew about Ryan, and it's not going to be easy."

Carrie's dark eyes were red rimmed. Celeste suspected that either she hadn't slept much the previous evening or she'd been crying. "Did Drew stay with you at Ethan and Harper's house last night?"

"No, he must have stayed here at the lodge. See? He was so mad at me he couldn't even stay in the same house."

"I don't think he's mad at you." He was likely worried, confused and probably dumbfounded by Carrie's behavior. She didn't know Drew well, but she was reasonably sure he was more concerned about Carrie's welfare than angry with her.

Carrie bit her lip. "I'm afraid I'm going to mess things up. What if I say something that makes Drew hate Ryan?"

"If you don't say anything, you're going to make Drew wonder what you're hiding. You need to tell him before he finds out on his own." Celeste glanced at the other line cooks in the kitchen and lowered her voice. "If you really want to be with Ryan, you'll have to be prepared to answer questions about your relationship. If you find it's too difficult to answer those questions, maybe you need to tell Ryan now, before you both get in too deep."

Carrie's eyes filled with determination. She straightened her shoulders and stood a little taller. "I'm going to talk to my brother. But for this one time, will you come with me?"

Celeste hoped Carrie had the guts to make her relationship work, because she was afraid it wasn't going to be easy for her and Ryan going forward. "Okay, I'll come with you this once. But I'm not going to say anything. It's all up to you."

"Thanks Celeste. Do you think we can go now? It's pretty quiet in the restaurant."

"Sure." Celeste turned down the heat on her tomato sauce and pulled her apron over her head. "Let's go."

They crossed the hotel lobby and when they reached Harper's office, Carrie knocked on the closed door. "Drew, it's me. Can we talk?"

"Come in."

Celeste put her hand on her back in support. "It's okay," she whispered. Carrie took a fortifying breath and opened the door.

Drew stood as they entered. There was a half-eaten sandwich and a bottle of cola on the desk along with several neat stacks of paper. He'd obviously been eating his lunch. Celeste wondered if he had a lot of work to do, or if he didn't feel comfortable eating by himself in the restaurant. For some reason, she got a lonely vibe from Drew. Loneliness was an emotion she was well acquainted with.

Maybe Drew needed to mend this relationship as much as Carrie did. Maybe more so.

Carrie placed her hand on Celeste's shoulder. "I brought Celeste along for moral support. I'm ready to talk to you about my friend."

Drew gave Celeste a nod, and she was relieved he didn't appear upset by her presence. He turned his attention to his sister. "If you're ready to talk, I'm ready to listen. Why don't you both have a seat?"

Celeste and Carrie sat in the chairs in front of the desk. Drew resumed his seat and pushed his lunch to one side.

Carrie breathed in deeply before beginning. "I met Ryan here at the lodge. He works for Luke's dad at Fields Digital Solutions and they look after all the computers, point of sale terminals and networks here. Ryan is a whiz with computers, and he's super smart."

"What's his last name?" Drew asked.

"Walters. Ryan Walters."

"Is he from Minnewasta?" he asked, naming the closest small town, some ten miles down the road.

"No, he's originally from Indiana. His parents and his brother and sister still live there. I've only met them over Zoom so far."

"How old is Ryan?"

When Carrie hesitated and glanced at Celeste, she understood this was the question the girl had been dreading. Or at least one of them. She gave Carrie what she hoped was an encouraging smile.

There was no denying the worry on Carrie's face as she turned to her brother. "He's twenty-eight."

Drew blinked a couple of times, clearly surprised by this information. Shocked might be a better word. But to his credit, he kept his concern out of his voice. "He's ten years older than you?"

"Closer to nine." Carrie's voice was defensive. "I'm going to be nineteen in January, remember? Ryan only turned twenty-eight a couple of weeks ago."

"So why do you like Ryan so much? What do you two have in common?"

"Lots of things. We both love video games and reading. We love watching sports. When we're together we often play board games." Carrie shook her head. "But it's not only games we have in common. We have similar world views. Ryan feels as strongly about preserving the environment as I do. He's a veteran and is involved with veteran's groups in the area. I've gone to a couple of events with him and met some amazing people."

"I see." Drew tapped his fingers on his desk. Celeste guessed he was considering his words carefully. "Does Ryan know about the money?"

"The money? You mean the money Uncle Ethan won in the lottery?" Carrie asked. When Drew nodded, she continued. "Yeah, he knows. It's common knowledge around here. He knows the money doesn't have anything to do with me. And anyway, Ryan isn't interested in money."

Celeste wondered about that. Ryan certainly didn't strike her as a greedy person, but she was sure that money could make his life a whole lot easier. When Drew glanced at her, she put a neutral expression on her face, hoping he couldn't read her thoughts.

"Even if it's not your money, it's in our family. Money like that can make people do some crazy things."

Carrie sat up straighter, her chin tilting at a defiant angle. "You mean crazy like dating someone ten years younger? Do you think Uncle Ethan's money is the only reason Ryan would want to be with me?"

"No, of course not. You're young and beautiful and sweet. I want to know what's in it for you. Why would you want to date someone so much older?"

Carrie lifted her hands in a helpless gesture. "Because when we're together we're not two people with a big difference in age. We're just Carrie and Ryan."

For a long minute, Drew simply stared at her. Celeste offered Carrie her hand and the younger woman squeezed so tight her fingers ached.

Finally, Drew leaned back in his chair. "So, when do I get to meet this guy?"

Carrie loosened her hold on Celeste's hand. Celeste let out the breath she'd been holding, relieved that Drew was trying to keep an open mind, even though he was obviously concerned about this relationship. It spoke of his deep connection to his sister and his inherent fairness.

She liked that about him. She liked *him*.

"He'll be coming to the lodge in a couple of days to do some work," Carrie said. "You can meet him then."

"All right." Drew got to his feet. "Can I stay at Ethan and Harper's house with you? The hotel room is nice, but I don't want to live there."

"Of course, you can, you dork." Carrie let go of Celeste's hand and came around the desk to hug Drew. "I missed you."

"I missed you, too."

As he hugged Carrie, Drew's gaze met Celeste's. She read the worry in his eyes. Celeste did her best to reassure him with a smile, but she was worried, too. Carrie had only told her brother part of the story.

Their relationship would be tested by what was to come. For both their sakes, she hoped it could withstand the strain.

LATER THAT AFTERNOON, Drew sipped his coffee as he waited in the restaurant at a table facing the door to the kitchen. The staff schedule told him that Celeste's shift ended at three. It was five minutes after. She should be leaving any moment. He only hoped she didn't exit through the service entrance.

He breathed a sigh of relief when she emerged through the kitchen door with one of the line cooks he'd been introduced to. Celeste laughed at something the other woman said, and for a moment, Drew was struck by her smile and the sound of her laughter. But even when she was laughing, Celeste had a restrained manner. She was holding herself back, not wanting to show the world the depths of her emotions.

He shook his head, not sure where the thought came from. After all, he barely knew her. He simply needed to talk to Celeste about Carrie, not analyze her personality.

He walked toward her. "Celeste, can I speak to you for a minute?"

She turned to look at him, clearly surprised by his presence. She turned back to her co-worker with a smile. "I'll see you tomorrow, Sue."

Sue glanced at him before responding. "See you later."

Celeste watched her friend leave, waiting until she was out of earshot before speaking. "What can I do for you, Drew?" Though her tone was calm, her eyes were alert and her body language wary.

It bothered him that she felt she had to be watchful around him. He summoned his most non-threatening smile, hoping to reassure her. At least he hoped his smile was non-threatening and didn't come off as stalker-like. "I was hoping to talk to you about Carrie. She trusts you, and I can tell you've got her best interests at heart. I want to know your honest feelings about this Ryan guy."

"I'm sorry, Drew. You and Carrie need to work this out between you. It's a family matter that I shouldn't interfere in."

Celeste turned to leave. Drew grasped her arm, dropping his fake smile and all pretenses in his desperation. "Please Celeste. Talk to me. Is she making a big mistake getting involved with him? Is he going to hurt her? If I stood by and did nothing while he took advantage of my baby sister, I couldn't live with myself."

She glanced around the restaurant. Drew followed her gaze. Staff members were bustling around, getting tables ready for the dinner rush, some of them watching their exchange with open interest.

He withdrew his hand. He had no business accosting her and embarrassing her in front of her co-workers. "I'm sorry. I shouldn't have—"

"Why don't you come over to my apartment? I'd like to be there when my daughter gets home from school, and we can talk privately. I'll make you a cup of coffee, if you like."

Drew blinked at her surprise offer, then quickly accepted. "Sure. Thanks."

He followed her outside and over to the event center, the large building next to the lodge where weddings and other events were held. The building had been clad in weathered barnboard that gave it the appearance of being the same age as the lodge's seventy plus years instead of less than three years old. An owner's apartment had originally been built for Harper on the second floor, but after she'd married Ethan, Drew heard that the small two-bedroom apartment had been given to Celeste and her daughter.

They climbed the enclosed outdoor stairs to the second-floor apartment, with Celeste leading the way. At the top of the stairs, she unlocked the door and stepped inside, turning to him as she held the door open.

"Please come in."

The apartment was small, but the sun streaming through the large windows made it feel bright and airy. Celeste put their coats in the closet and then stepped behind the kitchen island and poured water in the coffee maker. Drew sat on one of the stools at the island and watched her. Every movement Celeste made was graceful. The word regal popped into his mind when he looked at her. The way she moved, even the way she held her head, spoke of quiet elegance.

She measured coffee into the basket and started the machine. "It'll be ready in a few minutes. What do you take in your coffee?"

"I'll have milk, please."

She retrieved a carton of milk from the fridge and set it in front of him. She paused, both hands resting palm-down on the counter. "Carrie's a sweet girl, but she's no pushover. I think you should trust her."

"I *do* trust her. It's Ryan I don't trust. Despite Carrie's mathematical gymnastics, he's ten years older. He's been in the military. He's probably seen things, and done things, that a sheltered girl like her can't even begin to fathom. What's in it for him if it's not to use her for sex?"

To Drew's surprise, she laughed. "For heaven's sake, Drew. You make Ryan sound like some sex-crazed monster. Don't let your imagination run away with you."

"I can't help it. I don't know anything about him, so my imagination goes wild. Nobody will tell me anything, not really."

Her expression softened. "I understand. You'll meet him in a couple of days, and you'll be able to judge for yourself. Just keep an open mind, okay?"

"Why do I need to keep an open mind?"

Celeste frowned. "You're so suspicious. No wonder Carrie kept Ryan under wraps."

Drew threw up his hands. "Fine! I'll keep an open mind."

"Good."

The coffeemaker made some spitting sounds, signaling it was finished brewing. Celeste pulled a couple of mugs from a cupboard and filled them with coffee. Drew added milk to his mug, and she put the carton back in the fridge.

"Why don't we take our coffee to the living room?" she said.

They sat next to each other on the sofa. Drew set his mug on a coaster on the coffee table. "You really think Carrie's okay?"

"I do." Celeste sipped her coffee before putting it on the table. "Considering her age, I think your sister is a remarkably mature young woman. She's not stupid, Drew. She knows what she wants."

"If she's been seeing this guy for weeks, why is this the first I've heard of him? As far as I know, she hasn't said anything about him to our parents, either. Why the secrecy?"

"Maybe because of their age difference, she didn't want you and your parents to judge him before she had a chance to figure out her feelings."

Judge. There was that word again. Why did Celeste, and Carrie, feel they had to protect Ryan? Why did they believe he'd be judged? The thought made him uneasy.

"I think Carrie is trying to assert her independence." Celeste reached for her coffee and took another sip. "She's at a difficult age. She thinks of herself as an adult. She's finished high school, she's holding down an adult job, and she's learning about the responsibilities that go along with being a grownup. But her immediate family still thinks of her as a kid. Maybe that's why she didn't want to tell you about Ryan."

Celeste's thoughts had merit. Because Drew was six years older, he thought of Carrie the way he had when she was ten. The baby sister he needed to protect. Now that she was nearly nineteen, perhaps his thinking needed to change.

Maybe his attitude toward Ryan needed to change as well. He certainly knew what being judged felt like.

Celeste stared into her coffee mug. "I can understand why Carrie wants to be independent. I know what dependence feels like, and it's not good."

"What do you mean?"

Before she could answer, the door swung open and Celeste's daughter burst inside, dragging her backpack with her.

"I'm home, Mama!"

When she saw him sitting beside her mother, she stopped in her tracks and went silent, her dark eyes widening in surprise.

Celeste rose and went to her. "Hi, sweetie." The little girl glued herself to Celeste's side, her hand in hers. "We have company. This is Drew. He's Carrie's brother. He's going to be working at the lodge for a while, filling in for Miss Harper till she has her babies. Drew, this is my daughter, Hope Bishop."

Drew got to his feet and extended his hand to the little girl. "Nice to meet you, Hope. You probably don't remember, but we met three years ago at my uncle Cam's wedding to Scarlet. You were with my cousin Tessa. She's your friend, right?"

Hope solemnly shook his hand, her expression wary. "Tessa's my best friend. But I don't remember you."

"That's okay. I haven't come here for a visit since then. I live in Minneapolis."

She was maybe four feet tall and had the same café au lait complexion as her mother. The shape of her face—a perfect oval—was also much like Celeste's. She was going to be a beauty when she was older. Just like her mother.

Hope pulled an envelope out of her backpack and handed it to her mother. "Mama, I got an invitation to Charlotte's birthday party after school next Wednesday! Can I go? She's having games and hot dogs and cake. All my friends are going."

The look of distress that crossed Celeste's face alarmed Drew. "I don't know, Hope. I'll have to talk to Maggie."

"Please, Mama?" Hope appeared nearly as distressed as her mother. "I never get to go anywhere."

"I said I'd talk to Maggie. But you know I can't promise anything."

Hope's shoulders slumped as she stared down at the floor. "I know. Can I be excused, please?"

"Yes, of course."

As Celeste watched her daughter head to her room, Drew watched Celeste. She blinked rapidly, and he was afraid she was on the brink of tears. "Celeste? You okay?"

She stared at him as if she'd forgotten he was in the room. Then she straightened her shoulders and attempted a smile. "I'm fine. Can I get you more coffee?"

"No, thank you. What did you mean when you said you had to talk to Maggie?" It was none of his business, but he felt compelled to understand what distressed both of them like this.

Celeste sighed and sat on the sofa once more. Drew took the seat beside her. "Unless Maggie or Luke can drive Hope home, she can't go to the party. It's what I mean by being dependent."

"Because you don't have a car?"

"Yeah." She lifted her gaze to his, the frown between her brows marring her perfect complexion. "Don't get me wrong. I love working at the lodge, and I'm grateful every day for the opportunity I've been given." She swept out her hand to encompass the apartment. "And look at this place. It's beautiful. Ethan and Harper have given it to me rent-free. It's meant the world to me to have such a wonderful home to raise my daughter in."

Drew sensed her frustration. "But...?"

"But the lodge is ten miles from Minnewasta. Brainerd is even further. Every time I need something, I have to bother someone, usually Maggie, for a ride, or ask her to pick up things for me in town. A couple of weeks ago, I missed Hope's parent-teacher interview because I had no way to get to the school in town. I spoke to her teacher on the phone, but it's not the same as a face-to-face meeting."

"Have you thought about buying a car?"

"Yes, I've thought about it. But buying a car wouldn't do me much good."

"Why not?"

"Because I don't know how to drive. I've never been behind the wheel of a car."

Her confession shocked him. "Really? Never?"

"Never."

Celeste looked embarrassed. Drew immediately regretted his words. "I'm sorry. I guess I assumed everyone could drive. But it's not like we come out of the womb with a set of car keys in one hand and a gearshift in the other."

That made her smile. "If only. I've actually been searching online for a good used car for some time. I found a couple I like at a dealership in Brainerd, but it seems pointless to buy when I don't even have a learner's permit."

"How come you never had a chance to learn to drive?"

She turned toward him, resting her elbow on the back of the sofa and her chin in the palm of her hand. "When I was a kid, my dad had a car. He was the only one who drove it since my mom doesn't drive, either. He and my mom divorced before my sister and I were old enough to get learner's permits. We didn't see him a lot after he left. My sister Gloria's husband eventually taught her to drive."

Drew nodded. His parents had put up with his mistakes and his cocky adolescent attitude as they taught him to drive. He knew he was exceptionally lucky to have parents who were still together and still loved each other. Not all his friends could say the same.

Celeste straightened and reached for her coffee again. "When I got married, my husband promised to teach me. But he died in a car crash before he had the chance. For a long time after that I wasn't keen to get in a car, let alone drive one."

Hearing her story and what she'd been through made Drew respect her even more. "I'm sorry. That must have been very hard for you."

She gave him a sad smile. "It was. We were a happy family. But it's been six years, and I've learned to move on."

"Was that the reason you decided to take the job here at the lodge, to move on?"

Her smile disappeared and she turned her face away. "One of the reasons."

He waited for her to elaborate, but she remained silent. As Drew finished the last of his coffee, he came to a decision.

"Would you be comfortable with me picking Hope up from her friend's house after the party and driving her home? I'm happy to do it."

She started shaking her head before he finished talking. "I didn't tell you my story of woe so you'd feel sorry for us and volunteer to be our chauffeur. Thank you, but we'll be fine."

"Do you really want Hope to miss out on her friend's birthday party?"

The look of distress was back in her eyes. "No, of course not."

"Then quit being so proud and stubborn and let me pick her up."

She gave him an indignant glare. "You don't know anything about my life or my daughter's."

"No, I don't. But I can see how much it hurts you to say no to Hope."

Celeste stared at her hands folded in her lap. "I didn't know any of this was going to happen. I wasn't angling for a ride for Hope. Maybe you can help this time, but the next time, maybe you won't be around and we'll be in the same situation again."

She was right. Until Celeste was able to drive her own vehicle, she couldn't be fully independent. And until she was independent, neither she nor Hope could be truly happy. Drew wanted that for them.

"I'll tell you what. We're going to get that car for you. I'll help you study for your learner's permit and then I'll teach you everything I know. Or you can hire a driving teacher in Minnewasta or Brainerd. Whatever you want to do, I'll help you get there."

She turned to face him once more, shock evident on her face. "Are you serious?"

To his surprise, Drew realized he was completely serious. "Yes, I am."

"I can't ask you to do that."

"You're not asking. I'm offering."

"Why would you do that?"

He wasn't entirely sure himself. All he knew was that she needed help and he wanted to be the one who gave it to her. He settled for a half-truth. "You're an integral member of the staff here at the lodge. I don't want frustration with the isolation here to be the reason you decide to move somewhere else. You're needed at the restaurant, and I want you to be happy living here."

Her expression told him she wasn't sure if she should believe him. Or trust him. "You have to understand I can't—I won't—give you anything in return."

She was warning him that he shouldn't expect her to fall into his bed in gratitude. He held up his hands in a gesture of surrender. "I don't expect anything in return."

"That's very generous of you."

"Not entirely generous. I don't have much to do here in my off hours, especially since Carrie isn't happy with me right now. I'm going to have a lot of time on my hands."

A sudden grin blossomed on her face. "So, you thought you'd amuse yourself by laughing at me as I learn to parallel park. Is that what you're saying?"

Drew crossed his heart. "I swear I won't laugh at you. Even if you do something hilariously dumb, I'll keep it down to a small smirk."

She laughed. "I'm afraid you're going to be smirking a lot." Her smile disappeared, and her expression grew cautious once more. "Are you sure you want to do this?"

"Absolutely."

Her eyes filled with tears. "Thank you. You have no idea what this means to me."

"Hey. Don't cry."

Without thinking, Drew pulled her into a hug. His intention had been to soothe, but once Celeste was in his arms, her scent surrounded him, reminding him of flowers. She was soft and warm, and he was aware of her on a whole new level.

As a beautiful, desirable woman.

She quickly pulled away, and he let her go. Her gaze didn't quite meet his. "I'm sorry. I don't usually get so emotional, but your offer caught me by surprise."

She'd caught him by surprise, too. "You have nothing to apologize for."

Again, he sensed she was holding back. There was a great deal about Celeste he didn't know.

A great deal he wanted to know.

Celeste rose and reached for a tissue from a box on the counter. She wiped her eyes as she tried to compose herself. "Where do we start?"

"With the learner's permit, I guess."

"Okay." Celeste clutched her hands together, twisting the tissue. "I don't know exactly why you're doing this but thank you. I can't tell you how much I appreciate it."

As Drew acknowledged her statement with a smile, he had the oddest sensation that his decision to help Celeste be more independent was going to have as much impact on his life as it would have on hers.

Chapter Four

"MAMA, TELL ME THE STORY about how you met my daddy again."

Celeste smiled into her daughter's shining eyes. Hope had heard the story many times of how she met Easton Bishop at culinary school and immediately fell head over heels for him. But it was a happy story, and she was pleased to share it once again, especially since it delighted Hope so much.

She snuggled next to her daughter on the twin bed. "I spoke to your daddy for the first time the day our soups, stocks and sauces class began. I'd noticed him right away because he was so good-looking, but I was at culinary school to learn to cook, not to find a date, so I'd kept my head down and studied."

Celeste was eighteen and eager to set the world on fire with her culinary creations. From the time she was twelve, she'd baked cookies and cakes in her mother's old, unpredictable oven and knew she wanted to be a chef. More specifically, a baker. She saved for years for culinary school, from babysitting jobs and summer employment at fast food restaurants. Her mother, a primary school teacher, worked summer jobs and took on occasional weekend jobs to help pay for her and her sister's post-secondary education. They'd all worked too hard for her to mess it up by getting distracted by a handsome face.

Because, oh goodness, what a handsome face Easton Bishop had.

Hope poked her in the ribs. "And then what happened, Mama?"

Celeste dragged herself away from the old memories to concentrate on her daughter. "Well, my hollandaise sauce turned into a disaster. I made a dumb, rookie mistake and accidentally turned the burner on my stove too high. As I was processing the egg yolks and lemon juice in the blender, the butter I was melting in a saucepan overheated and started to smoke. If your daddy hadn't pulled the pan off the stove before the instructor saw what happened, it could have been a disaster. I might have flunked out of school. But he saved the day."

He'd saved her career that day, at least in her eyes. After that, they were inseparable. When they graduated from culinary school, they both got jobs at an upscale French-style restaurant in Myrtle Beach called Chez Henri, with Easton as a sous chef and Celeste as an apprentice baker. They married a few months later.

"What did Daddy say the day I was born?" Hope asked.

Celeste cupped her daughter's cheek. "He said you were the most beautiful baby he'd ever seen. He fell in love with you the minute he saw you. He'd be so proud of you, baby."

Hope reached for the picture of Easton on her night table. She gave his smiling face a kiss. "I love you, too, Daddy."

Celeste carefully put the picture back in its place. "Time to sleep, sweetheart. You've got school tomorrow."

Hope burrowed under the covers. ""Night, Mama."

Her eyes were already closed. By the time Celeste turned off the lights and closed the door, Hope would be asleep. She was like her father in that way. Easton had fallen asleep every night as soon as his head hit the pillow, while Celeste often tossed and turned, the day's events rolling around in her head for hours before she was able to succumb to sleep.

She was afraid tonight would be one of those nights. That afternoon, when she'd been in Drew's arms, she felt something for the first time in a very long time.

Desire.

It felt good. Really good.

She'd loved Easton with her whole heart and soul and every cell of her body. When a drunk driver blasted through a red light hitting Easton's car and killing him instantly, a part of her had died, too. For a long time, she couldn't face living her life without him. But with the encouragement and help of her mother and sister and knowing that Easton would want her to live for Hope, she was able to carry on.

When she'd called Hope back into the living room to ask her if she'd be okay with Drew picking her up from Charlotte's house after the party, Hope had been practically incandescent with joy. She'd looked at Drew like he was her personal hero.

Her daughter deserved a hero in her life.

For six years Celeste had carried on the best she knew how, for Hope's sake. She'd accepted Easton's death, though a day didn't go by that she didn't think about him. The idea of another relationship, another man in her life, had never occurred to her. She couldn't imagine being with anyone but Easton. The very idea felt wrong. And disloyal.

So why was she thinking about it now?

BY THE NEXT AFTERNOON, after the mostly sleepless night Celeste had predicted, she convinced herself that the stirrings of desire she experienced were simply normal reactions to being in close proximity to an attractive man. She was human, after all. A human woman who hadn't had sex in a very long time.

Celeste did her best to concentrate on the triple layered chocolate cake she was icing, but thoughts of Drew kept interrupting. Why had he offered to teach her to drive? What did he want? Was he looking for sex? She'd made it clear she wasn't offering, and he seemed to accept it. So, why?

Her mind drifted as she wondered what making love to Drew would be like. Was he simply looking for quick gratification to scratch an itch, or would he be the kind of lover who took his time, willing to make the effort to please them both? He struck her as the kind of man who wouldn't rush. If he asked her, maybe she should just go for it. It had been so long...

She shook her head. *Good lord*. She hadn't thought about sex so much since she'd first met Easton.

Get a grip, Celeste. The idea of having sex with Drew was a non-starter. She wasn't a casual sex kind of woman. She could never be intimate with a man she barely knew, a man she didn't have a loving relationship with. And since Drew was nine years younger, they couldn't possibly have a relationship.

Could they?

"Celeste, what are you still doing here? Your shift was over almost twenty minutes ago." Cheryl tied an apron around her waist.

"I know. I need to finish this cake." She slowly spun the turntable the cake sat on and smoothed the icing on the sides with her palette knife. *Enough.* When her fantasies started interfering with her work, it was time to get herself under control. She filled a piping bag with chocolate frosting and created elaborate rosettes on the top.

As she finished the last rosette, Drew entered the kitchen carrying a green binder and a large brown envelope. "Hey, you're still here. I thought your shift was over."

"That's what *I* said," Cheryl chimed in.

Celeste felt her face flush. "I had to finish the cake. It's on the menu tonight."

"It looks great," Drew said. "If you're done now, are you ready to study?"

"Study?" Cheryl diced an onion at the chopping block. "What are you studying for?"

"My learner's permit." Better to be upfront about what she and Drew were doing rather than have people speculate. "I need to learn how to drive, and Drew has generously offered to help me with the test and driving lessons."

"Good for you, Celeste. I know learning to drive is a big deal for you," Cheryl said. "Have fun."

Celeste pulled her apron over her head. "As much fun as I can have studying the rules of the road in Minnesota."

Cheryl chuckled. "See you two tomorrow."

They left the kitchen together in silence. Celeste tried to think of something to say. "Are you finished for the day, too? I thought Harper usually worked till five."

Drew shrugged. "She may have, but no one told me what hours I had to work. I figured that until you get your driver's license, I'd work the same shifts as you. So I started at seven, same as you."

She stared at him. "How did you know what shift I was working?"

He gave her a charming grin. "Luke and I made the schedule. I know when everyone's working."

"You didn't have to go to such trouble."

He shrugged again. "How are we going to study together if we don't work the same hours?"

"I guess you're right." She hadn't expected him to take his promise to help her so seriously.

"Let's get our coats." Drew halted his steps and frowned, suddenly looking unsure of himself. "Unless you'd rather study here at the lodge. Or you've changed your mind about this whole idea."

Celeste searched his face for any trace of deceit, but all she saw was complete openness. "I haven't changed my mind. My laptop and study materials are at my apartment. Besides, Hope will be home from school soon. Come on. I'll make you a cup of coffee. I might even have a cookie or two for you."

His sudden grin made him look boyish and carefree. "Best offer I've had all day."

After retrieving their coats from the staff lounge, they made their way to the event center and up the enclosed outdoor stairs to Celeste's apartment. Inside the apartment, she unwrapped the scarf from around her neck and gestured toward her laptop sitting on the coffee table. "Why don't you fire up the laptop and I'll start the coffee."

"Sure." Drew removed his coat and hung it in the closet. He held up the binder. "I printed off a copy of the Minnesota learner's permit study manual in the office in case you find it easier to study from a hard copy."

"Thank you. I think I would find that easier."

Though touched by his thoughtfulness, she still wondered why he was doing this for her. Visions of tangled sheets swept through her head and she blinked to dispel them. Why couldn't she get sex off her brain?

Once she had the coffee brewing, and thoughts of tangled sheets and hot sex under control, she joined him on the sofa.

He handed her the binder. "I printed some sample exams they had on the website, too. They're in the envelope. For today, I figured I'd make up an exam and you can use the quizzes in the envelope to study on your own."

"Sounds like a plan."

She opened the binder, noting that he'd collated the pages and punched three holes on the left-hand side so they could fit in the binder. For some reason, those three holes got to her. It showed the effort he'd gone through to help her.

"Thanks, Drew." Celeste tapped her fingers on the binder. "This is very considerate of you. I couldn't do this because I don't have a printer."

"You're welcome. I wanted to make studying as painless as possible for you because we're going to nail this thing on the first try."

She laughed. "Damn straight, we are."

Drew laughed with her. "Damn straight. Why don't you get started and I'll bring you a cup of coffee?"

"That would be great. Thank you."

For the next twenty minutes Celeste curled up on the couch with her coffee mug and read through the manual, trying to commit to memory the rules of the road. How many seconds she needed to stop at stop signs, the meaning of different traffic sign colors and shapes, and the speed limits on various kinds of roads and streets. She'd gone through the manual in the past and had been confident she could pass the learner's test, but she always got stuck on what to do next. Even if she purchased a car, she couldn't drive it with only a learner's permit. She needed someone with a regular license to be in the car while she learned to drive. Hiring a driving instructor meant she'd have to go all the way to Brainerd for lessons. She'd thought of asking Maggie to drive her, but it would have been a big ask. Maggie had already done so much for her and she didn't want to make her feel obligated to do even more. So, she'd been stuck in place. Until Drew had offered.

Every once in a while, she glanced over at him intently studying something on her laptop and taking notes on a pad of paper. His long lashes swept his chiseled cheeks and his beautifully shaped lips pursed in concentration. His dark hair fell over his forehead and he often pushed it off his face with an impatient hand. How silky would his hair feel if she ran her hands through it?

At precisely ten minutes after four, Hope burst through the apartment door. "Mama, I'm home!"

"Hi, baby." Celeste gave Hope a hug when she rushed into her arms. "Say hi to Drew. He's here to help me study for my learner's permit."

Hope was normally a shy child, at least until she knew a person. They didn't often have company in their apartment, and Celeste had never brought a man here before.

But she didn't seem shy around Drew at all. She greeted him with a broad smile. "Hi Drew!"

Drew gave her a friendly grin in return. "Hello, Hope. Do you want to help me quiz your mom for the driving exam?"

"Sure!" Hope's eyes lit with excitement. "Mama, are we going to get a car?"

"If everything goes the way I want it to, yeah, that's the plan. But that's sometime down the road."

"If we get a car, can I join the Girl Scouts?"

"You want to join the Girl Scouts?"

Hope shrugged. "All my friends go. Their meetings are after school, but I have to take the bus home, so I didn't join."

Celeste's heart fell. Hope hadn't even mentioned wanting to join. Was she trying to spare Celeste's feelings, or had she thought the idea was so outrageous there was no point talking about it? The last thing she wanted was for her daughter's life to be limited by the things she couldn't give her. Her gaze met Drew's.

He gave her a reassuring smile before turning his attention to Hope. "You and I are going to help your mom study, and she's going to ace that exam. Okay?"

"Okay! And then we'll get a car!"

He laughed. "One thing at a time. Come on. I'm making up an exam. You can help me pick out questions."

The two of them whispering back and forth distracted Celeste from her studies. When Hope cupped her hand against Drew's ear to tell him something, his answering grin and thumbs up made Hope giggle. Drew had charmed her daughter as easily as he'd charmed her. She wasn't sure if she should be happy about it or worried.

Celeste forced herself to concentrate on the manual once more. After another twenty minutes, she'd read through the whole thing and felt ready to challenge herself.

"Okay, you two. Time to quiz me. Do your worst."

"Let's see if we can stump her, Hope." Drew handed Hope the pad of paper he'd been writing on. "You can start. If you can't read my writing, let me know."

Hope slowly read the question, sounding out a couple of words as she read. "In what conditions can you not pass another vehicle when driving in the same direction?"

Celeste closed her eyes in concentration. "I know this one. You can't pass where there is a 'No Passing Sign" posted. You can't pass if there is a solid yellow line in your lane or when you're going around a curve or up a hill and can't see the road ahead clearly for at least seven hundred feet in front of you. You can't pass within a hundred feet of an intersection, tunnel or railroad crossing. And of course, you should never pass a car if there's another car coming towards you in the other lane."

Drew pumped his fist. "Correct!"

"Yay, Mama!"

They fired more questions at her, and she answered back. In the end, she scored twenty out of twenty.

"You did great, Celeste," Drew said. "Do you think you're ready to book your exam?"

The prospect of failing terrified her. The expectant look on her daughter's face told her failure wasn't an option. She *had* to take this first step, and then every step after that until she was legally driving her own car.

She blew out a breath. "I'm ready. Let's do this."

AFTER MAKING THE FIVE-minute drive from the lodge, Drew paused in the driveway of Ethan and Harper's house, a sprawling ranch-style home with a stone front and earth-toned siding that fit in with the surrounding forest. The lights were on, indicating Carrie was already home, but he sat, reflecting on the last couple of hours spent with Celeste and Hope. He was impressed with Celeste's quick recall, and he was confident she'd have no trouble with the written exam. Before he'd left, she pulled the trigger and booked her exam for two weeks from today. She'd told him she'd studied for the exam before, but never actually took it because she didn't know how to take the next steps.

He offered to let her practice driving with his car once she had her learner's permit, but she pointed out that

Minnesota law said she needed to take the road test for her license with her own vehicle. She had to be comfortable and familiar with the car in which she'd be taking the test.

Celeste had showed him and Hope a couple of used cars online on the website of a dealership in Brainerd. Hope was almost giddy with excitement at the prospect of buying a car. He and Celeste decided to look at used cars in Brainerd right after she took her learner's test.

Celeste wanted her driver's license as much for Hope's independence as her own. Perhaps even more. There was no mistaking the devastation on her face when Hope mentioned she couldn't join the Girl Scouts because she had no way to get home from their meetings. Maybe there was something he could do to help till Celeste could drive herself. He'd speak to her about it next time they were together.

Drew tapped his finger against the steering wheel. Spending time with Celeste and Hope had been fun. He hadn't spent much time with kids, aside from his little cousin Tessa and his own sister, back in the day. But Carrie wasn't a kid anymore. She'd made it abundantly clear that she considered herself an adult, and he had to start treating her accordingly.

With that thought in mind, he got out of his car and entered the house.

"Hello! You here, Carrie?"

Carrie's voice came from the back of the house. "In the kitchen."

Drew placed his jacket in the closet along with the leather briefcase he used to transport Harper's password notebook home with him every night. He then followed his nose to the kitchen where Carrie was cooking. The smells were glorious.

"Wow! Something smells great. What are you making?"

"Eggplant and mushroom pasta." Steam rose as Carrie drained a pot of pasta into a strainer in the sink. "It's almost ready. Are you hungry?"

"Starved."

"Good. You can set the table."

Drew threw plates and utensils on the kitchen table along with glasses and some orange juice he found in the fridge, while Carrie poured the pasta on a serving dish and covered it with her eggplant and mushroom mix. She brought the dish to the table, sat across from Drew and set her phone next to her plate.

"Bon appétit. I hope you enjoy it."

"If it tastes half as good as it smells, I'm going to love it."

Drew took a mouthful of the eggplant and moaned in ecstasy. "You really have talent, Carrie. This is what you're meant to do."

She smiled. "I'm glad you like it."

"I could get used to you cooking for me."

"This definitely won't happen every night."

"A man can dream, can't he?"

They both laughed. Drew saluted her with his orange juice. "To my sister, and her skills in the kitchen. May she never be too ticked off to feed me."

Carrie clinked her glass against his. "I'll drink to that."

They'd just finished eating when Carrie's phone rang. She snatched it up, smiling as she did so.

"Hey. I was just thinking about you." She glanced at Drew as she got up from her chair. "I'm having dinner with my brother."

Though she hadn't said his name, it was obvious that Ryan was Carrie's caller. Drew sipped his orange juice and watched as she walked back and forth behind the kitchen island, her face wreathed in smiles. She laughed at something Ryan said. Drew wasn't sure he'd ever seen her so happy. He wanted to be happy for her, and he wanted to give Ryan a chance, but his gut told him something wasn't right.

"Okay. See you tomorrow." She glanced at Drew before looking away. "Yeah, me too. Bye."

Carrie ended the call and set her phone on the table before sitting once more. "That was Ryan."

"I gathered." Drew chose his words carefully. "So, he'll be at the lodge tomorrow."

"Yeah, he will." Carrie lifted her chin in warning. "And I want you to be civil to him."

"I'll be civil. I'm always civil." He was annoyed to be painted as the bad guy when he was only looking out for her. "I've never seen you so crazy about a guy before, that's all."

"Ryan's a very special person."

"I'm sure he is, but I just want you to be careful. Because he's so much older than you, you two are at different stages in your lives. You're just beginning a career, and he's already established a second career. And you've never lived on your own. You went from our parents' house to our aunt and uncle's house."

"Look who's talking," she countered. "You only got your own place a few months ago."

"Yeah, and it's been a real adjustment for me. I'm simply saying you and Ryan have different life experiences. He's been in the military, he's traveled. Maybe he's decided he wants someone to settle down with. You've still got school and a career to begin."

She gave him an icy stare. "How do you know I'm not ready to settle down, too?"

"For Christ sake, Carrie. You're eighteen. You're nowhere near ready to settle for anything. This guy is ten years older than you. What do think is going to happen when you go back to school in St. Paul? Do you think he's going to sit around and wait for you?"

"I haven't made any commitments. Maybe I don't want to go to school in St. Paul. Maybe I don't want to go to school at all."

"Are you kidding me?" Drew couldn't believe what he was hearing. "Are you planning to throw away your future for this guy? Don't be crazy."

"Just because you think your age difference with Maggie is the reason a relationship didn't work between you doesn't mean it won't work for me and Ryan." She rose to her feet. "In case you haven't figured it out, your age difference had nothing to do with it. She was in love with Luke all along. She barely noticed you and when she did, it was because you kept pestering her."

Her words hit him like a slap to the face. Hearing her say Maggie had only seen him as an annoyance stung. Hard.

She marched out of the kitchen. "You can do the dishes."

A bedroom door slammed shut. Obviously, his sister could give as good as she got, something he never realized before. Maybe he should have kept his opinions to himself, but Carrie was his only sibling and he wanted what was best for her. He hoped Ryan was as great as everyone said he was because he couldn't stand the thought of her being hurt.

DREW'S STOMACH WAS tied in knots from the moment he woke the next morning. Ryan was coming to the lodge today, and he'd meet him for the first time.

At least he hoped he'd meet him. After their confrontation last night, Carrie left the house early without speaking to him.

For most of the morning, he immersed himself in spreadsheets and accounting data, and tried not to think about Ryan and his sister. He also searched through every drawer and folder in the office for the missing purchase order but came up empty. He considered simply paying the damn invoice since Maggie already said she'd ordered extra baking supplies. But he couldn't let it go. The idea of messing up at the family business within the first week was a non-starter. He'd have to investigate further.

Luke and Maggie provided a welcome diversion when Drew met with them in the restaurant for a late lunch. They updated him on preparations for the Christmas party. The live band had been booked, food ordered, and tickets were on sale on the lodge's website. Scarlet Hainstock, the lodge's marketing guru, had begun spreading the news of the Christmas dance on social media and would soon go on local and statewide radio and TV stations.

"Scarlet figured we needed a catchy name for the party before we started advertising it, so she came up with The Mistletoe Ball," Maggie said.

"Works for me. Scarlet's the marketing expert so if she thinks the name will sell tickets, I'm all for it."

"By the end of next week, ticket sales will tell us what kind of shape we're in," Luke said. "Scarlet's emphasizing the outdoor winter activities at the lodge, and the amenities like the spa in her advertising. We're hopeful that guests will make a weekend out of attending the Christmas Ball." He held up his hand. "Sorry. The Mistletoe Ball."

"Is there anything I can do?" Drew asked.

"Just keep us updated on the numbers. We need to keep a close eye on our budget." Luke got to his feet. "I've got to get back to work. If you have any questions, let me know."

"I will." Drew put his laptop back in its case. "I'll see you later."

"Drew, wait," Maggie said. "I heard that Ryan was going to be here today. Have you met him yet?"

"No. Carrie said she'd introduce me today."

"Okay, good." The nervous glance she sent Luke put Drew on high alert.

"What is it?"

Maggie clasped her hands in front of her. "I only want you to keep an open mind when you meet Ryan, that's all."

"I'll do my best, for Carrie's sake. She's already told me he's ten years older."

"Right. Well, I hope you have a good meeting. I'd better get back to the kitchen."

That was the second time someone had told him to keep an open mind where Ryan was concerned. Why did everyone assume he was so close-minded?

He went back to his office and worked for another hour. When a knock sounded at his door and Carrie stuck her head inside, his heart lifted. He'd been afraid she wouldn't speak to him today.

Drew got up from his chair and walked around his desk. "Hi! Come in!"

"Hey," Carrie said as she stepped inside the office.

"Hey yourself. Listen, I'm sorry I went all big brother on you last night. I only want you to be happy."

"I know. I'm sorry, too. What I said about you pestering Maggie was uncalled for."

"Apology accepted."

"Good, I'm glad. I hate fighting with you." Carrie reached for Drew's hand. "Ryan's here, and I want you to meet him. He's looking forward to meeting you."

Carrie looked apprehensive, and again he wondered why everyone felt they had to protect Ryan from him. Though the idea rankled, Drew smiled to reassure his sister.

"I'm looking forward to meeting him, too."

"Come on. I'll introduce you."

She led the way to the staff lounge and the small office next to it. Carrie opened the door and Drew followed her inside. A man with dark blonde wavy hair sat at a desk in front of a laptop. He turned to look at him, a tentative smile on his face. Drew returned the smile. And then he realized the man was in a wheelchair.

"Drew, I'd like to introduce you to my friend Ryan Walters." Carrie stepped closer to Ryan and put her hand on his shoulder. "Ryan, this is my brother, Drew Barnes."

Drew did his best to hide his shock. He put a polite smile on his face and extended his hand. "Good to meet you, Ryan."

"I'm happy to meet you, too. I've heard a lot about you and your parents." Ryan shook Drew's hand, then looked up at Carrie. "You didn't tell him, did you?"

She shook her head. "I wanted Drew to meet you and get to know you first. I'm sorry."

Ryan grasped her hand. "It's okay, sweetheart. But I don't think it was fair to your brother not to give him a heads-up about Ole Faithful here." He patted the arm of the wheelchair.

Drew stared at the chair. Suddenly, the way everyone kept telling him to keep an open mind made sense.

"I'm sorry, Drew," Carrie said. "I know I should have told you, but I didn't want you to make up your mind about Ryan before you met him."

"I get it." But he was disappointed Carrie felt she couldn't trust him with the truth.

"Did Carrie tell you I was in the military?" Ryan asked.

"Yeah, she mentioned you were a veteran."

"I was in Afghanistan. I was at a forward operating base in Taliban controlled territory when I was shot in the back. When they were able to get me to medical help, they discovered that my spine had been partially severed in the lower lumbar region. That means that while I don't have the use of my legs, I can still use my arms." Ryan patted the armrest of his chair once more. "Comes in handy for getting around."

"I appreciate you telling me."

"I want to be upfront with you, and your parents."

"Have you told our parents..." Drew gestured toward the wheelchair. "...about Ole Faithful?"

When Carrie shook her head, Ryan smiled up at her. "We'll tell your parents together. No more surprises, okay?"

"Okay." Carrie smiled at Ryan and then turned to Drew. "I've been trying to convince Mom and Dad to come here to the lodge for Christmas. I want them to meet Ryan."

"Yeah, good idea." Drew didn't know what else to say. Questions exploded in his head but everything he wanted to ask seemed too personal or bordered on being rude.

Seeing his sister with Ryan as she smiled into his eyes, her hand protectively on his shoulder, Drew couldn't help thinking their relationship was far more serious than he'd imagined. And he was afraid his sister was in way over her head.

Chapter Five

"TAKE THAT!" HOPE CROWED in satisfaction.

"I can't believe you beat me again!"

"That's okay, Drew." Hope grinned and patted his shoulder. "I'll bet you're good at other things, beside video games."

Drew laughed ruefully. "Gee, thanks Hope."

Celeste looked up from studying to watch them. Hope had her arm draped casually over Drew's shoulders, and they were laughing and teasing each other like old friends, even though they'd only really met a few days ago. They'd been playing video games since after dinner when Celeste had parked herself on the sofa to study.

It was Hope's idea to invite Drew for dinner. He was at the apartment quizzing Celeste when Hope arrived home from school, and she'd been excited to see him again. Her daughter's sudden attachment to Drew was beginning to worry her. What happened when he left the lodge in a few weeks? Despite her worry, she didn't have the heart to keep them apart. Hope was genuinely happy to be in Drew's company and, surprisingly, he seemed happy around her, too.

Celeste studied Drew's face. Though he did his best to disguise it, especially around Hope, she'd known he was upset the moment he'd arrived at her apartment after work. She didn't have to be a mind reader to know why. Ryan had been scheduled to be at the lodge today.

A quick check of the clock on the stove told her it was nearly eight. "Time for bed, Hope. Go change into your pajamas and brush your teeth."

Hope slid off her stool at the kitchen island and turned to Drew. "Will you say goodnight to me before you leave?"

"Of course, I will."

Hope hurried off to her room. Celeste collected the binder and the quizzes Drew had printed for her and tucked them into a drawer in the coffee table. She'd practically memorized the handbook. She was going to pass that test if it killed her.

Maybe one of the reasons Hope enjoyed having Drew visit was because they didn't get much company. It bothered Celeste that she rarely got the chance to play with kids her own age after school. The only playmate Hope saw regularly was Tessa Hainstock, Cam and Scarlet Hainstock's daughter. They knew Celeste didn't drive and were great about driving the kids to each other's house. But Celeste was afraid Hope was missing out on making more friendships.

Her stomach clenched. She had to pass this damn test.

"You okay?" Drew watched her from his stool at the kitchen island. "You're holding your stomach."

"Oh." Celeste looked down to see her hand covering her abdomen. "Just thinking about the exam. So much is riding on it."

"You're going to do great. You know this stuff cold." He tapped his fingers against the countertop. "Listen, I was thinking, what if I drove Hope home from Girl Scouts until you're able to do it yourself? It's not a big deal."

Celeste stared at him. "I thought you were only at the lodge temporarily."

"I am, but I'll likely be around for a few weeks after Harper's babies are born."

She was humbled by his generosity but knew she couldn't accept. "Drew, that's incredibly kind of you, but it won't work. I could enroll her in Girl Scouts now and she could go for a while, but once you're gone, she'd have to quit. I can't take the driving test for six months after passing the written exam, so even if everything went perfectly, the soonest I could get my license is May. And what do I do when I'm working an evening shift? I really appreciate your offer, but it simply won't work."

Drew looked like he wanted to argue, but finally he sighed and looked away. "You're right. It would be cruel to let her join and then snatch it away."

"Yeah. Someday, once I get my license and a vehicle, I'll find a place in Minnewasta to rent. Then Hope can do all kinds of after school things. But until then..." She shook her head.

Drew slid off his stool and moved closer. He reached for her hand, giving it a reassuring squeeze. "Don't worry. Everything's going to work out."

Nerves danced in her stomach as she stared into his eyes. She carefully pulled her hand away. "I could say the same to you. Carrie introduced you to Ryan today, didn't she?"

Drew frowned and ran a hand through his thick, dark hair. "Yeah, she did, and it was a shock. You knew about Ryan. Why didn't you say anything?"

Before Celeste could form an answer, Hope ran into the living room. "Mama, I've brushed my teeth. Can you and Drew tuck me in now?"

Drew answered for her, smiling at her daughter. "Coming right up, Hope."

Celeste trailed behind them as they headed to Hope's room. Hope jumped into her bed and stuck her feet under the covers. Drew pulled the blankets up over her head and she giggled.

"Too far, Drew!"

He laughed as he folded the blankets under her chin. "Is this better?"

"Much better. Drew, are you still going to pick me up after Charlotte's party?"

"Of course I am. Nothing could stop me."

"Mama said she's going to Brainerd tomorrow with Miss Cheryl to get a birthday present for Charlotte."

"Good plan." Drew nodded sagely. "Can't go to a birthday party empty handed."

Hope yawned, her eyes at half-mast. "That's what Mama said."

"Time to say goodnight, Hope. Sleep well."

"Goodnight, Drew. Thanks for tucking me in."

"You're welcome."

Celeste kissed Hope goodnight and she and Drew left the bedroom. When they reached the living room, Drew grabbed his jacket from the closet.

"I should go."

"Wait." Celeste put a hand on his arm. "I couldn't tell you about Ryan being in a wheelchair because it wasn't my story to tell. Maybe I was wrong, but it didn't feel right for me to be the one to give you news like that."

Privately, Celeste believed Carrie should have told Drew that Ryan was a paraplegic before he met him. It had obviously been a shock.

Drew blew out a breath and tossed his jacket over the armchair. "You're right. It wasn't your responsibility. I can't believe Carrie blindsided me like that. It makes me think that on some level she's ashamed of Ryan's disability. If that's the case, what's she doing with him?"

"I'm making tea. Would you like some?" At Drew's nod, Celeste put water on to boil and prepared a teapot with two bags of herbal tea. "I agree that Carrie should have been upfront with you. But she's not ashamed of Ryan. Just the opposite. She's proud of him, and I think she feels very protective of him."

"Protective? Do you mean she's trying to 'save' him?" Drew made air quotes with his fingers. "I'm worried he's got some kind of hold on her."

"I think he does. It's called love."

"Love?" Drew scoffed. "It was one thing to find out that Ryan is ten years older than Carrie, but then to learn he's a paraplegic...I don't know what to think. Carrie is so young."

"Carrie may be young, but she's what my mother would call an old soul. She knows what she wants. I think you need to respect her choices."

Drew took out his phone and scrolled before handing it to her. "Here, look at this. I've been checking out websites about paraplegics. They talk about loss of bladder and bowel control, and sexual disfunction. If they stay together, would they be able to have a normal sex life? Children? As heroic and impressive as Ryan might be, I want my sister to have a normal life. She's even talking about not going to culinary school in St. Paul because she wants to stay here with Ryan."

Celeste lifted the whistling kettle from the stove and poured hot water into the teapot. Did he have an issue with disabled people in general or was it just Ryan? "I don't want Carrie to make a decision that will have a detrimental effect on the rest of her life either. But in the end, it's not up to us. It's up to Carrie and Ryan to decide whether they want to be together and face life's challenges as a couple."

Drew sat at the island once more. "As her brother, don't I have an obligation to point out the problems she's going to face if she gets even more deeply involved with Ryan?"

"Harping on her will likely only alienate Carrie. I doubt she'd listen to you." She brought out two mugs from a cupboard and poured tea into them. "I sure didn't."

"What do you mean?"

Celeste sat on the stool next to Drew. "I know a little something about defying the wishes of my family. My husband's father and brother had both been in jail, so a lot of people, including my mother, wrote off the whole family. But I knew Easton wasn't like them. He was a good, honest person, and he was going to make his dream of being a famous chef come true. He would have done it, too, if he'd lived."

"I'm sorry Celeste."

She waved away his sympathy. "My point in telling you this is that no one was ever going to convince me not to be with Easton. Believe me, my mother tried. Eventually she and my sister figured out what I saw in him because they saw it, too. Maybe that will happen with you and Ryan."

Drew shook his head. "I don't know."

"Don't make Carrie choose between you and Ryan because if you present her with that ultimatum, you're going to lose. I think the best thing you can do is to show her that you're making an effort to get to know him."

Drew silently sipped his tea and stared across the room. Celeste watched him, admiring the perfection of his profile, the strong chin, the beautifully sculpted lips, the perfect cheekbones. He was possibly one of the most beautiful men she'd ever met.

She was so deep in thought she almost missed his quietly spoken words.

"How do I do that?"

"Well, being a chef, my mind immediately goes to food. What if you invited them to join you for dinner? It would give you a chance to get to know Ryan and observe him and Carrie together. But not at the lodge restaurant. Somewhere private, like maybe Ethan and Harper's house."

"Sounds like a good idea. Only one problem. I can't cook. Would you help me?"

She blinked. Did she really want to get so deeply involved in Drew's private family business? Perhaps not, but he'd gone out of his way to help her gain independence. The least she could do was to cook one meal. And besides, she didn't want to see either Carrie or Drew get hurt. Especially Drew.

Why should his happiness matter so much to her?

"Please?"

"Sure. We'll figure out what to make and I'll give you a grocery list. When do you want to do this?"

"As soon as we can arrange it." He put his hand over hers and squeezed her fingers. "Thank you. For everything."

Celeste stared into his dark brown eyes with their ridiculously long lashes. Warmth spread from the hand he placed on hers to the rest of her body. She wanted to stay like this, just being with him, touching him, all night.

No. It was dangerous to think that way. She wasn't ready. She might never be ready.

Extricating her fingers from beneath his, she picked up her tea with a trembling hand and made herself smile. "You're welcome."

Chapter Six

AT EXACTLY SEVEN O'CLOCK, Drew pulled up to the address in Minnewasta Celeste had given him. He knew he was at the right house when he saw a woman and a little girl walking away from the house. The girl was holding a sparkly pink gift bag and skipping alongside the woman while making excited gestures with her hands. *Good luck, Mom.* The child was likely hyped up on sugar and would be bouncing off the walls for a while.

Looked like Hope's friend's birthday party was a big success.

He walked to the front door and rang the bell. A large man wearing a white, faux-fur bunny suit, complete with enormous pink ears and giant feet, answered the door. Drew took a step back in surprise. "Ah...Hi. I'm here to pick up Hope?"

"And what's your name?" The bunny used his bulk to block the door.

"It's Drew. Drew Barnes."

The wide smile on the bunny's face made his fake whiskers twitch. "Good answer! Hope's mom told us she was sending you to pick her up."

"Right. Celeste and I both work at the lodge."

A much smaller woman came to stand beside the bunny. She put her hand on his arm. "Jack, quit blocking the door and invite Drew inside. It's cold out there!"

"Where are my manners? I'm Jack, Charlotte's dad, and this is my wife Daisy. Please come in and I'll call Hope."

Jack stepped aside to let Drew enter, then opened a door and called down the stairs. "Hope! Your ride is here!"

A moment later, Drew heard footsteps clambering up the stairs. Six little girls, including Hope, emerged through the basement door on a wave of giggles.

"Drew!" Hope vibrated with excitement, and likely an overdose of sugar. "We had so much fun!"

He couldn't help but grin at the exhilaration in her eyes. Seeing her so happy made him grateful he'd been able to convince Celeste to let him pick her up. "That's great. You can tell me all about it on the way home."

"Charlotte, help Hope find her jacket and make sure to give her a goody bag," Daisy said.

"Hop to it, girls!" Jack said.

All six girls bunny-hopped away, their high-pitched giggles bouncing off the walls. Daisy turned to him with a smile. "They had a lot of fun. Probably too much cake and way too many candies from the piñata, but lots of fun."

"Sounds like the party was a hit."

"I hope so. A little girl only turns ten once. We wanted to make it memorable."

Drew grinned at Jack. "I'm pretty sure they're going to remember this party."

"Hey, if a guy can't make a fool of himself at his daughter's tenth birthday party, when can he? The bunny suit isn't going to fly when she's fifteen."

"Probably not," Drew agreed with a laugh.

"Before Charlotte was born, if someone had told me I'd be wearing a giant bunny suit on her tenth birthday, I would have told them they were crazy. Turns out, you'll do just about anything for your kid."

Daisy put her arm around his padded waist and smiled up at him. "The kids loved it, especially Charlotte. Father of the year, right here."

The girls returned. Drew held Hope's goody bag in one hand and helped her into her coat with the other. After slipping on her winter boots, Hope turned to Charlotte's parents. "Thank you for inviting me."

"You are very welcome. It was a pleasure having you," Jack said. "Hop on over anytime!"

They said their goodbyes and made their way to Drew's car, Hope alternately skipping and running and twirling in circles. After buckling her into the front passenger seat, they headed back to the lodge.

"So you had fun?" Drew asked.

"So much fun! We played lots of games like pin the tail on the donkey and musical chairs and had prizes and everything. Charlotte's dad played some of the games with us, like Bingo. He taught us how to play five card stud, too. We bet with buttons, then we traded them in for jellybeans when the game was over."

"Interesting." Maybe he wouldn't mention to Celeste that the kids had been playing poker.

"Charlotte's dad is so much fun." Drew heard Hope emit a long sigh. "I wish I still had a dad. I was only three when mine died."

Drew's heart broke for her. "I'm sorry you lost him, Hope."

"I'm sorry, too. Mama likes to tell me stories about him. I think he would have been fun, like Charlotte's dad."

"I bet he would have been."

"I wish I could remember him better," she said quietly.

Drew didn't know what to say to that. It wasn't fair that a child should lose her father in a senseless accident. Hope was usually such a happy child, and Celeste such a wonderful mother, that it was easy to forget Hope had lost an important person in her life. And was missing him.

"I'm sure he loved you a lot," Drew said at last.

"That's what mama says."

"When someone loves you that much, they'll always be with you. So you'll never lose them, even if you can't quite remember them."

Hope turned to look at him. "You think so?"

Drew gave her a quick smile before turning his attention back to the road. "Yeah, I really do."

"EITHER I'M BLIND OR we're running out of strip loins steaks, Chef." Sue slammed the door of the cooler. "I can't find them anywhere."

"What? That can't be right," Maggie said. "Celeste, can you help Sue check the cooler? By my count, there should be one loin left."

Celeste wiped her hands on a towel. "Of course, chef."

Maggie liked to purchase the loin whole and cut it into steaks herself so she could control the size. It was a large chunk of meat, too big to be missed hiding behind a carton of milk. She and Sue took almost everything out of the commercial fridge, then double-checked the walk-in freezer to make sure it hadn't been put there by mistake, but the missing loin was just that—missing.

Celeste closed the door of the freezer. "I'm sorry, Maggie. There's no more strip loin."

"I don't understand." Maggie plated the two remaining steaks. "Did I cut the steaks too thick and use up all four loins without realizing?"

"I suppose it's possible." Celeste was doubtful. Maggie was very careful about portions and costs. She would have been very precise in the way she cut and weighed the meat. But she had no other answers.

"If we don't have any more steak, we have no more steak specials to offer. We'll need to come up with a different special," Maggie said. "Celeste, speak to the servers and tell them not to take any more orders for strip loin steak. We're going to use the veal I'd planned to have for tomorrow's special. Veal piccata. We can plate it up quickly and make it look and taste wonderful. Sue, bring out the veal from the cooler, and we'll start preparing it."

"Yes, chef," Celeste and Sue answered.

Celeste hurried off to speak to the servers and let them know about the change in the menu. When one of the servers asked what sides would accompany the veal dish, Celeste ran back to the kitchen to check with Maggie. On the fly, they decided to serve the piccata over pasta and use the asparagus they'd planned to serve with the steak as a side dish. She didn't know what they'd do with all the baked and mashed potatoes they'd already prepared and planned to serve with the steak.

But that was a problem for tomorrow. Right now, they needed to get through dinner.

Once she'd relayed all the information to the servers, Celeste returned to the kitchen and set to work. As Maggie sliced the veal into cutlets, she pounded them with a meat mallet until they were no more than a quarter inch thick. At this thickness they would fry up quickly—no more than three minutes in total. Orders soon began to come in for the piccata, and they struggled to keep up.

"Sue!" Maggie called. "Run to the bar and ask the bartender for a couple of bottles of his driest white. We need it for the sauce. Go!"

"Yes, chef!" Sue raced out of the kitchen.

The rest of the dinner rush flew by in a blur of activity. Celeste continued to cut and pound the veal while Maggie fried it and made the sauce. Sue and Barb, the other line cook, worked on the sides. Dinners were always busy, but they carefully prepared for them. They planned out menus and specials days ahead and prepped much of the food in advance so they weren't scrambling.

Finally, the rush died down and the last of the diners left the restaurant. Sue and Barb chopped leftover baked potatoes to make home fries for tomorrow's breakfast. The mashed potatoes would be made into soup for lunch the next day so they wouldn't go to waste. Celeste and Maggie brainstormed about tomorrow night's special. Only a tiny portion of the veal remained, so they'd need to come up with something else.

"Our butcher might have more veal to add to what we have left. We could do scallopini tomorrow," Celeste suggested.

"That's a possibility." Maggie paced in a tight circle in front of the grill. "But I think we'll have to go with something less expensive, like chicken or a cheaper cut of beef."

Celeste understood her reasoning. If the strip loin had been incorrectly cut, giving too much to each diner, they'd likely lost money on every meal. A snafu like this hadn't happened in the entire time Celeste had been at the lodge. It was out of character for the way Maggie ran her kitchen.

They all pitched in to clean the kitchen. When they were finished, Maggie thanked Sue and Barb for all their hard work this evening, hugging them both in turn. After they left, along with the dishwasher and the servers, Maggie leaned against the counter with her head bowed. "You should go home, too, Celeste."

"There's no rush. Mrs. Thompson is with Hope." Whenever she worked the dinner shift, she had a local woman stay with Hope from the time she came home from school until Celeste finished work. Mrs. Thompson had been with them for the last three years and Celeste didn't know how she'd manage without her, especially since she drove herself to the lodge and back home again. As an added bonus, Hope adored her.

Tonight's schedule was different since Hope was at her friend Charlotte's birthday party. Celeste asked Mrs. Thompson to come to their apartment around seven instead of her usual after school time. Drew had sent her a text around seven-thirty to let her know he'd dropped Hope safely at home.

Celeste was thankful to Drew for picking up Hope, but she was glad she'd been at work when he arrived at her apartment. She still felt unsettled from the last time she'd been with him. Despite restricting their contact to text messages the past few days, she couldn't stop thinking about him. And it scared her.

With an effort, Celeste pushed away thoughts of Drew. Right now, she needed to concentrate on her friend. "Are you okay?"

Maggie shook her head. "No, not really. How could I have made a mistake like that? I mean, to mismeasure so badly that I lost an entire loin? It's inexcusable."

"Don't be so hard on yourself." Celeste put her hand on Maggie's shoulder. "We should check your scales. Maybe they're not working properly."

Maggie looked skeptical. "Maybe."

Celeste put her arm around her and hugged. 'I've worked with you for three years and in all that time, you've had this kitchen running like a well-oiled machine. There has to be an explanation for what happened that was totally out of your control. I just feel it."

"I hope you're right." Maggie leaned her head against Celeste's shoulder. "I'm not looking forward to telling Luke what happened."

"He'll understand. He loves you."

"I know." Maggie straightened and stepped away from Celeste. "But if I wasn't married to the restaurant manager, if I was working in a kitchen that wasn't owned by my family, I'd likely be fired for messing up like this."

She was probably right. People were fired from kitchens for far less. She should know. But Maggie didn't need to hear that right now. "I still think there's another explanation. We'll figure out what really happened. You'll see."

Maggie tried to smile, but it didn't reach her worried eyes. "You're a good friend, Celeste. Thank you."

After everything Maggie had done for her and Hope, being a friend was the least she could do.

AFTER SEARCHING HARPER'S small office again for the missing purchase order, Drew came to the conclusion that he'd have to talk to Maggie. This time, he'd show her the invoice. Maybe seeing it would jog her memory and she'd be able to tell him why she hadn't created a purchase order when she ordered the goods.

Drew consulted the staff schedule and saw that Maggie would finish her shift at three today. He sent her a text asking to meet him in the restaurant at three-fifteen for a couple of quick accounting questions. When she responded she'd be there, he stuffed the invoice into a folder and made his way to the restaurant.

He'd just been served a cup of coffee when Maggie exited the kitchen and walked toward him. Drew rose to his feet.

"Thanks for meeting me. Would you like coffee?"

"Sure."

Drew signaled the server while Maggie sat across from him. The server set a cup in front of her and when she left, Maggie asked, "What can I do for you?"

He pulled the invoice from the folder and handed it to her. "I wanted to ask you about this. I mentioned a large order for flour and sugar to you previously, and you confirmed it, but I can't find any documentation that it was ever ordered or received." As she perused the invoice, saying nothing, anxiety made Drew's gut clench. "I'm probably being overly cautious, but it didn't feel right to pay this invoice before you actually looked at it."

Maggie looked up from the invoice, confusion in her eyes. "I didn't order this."

"What?"

"When you asked me about making a large order for baking supplies, I said yes because I did. But not from this company. We used to buy goods from them, but we got a better deal from our new supplier, so we switched."

"So you never received these supplies from this vendor?"

"No. I haven't ordered anything from them in over a year."

Drew sat back in his seat. "Are you sure?"

"Positive. You said you haven't paid this invoice, right?"

"Right. When I couldn't find documentation, I held back."

"Good thing you did." Maggie pulled out her phone. "I'm going to ask Luke to meet us here, if that's okay with you."

"Sure."

He sagged against his seat as Maggie sent her text. *What the hell was going on?*

Luke arrived a few minutes later and slid into the booth beside Maggie. "What's up?"

Maggie filled him in. "How did this happen?"

Luke turned to Drew. "Where did you find this invoice?"

"In Harper's desk drawer, inside a file called, 'To be paid.'"

"Good thing you questioned it. It's a lot of money." Luke gave him an approving nod. "The only thing I can think of is that Harper received this invoice and stuck it in her file, thinking it was legitimate. I've heard of invoice scams before. Bogus invoices are sent to companies. They look real, so sometimes people are taken in and they go ahead and pay them. I guess Harper was fooled."

Maggie frowned. "That doesn't sound like Harper."

"No, it doesn't, but look at this thing." Luke picked up the invoice once more. "It looks completely legit. They even use the name of a previous vendor of ours. It's not surprising that Harper got taken in."

"Don't you think it's suspicious that the scammers use the name of an actual former vendor of ours? I mean, what are the odds?" Drew asked.

"Scammers aren't stupid," Luke said. "Of course they'd use the name of a vendor in our industry. The fact that this is a business we've used in the past is likely a coincidence. If they'd sent us an invoice for car parts or something, Harper would have been immediately suspicious. But this thing got by her."

Drew felt compelled to come to Harper's defense. "She likely would have figured it out before she sent them a check."

"That's for sure," Maggie said with a smile. "Any time I've forgotten to create a purchase order in the past, she gave me the gears."

Drew wondered why Harper hadn't questioned Maggie this time. But then, with the complications in her pregnancy, her mind was likely elsewhere.

Luke's explanation made sense, but it still bothered him that the invoice had come from a vendor they'd used in the past. It could be coincidence, as Luke said.

Maybe *too* much coincidence?

Luke set the palms of his hands on the table. "So we're good? Mystery solved?"

"Yeah. I'm going to contact this vendor and let them know what happened. Maybe they had some kind of data breach."

"Sounds like a good idea." Luke got to his feet. "You ready to head home, sweetheart?"

Maggie rose. "I'm ready. See you later, Drew."

After they left, Drew tapped his fingers against the tabletop as he finished his coffee. Luke was probably right. Harper had been fooled by the realistic-looking fake invoice and stuck it in her folder. And since no money had changed hands, no real damage had been done.

But he couldn't shake the feeling something wasn't right.

Chapter Seven

DREW HAULED GROCERIES into the house and unloaded them into Harper's fridge and pantry. Dinner with Carrie and Ryan was arranged for tonight and he'd managed to find everything on Celeste's grocery list. He hadn't spoken to Celeste in person for a week, not since the previous Friday night when he'd last helped her study for her exam and tucked Hope into bed. Even though they worked in the same building, they'd communicated only by text and email all week. Celeste claimed to be too busy to study with him, as well. Her messages had been short and direct, without a single personal comment or question.

Had he done something to offend her? Was she angry with him?

The idea of Celeste being angry with him unsettled him. She was his friend, the one person here at the lodge he could really talk to. If he'd insulted her in some way, he was deeply sorry.

Not that he didn't have plenty to keep him busy this week. He'd contacted the vendor they'd received the fake invoice from and informed them what happened. It was the first they'd heard of such a thing happening, and they promised to check with their security people to see if there had been a data breach. Out of an abundance of caution,

Drew changed the password to the accounting system. When he let Ethan know of the change, he only told him it was good practice to change the password regularly. He didn't want to alarm his uncle. He had no proof there was a problem.

No way did he want to be in the middle of another large online security problem, and he sure as hell didn't want to be responsible for one again. He hoped he was overreacting.

He checked his watch; four-thirty. He'd arranged to pick up Celeste at the lodge at four forty-five so they could begin prepping dinner. Most days, Drew walked from the house to the lodge. It was a twenty-minute walk to the lodge through a trail in the forest. Drew wished he could walk the trail now. It was peaceful in the forest. The pine scented air calmed him and helped him think.

But Celeste was making a dessert at work for dinner tonight, so he wasn't going to make her carry it. Besides, she'd been on her feet working all day. She deserved five minutes of rest before he made her work again.

He shook his head as he closed the front door of the house behind him, disgusted with himself. No wonder she was annoyed with him. She'd worked all day and now he was expecting her to cook a special dinner for him.

Drew drove the short distance to the lodge. The front porch and lobby were now decorated for Thanksgiving with horns of plenty and colorful fall leaves. He'd have to tell Scarlet how lovely her decorations were.

As he walked by the restaurant, he noticed Ryan and Carrie having coffee at one of the tables near the entrance. Hope sat with them, drinking a soft drink through a straw.

"Do your legs hurt, Ryan?" Hope asked.

Drew stopped dead in his tracks at her innocent question. He ducked around a half wall, hoping he hadn't been seen. He wanted to hear the answer, too.

"No, they don't hurt. In fact, I can't feel anything at all. My spinal cord is damaged and that's why my legs don't work."

"Is it hard to push your wheelchair?"

"Sometimes I get tired," Ryan admitted. "See these? They're padded on the palms so I don't hurt my hands when I push my chair. But you know what? Pushing my chair helps keep me in shape and makes my heart strong. Ole Faithful is a good friend to me."

Ryan must have lifted his hands to show Hope the fingerless leather gloves he wore to protect his hands. Drew couldn't imagine how tough it must be to lose the ability to walk. And if those things he'd read about—incontinence and sexual dysfunction—were also true for Ryan, it was remarkable he could keep a positive outlook. Drew wasn't sure he could.

"Drew!"

He turned around to see his little cousin Tessa barreling toward him. When she reached him, he lifted her and swung her in the air before setting her back on her feet. They'd been greeting each other that way since she was two years old.

"Tessa, you're getting so big I can hardly lift you anymore. How old are you now, twenty?"

"No, silly. I'm only eight!" Tessa giggled. "Guess what? Hope is coming to my house for a sleepover tonight!"

"That's great. Have fun but try not to giggle too much. You two need to get some sleep."

Tessa responded with more giggles. "Okay."

Scarlet and Cam caught up with them, Cam holding their two-year-old son Jackson. He wriggled in his father's arms, trying to get to his big sister.

"Oh no you don't," Cam said with a smile. "We've already chased you half-way across the lodge."

Scarlet stepped up to Drew and kissed his cheek. "Hi, Drew. I hear you're hosting dinner tonight."

"I guess you could call it that, although it's not my house and I'm not doing any of the cooking. Celeste volunteered to help."

Scarlet shared a glance with Cam and turned back to him with a smile. "So I heard. Isn't that interesting."

Drew shrugged. "What's so interesting about it? I can't cook, so Celeste is helping me out." He didn't want them, or anyone else, to get any ideas about him and Celeste. He knew instinctively that Celeste wouldn't like anyone speculating about their relationship. Besides, after not speaking to him the last few days, he wasn't sure if they were even friends anymore.

The thought saddened him. And it confused him, too. What had he done?

Tessa tugged on Cam's arm. "Come on, Daddy. I see Hope in the restaurant with Carrie. Let's go!"

They walked around the half wall into the restaurant. When Hope saw Tessa, she ran toward her and they hugged and greeted each other with more giggles. Drew had to smile. Scarlet and Cam would have their hands full tonight.

Carrie rose to her feet as they approached their table. "Hi, Auntie Scarlet. Uncle Cam." She gave each of them a hug and then ruffled Jackson's hair. "And hello to you, too, little man." When Jackson reached for her, Carrie took him into her arms and kissed his cheek.

Cam leaned over the table to shake Ryan's hand. "Good to see you again, Ryan."

"Good to see you, too, sir."

"Remember I told you it's just Cam. No need to stand on ceremony."

Ryan smiled. "Okay. Cam."

After Scarlet greeted Ryan, Tessa tugged on her hand. "Can we go home now, Mommy?"

"As soon as Hope's mom brings her overnight bag we can go."

Right on cue, Celeste emerged from the kitchen carrying a cardboard bakery box and an overnight bag slung over her shoulder.

Drew hurried toward her and took the box. "I can carry that for you."

Celeste briefly lifted her gaze to his, then looked away. "Thanks."

They walked back to the rest of the group together. Celeste slipped the overnight bag from her shoulder and handed it to Cam. "Thanks for letting Hope stay with you tonight."

"It's our pleasure. The girls always have a lot of fun together," Scarlet said. "We'll bring Hope home right after lunch tomorrow, if that's okay."

"It's perfect." Celeste bent to hug Hope. "See you tomorrow, sweetheart. Be a good girl for Mr. Cam and Ms. Scarlet."

"I will, Mama."

With that, Scarlet and Cam said their goodbyes and left the restaurant, with Hope and Tessa skipping behind them.

Carrie turned to Celeste. "Is our special surprise in the box?"

"It is. I put the finishing touch on it after I finished my shift."

"What's the special surprise?" Drew asked.

Celeste smiled. "Well, it won't be much of a surprise if I tell you."

Her eyes sparkled with humor. Drew hoped it meant that whatever had been bothering her had passed.

"I can't keep a secret," Carrie blurted. She turned to Ryan. "You said it was your favorite dessert."

"Carrot cake with cream cheese frosting?" he asked.

"Yes! I made the cake and Celeste made the frosting. She makes the best cream cheese frosting. You're going to love it!"

"I know I will. Thank you, Carrie." He held Carrie's hand and smiled into her eyes.

Once again, Drew had the uncomfortable feeling that Carrie was in over her head with Ryan. He cleared his throat. "Celeste and I will head over to the house now and start prepping for dinner. Why don't you join us in about an hour? We can have a glass of wine before dinner." He turned abruptly to Celeste, suddenly aware he hadn't asked her how much time she needed to prep. "Is that okay with you?"

"Yes, it's perfect."

Again, she smiled briefly before glancing away. For one second, he wished Celeste would look at him the way Carrie looked at Ryan.

Where had that thought come from? He needed to get a grip.

"All right. We'll see you two in about an hour."

Drew walked silently beside Celeste as they made their way to his car. He struggled to come up with something to say that didn't sound stupid or banal. What he really wanted to ask was if they were still friends.

Finally, Celeste broke the silence. "Were you able to get everything on my grocery list?"

"Yes. At least I think so. You can look things over when we get to the house. If you don't like something I bought, I can run into town and get something else."

"I'm sure it'll be fine, Drew."

"Okay." He hoped that was true. The last thing he wanted was to disappoint Celeste.

Fat flakes of snow began to fall. Celeste held out her hand and let the snowflakes melt on her bare palm, a look of wonder on her face.

"It's like being in a snow globe." She tipped her head skyward and smiled. "I love the first snow. It always feels like magic."

"It kind of loses its charm after the thirtieth snowfall in January." Drew unlocked the car and set the cake box on the back seat. "The weather must have been a shock to you when you first came to Minnesota."

"It was." Celeste slid into the passenger seat. "It was so cold the day Hope and I arrived. I was afraid I'd made a huge mistake. But Maggie and Luke were so kind to us. They even brought us parkas to wear that first day. I knew then I'd made the right decision in trusting them. I've never regretted it."

"What made you decide to take the job at the lodge?"

Her smile disappeared. "The usual thing. I needed a job, and Maggie offered me one."

Drew was certain there was much more to the story, but he didn't push. "Do you ever miss South Carolina?"

"Sure, sometimes. My family is there. And I have to admit that when it's twenty below here, I dream about warm ocean breezes."

"So do I, and I was born in Minnesota."

Celeste chuckled. "Glad I'm not the only one."

Drew put the car in gear and drove out of the parking lot and onto the main road. It occurred to him that work was the only thing keeping her in Minnesota. He knew she liked her job, her apartment and the people she worked with, but the lodge couldn't compete with the pull of family. If a good job in Myrtle Beach presented itself, would she go?

The idea of Celeste leaving gave him an empty feeling in the pit of his stomach. Though he'd known of her the last three years, they'd only become friends in the last few weeks. She had to do what was best for her and her daughter. His feelings didn't fit into the equation.

Still, he hoped she'd stay. Maybe learning to drive would help to keep her here.

They arrived at the house a few minutes later. So far, the snow was melting as it landed, but the temperature was dropping. There could be a thick layer of snow on the ground by morning. Would the slippery, snow-covered roads scare Celeste and keep her from practicing her driving? How would she ever get her driver's license if she never actually drove?

Stop. He had to quit worrying about the future and to try to enjoy his time with Celeste today.

As soon as she arrived in Harper's spacious kitchen, Celeste set to work. She filleted the fresh whole salmon that she'd had him purchase, not an easy find in November in Minnesota. He'd gone to several stores in Brainerd and was contemplating a trip to Minneapolis when he finally found a shop that carried fresh salmon.

"How can I help?" he asked.

"You can start prepping the Tabbouleh salad. Give the tomatoes a good wash and then cut them into quarters. After that you can slice the red onion and halve the olives."

Drew carried out her instructions while she got the fish ready and put water on to boil for the bulger. They stood side by side at the double sink washing salad greens and mushrooms, and snapping the woody ends from the asparagus.

"Are you nervous about this dinner?" Celeste asked.

"Yeah," Drew admitted. "Nervous, excited, worried. I honestly want to like Ryan. I want to believe he has Carrie's best interests at heart and that he wants her to be happy. But what if I say the wrong thing? Carrie is sensitive about everything I say, and she's very protective of him."

"She is. She's a woman in love, Drew. To her, Ryan is perfect and you're not going to convince her otherwise. You have to let her make her own decisions about him."

"She's too young to be in love." Drew twisted an asparagus spear in half, sending the tip flying across the counter.

"No, she's not. Don't say something like that to her unless you want her to get her back up." Celeste handed the asparagus back to him with a smile. "For tonight, just enjoy having a nice meal with your sister and her friend and don't worry about the future. Try to get to know Ryan. I think you'll be happy with what you find."

"I hope so." The idea of someone taking advantage of Carrie caused a ball of anger to form in his gut. He tried to concentrate on Celeste's words and hoped she was right about Ryan.

When they were done getting the vegetables ready, Celeste dried her hands on a towel. "I'll mix the dressing for the salad and put together the mushroom appetizers. If you get out water glasses and utensils for three, I'll help you set the table."

"What do you mean for three? There's four of us."

"I'm going to head home as soon as I plate your dinners and bring them to the table."

"Why do you have to leave?" Drew panicked at the thought of her going. "There's plenty of food, and Hope's at a sleepover so you don't have to hurry home. Besides, it's dark and cold out there. You shouldn't be walking at night by yourself."

"I'll use the flashlight on my phone. I'll be fine." She took the boiling water off the stove, added a cup of bulger and set it to one side. "This is a family dinner, Drew."

"Ryan's not family."

"Carrie doesn't feel that way. I'll only be in the way. I should go."

"You can't go," he blurted. "I need you."

Celeste stared at him, her eyes wide in surprise. Drew stared back. His words hung between them as if carved into the air. He hadn't consciously intended to say them. Hell, he hadn't even known he'd meant them.

But now that they were out there, he realized he did.

She looked away, turning the handle of the bulger pot one way and then the other. "If you're feeling that uncomfortable, I guess I could stay. For moral support."

"Yeah." Relief flooded over Drew. "For moral support."

"All right." Celeste gave him a half-smile. "You can bring out four place settings. Leave the plates here by the stove."

Drew grabbed four water glasses from the cupboard before she could change her mind.

Celeste prepared the dressing for the salad and stuffed mushroom caps with the bread crumb and cheese mixture she'd made. Then she helped him with the table. She found a tablecloth and some placemats in the dining room buffet that made the table look festive and pretty. She even moved the candleholders with their long tapers from the fireplace mantle onto the table.

"Don't forget to remove that chair for Ryan," Celeste said. Drew set one of the chairs to the side of the room. He didn't want to draw attention to Ryan's disability by having to move a chair in his, and Carrie's, presence. The reality of having a disability such as Ryan's was hard to ignore. But for tonight, he was going to try to get to know Ryan as a person, not as someone with a disability.

"This looks beautiful," Drew said as he lit the candles with a wooden match from the fireplace. "Thank you."

She smiled. "You're welcome."

He loved her smile. When Celeste smiled, her face lit up. He stared into her eyes, their dark brown depths pulling him in. Neither of them moved, or even breathed. Did she realize how beautiful she was? Perfect oval face, gorgeous almond-shaped eyes, lovely coffee colored skin. He couldn't look away.

The doorbell rang, breaking the spell.

Celeste looked away, gesturing toward the door. "They're here. Remember. Open mind. Get to know Ryan."

"Got it." He vowed not to let either Carrie or Celeste down.

"Hello! We're here!"

Before Drew even said hello, Ryan had grabbed hold of the door frame, tipped his chair back and boosted himself over the threshold of the front door and into the foyer.

"I'll put the ramp on the front porch under cover so it doesn't get slippery. It's really snowing out there right now," Carrie said.

"What ramp?" Drew asked.

"I have a portable six-foot aluminum ramp that I keep in my truck," Ryan said. "It folds up like a suitcase and I can use it in a lot of places that don't have permanent ramps."

Drew hadn't even considered the accessibility of the house. "I'll give you a hand, Carrie."

As he grabbed his jacket from a hook near the front door, he heard Celeste speaking to Ryan. "I'll take your coat and then we can warm up by the fire."

By the time he got outside, Carrie had already folded the ramp in half. "It's not very heavy, so I have no trouble handling it. Comes in handy for situations like this."

Drew clicked the locks on the sides of the ramp to keep it folded securely together and then used the handle to carry it up the two front porch stairs. He propped it against the wall near the door under the covered porch where the snow couldn't reach it. "What happens if there's more than two stairs? Wouldn't this ramp be too steep?"

"Yeah, possibly," Carrie agreed. "In situations where there's no permanent ramp and Ryan's ramp won't work, we usually just don't go in. If a business can't be bothered to be accessible, then we can't be bothered to spend money there."

Drew still had questions. What if the building contained a business Ryan really needed to visit? If Carrie and Ryan stayed together, would she be lugging around that ramp for the rest of her life? Why should her life be limited because of Ryan's disability? Did she know what she was getting into?

He kept his thoughts to himself. He promised Celeste and Carrie that tonight was for getting to know Ryan, and that's what he intended to do.

But he couldn't stop worrying.

Drew followed Carrie inside, and they hung their coats at the front door. He heard Ryan's deep voice and the sound of Celeste's laughter. Her melodic laughter eased Drew's mind. He was grateful and relieved she'd stayed.

When they entered the living room, Celeste and Ryan were sitting near the fire, each holding a wine glass.

"You're starting without us!" Carrie said with a laugh. She went over to Ryan and dropped a casual kiss on the top of his head.

He smiled up at her. "I can't help it if you're a slow poke."

"Carrie, would you like white wine, too, or do you prefer something else?" Drew asked.

"Wine will be great, thanks."

Drew made his way to the kitchen on the other side of the house. The short walk gave him the opportunity to collect his thoughts. He pulled the wine from the fridge door and set it on the counter. Seeing Carrie and Ryan's casual affection and the way they looked at each other worried him. Ryan seemed like an upstanding guy, but did that make him right for Carrie?

Taking a deep breath, he pulled two wineglasses from the cupboard. As he was pouring the wine, Celeste entered.

"I'm going to heat the appetizers." She pulled the tray of mushroom caps from the fridge and popped them into the preheated oven. After adjusting the timer, she turned to look at him, her head tilted to one side. "You okay?"

He stood a little straighter, not wanting her to guess the direction of his thoughts. "Of course."

"You've got this, Drew."

"Thanks." Knowing Celeste believed in him calmed his nerves.

He made his way back to the living room with the wine and handed one of the glasses to Carrie. When Celeste rejoined them, he lifted his glass. "To new friends."

The others lifted their glasses in response. "To new friends."

"Are you going home for Christmas, Ryan?" Celeste asked. "Carrie told me you're from Indiana."

"Yeah, from a small town outside of Indianapolis," Ryan replied. "I'm going to visit my family at Thanksgiving, but I plan to stay here in Minnesota for Christmas. What about you? I hear you're from South Carolina."

"I am," Celeste replied. "I'm trying to convince my mother to come to the lodge for Christmas."

"Speaking of Christmas," Carrie said, turning to Drew. "Ryan and I video chatted with Mom and Dad the other day, and they plan to come to the Mistletoe Ball."

Ryan reached for Carrie's hand. "We took your advice, Drew. We told them about our age difference and my disability. I don't want to hide anything from them."

"I'm glad you talked to them."

Drew imagined his parents' decision to come to the party was prompted by their announcement that they were a couple. They'd want to meet Ryan and find out more about him. They were likely as concerned as he was about Carrie's future.

"Mom and Dad want us to come home for Thanksgiving, too. I'm off from Wednesday to Friday. How about you?"

Drew glanced at Celeste. He didn't like the idea of leaving her and Hope alone for the holiday, but he couldn't put off his parents either.

Celeste smiled at him. "Cheryl invited Hope and me to her house for Thanksgiving. Maggie's giving us the day off since the restaurant is closed that day, and Cheryl said her husband would even pick us up. Wasn't that nice of them?"

"Very nice." It was uncanny how she could read his mind. She knew he'd be reluctant to leave unless they had other plans. He turned to Carrie. "Tell Mom she better make my favorite pumpkin pie. We can drive together to Minneapolis."

"Great," Carrie said. "I'll let her know."

Celeste excused herself to get the appetizers from the kitchen and returned with a tray bearing the hot mushroom caps along with plates and napkins and the wine. Drew refilled their glasses, except for Ryan's, who declined because he was driving. As they ate, the conversation turned to the weather and the snow.

"I hope this snow doesn't stick around," Carrie said. "I hate driving in the snow."

"I'm afraid of driving in the snow, too." Celeste gave a worried frown. "Not that I've ever done it. But I'm writing my learner's exam next Thursday so someday I'll have to tackle winter driving."

"Good luck on your test," Ryan said, raising his empty glass to her.

Celeste returned the salute with a smile. "Thanks."

"She's going to ace the exam," Drew told them. "She knows the material cold. She's so confident, she's already picked out the car she wants to buy."

"I'm not worried about the written exam, but the road test scares me. I've never driven before."

Ryan blinked at her. "Never?"

"Never." She told him her story about growing up without a car.

"You're going to do great." Drew tried to give her a reassuring smile. "We won't practice on the snowiest days, and if you decide to wait till spring to start your driving lessons, that's okay, too."

She frowned. "I can't wait till spring. You'll be gone by then, won't you?"

Drew realized with a start that she was right. He'd never intended to stay at the lodge past Christmas. But now he wasn't so sure what he wanted. All he knew was that leaving Celeste in the lurch didn't feel right.

In fact, it felt very, very wrong.

"Yeah. Right. I'll be gone."

"We'll figure something out." Celeste smiled and got to her feet. "I think it's time to put the salmon on. Is everyone hungry?"

"Starved," Ryan said.

Carrie laughed. "You're always hungry."

"Good. I like a hungry crowd." Celeste gathered the dishes. "Why don't y'all keep me company?"

In the kitchen, she heated olive oil in a large non-stick frying pan. While it heated, she seasoned the salmon fillet with salt and freshly ground black pepper.

"Can I help, Celeste?" Carrie asked.

"No, I've got this. You sit back and relax tonight, sweetie. Drew, get this lady another glass of wine."

Carrie laughed as Drew pulled another wine glass from a cupboard and poured the last of the wine in it. "I could get used to being pampered like this."

Drew poured club soda over ice for Ryan while Celeste heated another pan to sauté the asparagus.

Carrie saluted her with her glass from her perch on a stool at the island. "Watching you work is efficiency in motion, Celeste. I want to be like you when I grow up."

Celeste laughed as she measured butter into the second pan. "Be careful what you wish for."

Carrie was right. Celeste was efficient, precise and no movement was wasted. She placed the salmon fillets, skin side up in one pan and the asparagus into the second pan. She turned the asparagus several times with her tongs, and when they were shiny with oil, she covered the pan with a lid. Then she turned her attention back to the salmon and turned the fillets, revealing a perfectly golden-brown exterior.

"That smells amazing," Ryan said.

"Thank you. I've always believed the eating experience should engage all the senses, not just the taste buds." She removed the lid from the asparagus, adjusted the temperature and turned the spears with her tongs. "Drew, can you bring the salad from the fridge? And a lemon?"

He brought her the bowl and a lemon, and she set the four plates beside the stovetop. "Cut that lemon into quarters, please."

"Yes, ma'am."

By the time he'd finished quartering the lemon, Celeste had divided the bulger and salad greens between the four plates, placed perfectly cooked salmon fillets on top the bulgar and added the asparagus spears. After setting a piece of lemon next to the salmon, she looked up with a smile. "Dinner is served. Let's take the plates to the dining room."

In the dining room, they dug into the delicious food. Celeste smiled at the praise the others lavished on her.

"This is wonderful, Celeste. It was amazing how you got everything to be ready at the same time," Carrie said. "I still have trouble with that."

Celeste shrugged. "You'll get it. I've just had more practice than you, that's all. You're going to be an amazing chef. You've learned so much the last few months."

"And you'll learn even more at culinary school," Drew added.

Carrie put her head down and stabbed at an asparagus spear. "I told you I haven't decided about school yet."

Drew set down his fork. "What's to decide? If you want to be a chef, you have to go to the culinary school in St. Paul."

"It's my decision, not yours." Carrie lifted her chin, a sure sign she was going to be stubborn.

Ryan reached for her free hand. "Your brother's right, Carrie. You need to go to school."

"But I don't want to leave you."

"I know," he said gently. "I don't want to leave you either, but it's not forever. We'll still see and talk to each other while you're in school."

Carrie acknowledged his words with a nod, but her frown told Drew she wasn't happy. It also told him how much influence Ryan had over his little sister. Ryan let go of her hand with a smile and they resumed eating.

Drew decided to steer clear of controversial subjects. "So, how did you come to work for Jerry Fields, Ryan?"

"I've always been something of a computer geek," Ryan said. "After my injury, I started looking for a new occupation. I stumbled upon a coding class and after that, I wanted to learn more. I went back to school in Indiana and became certified in network security. About the same time I finished school, Jerry was looking for help with his business. It had grown to the point where he couldn't handle it on his own anymore. I saw his ad and applied for the job. When we discovered we were both veterans, working together seemed like a natural fit. I haven't regretted moving to Minnesota for a minute."

Drew couldn't imagine how difficult it must have been to go from being able to use his body any way he wanted, to being confined to a wheelchair. Ryan had to reconstruct his life and start all over again. Drew admired the grace with which he'd made the change.

"I noticed your truck out there. It looks like a pretty sweet ride."

Ryan grinned. "Thanks. It's my pride and joy. It's changed my life since I got it."

"How do you mean?" Celeste asked.

Ryan turned to her. "Because it's made in such a way that I don't need my legs to drive it. It's all hand controls. The best thing is that the driver's seat swings out and lowers so I can easily slide into it. There's a lift in the truck bed that picks up my chair and secures it in the back."

"That sounds ingenious," Celeste said.

"It is. The first vehicle I bought after my injury was a car that had been retrofitted with hand controls. Up until a few years ago, a modified vehicle was the only option for a disabled person. I figured out how to slide myself into the driver's seat, but the problem was never about getting into the car and learning to drive it with the hand controls."

"What do you mean?" Celeste asked. Drew wanted to know the answer to that question, too.

"The real problem is transporting my chair with me. Unless I only plan to go to a drive-thru and never get out of my car, I had to figure out a way of bringing my chair with me once I was already in the driver's seat. Otherwise, I had no way of being mobile and independent."

Celeste nodded, and Drew knew she identified with Ryan's need for independence. "So, how did you manage to get your wheelchair in the car?"

"Fortunately, my chair's lightweight and small, and it comes apart easily. From the driver's seat, I was able to take off the wheels, and put them in the back seat. Then it was a matter of setting the cage beside me on the passenger seat. I had just enough room to get it over me and the steering wheel."

"And then, when you got to wherever you wanted to go, you had to put your chair back together again?"

"Exactly, only this time I went in reverse order."

"Wow." Celeste sat back in her seat. "And I thought *I* had problems learning to drive. You put me to shame."

"Your problems are as relevant to you as mine were to me. Everyone faces some kind of obstacle in getting what they want," Ryan told her. "Just know it can be done. If I can do it, so can you."

She smiled at him and lifted her wineglass in a silent salute. Drew was impressed, too. Ryan had amazing determination.

Celeste got to her feet. "Carrie, can you help me with dessert?"

"Of course." She put her hand on Ryan's shoulder as she rose. "Your favorite. The carrot cake."

He covered her hand with his and smiled up at her. "Can't wait."

They gathered the empty plates and went into the kitchen. Drew sipped his wine and contemplated the man across the table from him. He was beginning to see why everyone at the lodge sang his praises.

"Do you plan to stay in Minnewasta?" Drew had heard that Ryan was currently renting a house there.

"I don't have any immediate plans to move," Ryan said. "Aside from some of the things I do onsite at the lodge, most of my work can be done from any location as long as I have a good internet connection."

"So then why did you move to Minnesota instead of staying in Indiana? Did Jerry want to keep tabs on you?"

Ryan shook his head. "No, nothing like that. Jerry gave me the choice. I could have stayed in Indiana close to my parents and siblings and worked from there, but I needed to make my own way. I love my family, but after my injury, they smothered me with kindness. They wanted to do everything for me, to make my life easier. I know they did it out of love, but I had to learn how to live in this body as an independent, productive person."

Drew could respect that.

And he could respect Ryan. But he still didn't know if that made him right for his baby sister.

Carrie returned to the dining room with four plates of carrot cake on a tray, followed by Celeste with a carafe of coffee. Carrie set one of the plates in front of Ryan.

"There you go. Enjoy."

They shared a smile as he looked up at her. "Thank you. It looks amazing."

After passing out the cake and pouring coffee, Celeste and Carrie sat once more. Carrie pointed her fork at Drew. "You should see Ryan's new truck in action. It's awesome."

Drew swallowed a bite of his cake. He'd seen the truck outside when he'd helped Carrie fold the ramp. To his untrained eye, it looked like any other pickup truck made by that company. "Yeah, I'd like to see that."

"It's an amazing piece of engineering," Ryan said.

"For the price they charge, it better be amazing engineering." Carrie turned to Drew. "It was twice as much as the regular model. You'd think the government or the manufacturer would do something to make vehicles like this more affordable. A lot of people could gain their independence with a truck like this, but they're simply too expensive."

More affordable. Too expensive. Drew stopped eating and set his fork on the table.

In the end, it all came down to money. He swallowed a profound sense of disappointment. "Ryan, has Carrie told you much about our family?"

Ryan took a sip of his coffee before speaking. "Yes, some. You two grew up in Minneapolis and your folks are accountants and financial planners. Your mom has two younger brothers and your dad is an only child."

"Right. Did she tell you about Ethan?"

On his right, he heard Celeste's softly spoken, "Drew, don't." But he ignored her.

"You mean your Uncle Ethan? Sure, he owns the lodge." Ryan swept out his hand to encompass the room. "And this house."

"That's right. But did she tell you how Ethan came to own the lodge?"

Carrie's fork clattered against her plate. "What are you doing, Drew?"

Ryan put his hand over hers. "It's okay, sweetheart." He faced Drew once more. "Yes, Carrie told me about Ethan's lottery win and how he was able to rebuild the lodge."

"Money like that would make your life a lot easier," Drew said.

Ryan lifted his chin. "Money like that would make anyone's life a lot easier. But it has nothing to do with me. I've always worked for whatever I got, including that truck outside. I'll always work hard. That's one thing that didn't change when I lost the use of my legs. If you think the only reason I want to be with Carrie is because I believe I'll somehow get money out of Ethan, you're selling your sister very short." He released the brakes on his chair and pushed away from the table." I think I should go. Thank you for dinner, Celeste."

Carrie got up and followed him. "I'm not sure you could be more insulting, Drew. To me or to Ryan."

"Where are you going?"

"I'm going with Ryan. I sure as hell don't want to stay here with you."

Celeste rose and followed them to the front door. Drew heard their muffled voices as they put on their coats in the foyer. A moment later, he heard the door open and close.

Celeste returned to the dining room and sat beside him. "Carrie was very upset and I can't blame her. You basically told her the only reason Ryan would want to spend time with her was because of Ethan's money."

"That's not what I meant. You know that's not what I meant." He exploded out of his chair, knocking it to the floor. "Damn it, I only want to protect her."

"I know you do," she said quietly. "But all you're succeeding in doing is pushing her away."

Drew groaned and threw back his head. She was right. How had it gone so wrong so quickly? "I'm sorry. I shouldn't have yelled at you."

"It's all right. I understand."

"You're being too nice. The least you could do is tell me what a jerk I am."

She grinned. "Okay. You're a jerk. Feel better now?"

"Yeah. Much." Drew picked up his chair and slid it under the table. "Carrie's never going to forgive me. And Ryan, I'm sure he hates me."

Celeste got to her feet to face him. "Maybe with time, and a sincere apology, they'll get over it."

"Maybe."

He'd insulted Ryan's integrity, his honor. And he'd basically told Carrie she wasn't worth being with unless the promise of their uncle's money was dangled in front of a potential boyfriend.

He'd completely mishandled the situation. He should have been more subtle. He should have pointed out gradually to Carrie that her relationship with Ryan was a mistake, that the reality of living with Ryan's disability was more than she could handle.

Instead, he was abrupt and rude and had driven her directly into Ryan's arms. For that, he was very sorry.

"But it has to be a sincere apology, from your heart," she said. "Can you honestly say you believe Ryan is with Carrie because he cares about her and has her best interests at heart?"

When he hesitated, Celeste shook her head. "That's what I thought. You have no control over what they feel for each other. The heart wants what the heart wants. The more you fight against it, the stronger the feelings get."

Her dark eyes brimmed with emotion as she looked up at him. And suddenly it didn't matter that she'd been married before and had a child. Or that she was nine years older. Nothing mattered but Celeste.

The heart wants what the heart wants.

He pulled her against him, his mouth descending swiftly on hers. At first he read her surprise, but then she relaxed against him on a sigh and gave herself over to the kiss.

Drew lost control. He ravaged her mouth, his tongue sweeping hers over and over, the sweet taste of icing intoxicating him. She responded just as wildly, with thrusts of her own. Her hands wound around his neck, her questing fingers diving through his hair. But when he pulled her more tightly against him, and let her feel the evidence of his arousal, she pulled away.

The shock on her face told him he'd made a terrible mistake. "Celeste, I'm sorry."

She backed away and waved her hand, her gaze not meeting his. "I...I need to go home. I'll get my coat."

"I'll drive you."

"No, that's fine. I can walk."

"There's no way I'm letting you walk alone. It's cold and dark and it's snowing. If anything happened to you...I'm driving you."

Celeste looked up at him, her eyes bleak. He'd taken advantage of their friendship and manhandled her like a randy teenager. No wonder she was upset.

"I guess you're right." Her voice was heavy with resignation.

Silently, they put on their coats and headed outside to Drew's car. The temperature had plummeted and snow had begun to accumulate. Once inside the car, he turned on the heater and the seat warmers, and pulled out of the driveway.

The five-minute drive to the lodge was the longest of Drew's life. The silence inside the car was deafening. He didn't know what to say or do to make it up to her. He'd let his emotions, and pure lust, get away from him. He couldn't even say he understood exactly what happened.

All he knew was that Celeste was so beautiful and so completely appealing. When she'd looked up at him, her eyes shining with honesty, something had come over him. Something he was unable to resist.

He should have been able to control himself. Celeste was his friend. God, he was such an ass.

He brought the car to a stop next to the stairs leading up to her apartment. As she opened her door, he placed his hand on her arm, stopping her. "Celeste, I'm sorry."

She nodded, her forehead wrinkling with her frown. "I know. I'm sorry, too. But right now, I need to go home."

He removed his arm, and she got out of the car. Was this the end of their friendship?

Before closing the passenger door, she leaned inside to look at him. "I'll call you tomorrow, and we can talk."

His heart lifted. At least she didn't want to cut him off completely. At his nod, she shut the door. Drew waited until he saw her unlock the door and go inside the covered staircase before he drove away.

As he cleaned up and put leftover cake away, he wondered how he'd managed to so thoroughly mess things up this evening. And he wondered what Celeste would say to him tomorrow. He only hoped she wouldn't say she never wanted to see him again.

Chapter Eight

CELESTE PACED THE FLOORS of her apartment, her phone in her hand. Her mostly sleepless night made concentration difficult. She needed to call Drew before Scarlet and Cam brought Hope home from her sleepover, but she couldn't find the words to explain.

She didn't even know what she wanted to explain. Did she want to justify her enthusiastic response to his kiss, or the abrupt way she ended it? The truth was she couldn't account for either of her reactions to his kiss.

His kiss. Oh God, *his kiss.* It was tender and wild, passionate and arousing, all at the same time. She hadn't been kissed like that in a very long time. Not since...

Not since Easton.

She couldn't let Drew think anything could come of that kiss. There were too many differences between them. She was nine years older, for God's sake. She'd been married, she had a child. She had to think about Hope. Her daughter had to be her first priority.

And they weren't of the same race. It didn't matter to most people, but it did to some. The difference in the color of her parents' skin had caused most of the strife in their marriage, and she wouldn't subject Hope to that. She knew how hurtful it could be.

Satisfied she'd finally screwed her head on straight, Celeste hit Drew's number on her phone.

He picked up immediately. "Celeste. Hi."

The way he said her name, his voice deep and rich, felt like a caress. For a moment, Celeste lost her train of thought, and almost lost her resolve. Then she cleared her throat and pulled herself together. "Hi Drew. Listen, about last night. We were both feeling emotional because of what happened with Carrie and Ryan and things got away from us. Let's just forget it happened, okay?"

She clutched the phone as she waited for him to speak. After a pause, she heard him expel a breath. "If that's what you want."

She inhaled, relieved. "Yes, I think it's best for both of us if we can just remain friends."

"Your friendship means a lot to me, Celeste. I don't want to lose it."

"Your friendship means a lot to me, too." She was only beginning to realize how *much* it meant to her. The prospect of losing him frightened her. She quickly changed the subject. "So, have you talked to Carrie?"

She heard his frustrated sigh. "No. She's here at the lodge. I've texted her and apologized, but she hasn't responded."

"Give her some time. She was very upset."

"Yeah, well, patience isn't one of my virtues."

Celeste smiled at that. "You have other virtues." *Like the way you kiss.*

"Damned if I can think of any at the moment," he said. "Your exam is next week. Do you still want me to drive you to Brainerd?"

"Yes, please. I'll be ready to leave at two. Cheryl said she could come in an hour earlier on Thursday."

"Do you want to squeeze in one last study session before then?" he asked.

Celeste hesitated. Perhaps being alone in her apartment with Drew wasn't such a good idea. She wasn't sure she could trust herself. "Thanks, but I think I'm good. I've practically memorized the manual."

"Okay, then I'll talk to you on Thursday. Come to my office when you're finished work. I'll be ready to go."

"I really appreciate all your help, Drew. I'll talk to you later."

"Celeste?"

"Yes?"

"Thank you."

"For what?"

"For not being angry with me. I'd never do anything to hurt you. I hope you know that."

Emotion clogged Celeste's throat, making it difficult to speak. "I know. I have to go."

"Bye."

She stabbed at the button to end the call, her eyes filling with tears. Why was she crying?

She closed her eyes and concentrated on her breathing, counting the inhales and exhales until her heartrate slowed and she felt more in control. As she opened her eyes, a new resolve steadied her. They could never be more than friends, and she certainly couldn't kiss him again. She was far too old, and had too much pride, to make a fool of herself over him.

Celeste pushed aside the sense of loss. It simply wasn't meant to be.

WHEN DREW ENTERED THE house after work, the lights were on and sounds of dishes rattling came from the kitchen. He breathed a sigh of relief that Carrie had come home. She'd stayed away last night, and he assumed she'd gone home with Ryan.

He was such an idiot. He'd only succeeded in pushing her closer to Ryan. His first order of business was to apologize. Once they were on solid ground again, he could talk to her about Ryan and try to persuade her to see other people.

Carrie was busy making some kind of stir fry on the range and didn't look up as he entered the kitchen. It was going to be up to him to make the first move.

"I'm sorry, Carrie," he said. "What I said to Ryan was uncalled for."

"Yes, it was." She still didn't look at him.

"What I implied about you was even worse. You are a wonderful, beautiful girl. Any man would be lucky to call you his girlfriend."

"I'm only interested in one man calling me his girlfriend."

She wasn't making this apology easy. "In my defense, I'm worried about you. I don't want anyone to take advantage of you."

Carrie finally lifted her head and looked at him. "I keep telling you, Ryan's not like that. He's an honorable man, and he would never hurt me. If you'd bothered to get to know him instead of automatically judging him, you'd know that."

"You're right. I need to get to know him."

Carrie frowned. "You're going to have to apologize first. He tried not to show it, but he was really upset that you questioned his integrity."

"Yeah." Drew sat on one of the stools at the island. "But first things first. Do you forgive me?"

She rolled her eyes. "Of course I forgive you, you dork. You're my brother. I think forgiveness is baked into the genetic code."

Drew grinned at that. "Good." He sobered. "Now how do I apologize to Ryan?"

Carrie turned off the stove and set the stir fry pan to one side before reaching into her back pocket for her phone. "We'll give him a call right now. Okay?"

"Okay." Nerves danced in his gut. This wasn't going to be easy but at least Carrie was on his side.

Carrie hit Ryan's number and put the phone on speaker. He answered after a couple of rings. "Hey, baby. How you doing?"

"I'm great, Ryan. I'm here with Drew. He has something he wants to say to you."

She stuck the phone under his nose and looked at him with lifted eyebrows.

"Hi Ryan." Drew hesitated, trying to sort through his thoughts. "I'm sorry for what I said last night. It was uncalled for. Carrie says you're a man of honor, and I believe her. She knows you better than anyone."

"Yeah, she does," Ryan said.

He had to come clean and tell the whole story because he could sense that Ryan wasn't going to give his forgiveness easily. "I admit I'm paranoid when it comes to money. It goes back to when Ethan first won the lottery. Do you remember, Carrie?"

"Sure, I remember. It was exciting."

"It was, but it also got scary. When people found out about Ethan's big win, they started coming out of the woodwork. Everyone wanted a piece of the pie and some would do anything to get it."

"What do you mean?" Ryan asked.

"One of Ethan's former friends had a drug problem. When Ethan refused to give him money to feed his addiction, he threatened him. Ethan was worried enough that he went to the police. They discovered he'd been stalking Carrie and me, following us to school and other activities. When the police questioned him, he confessed he'd been planning to kidnap Carrie and hold her for ransom until Ethan gave him money. He figured Carrie, being only twelve at the time, would be easier to snatch than me."

"Oh, my God!" Carrie's eyes were wide with shock. "Why didn't anyone ever tell me this?"

"Mom and Dad didn't want to scare you," Drew replied. "They told me because I was already driving and out and about more than you. They wanted me to be careful. It scared the crap out of me."

She shook her head. "All I remember is that Mom and Dad made me change schools, and I was so angry I had to leave my friends."

"Yeah. They sent us both to a private school with better security. After that, everyone in the family took security far more seriously. Mom and Dad created the foundation to look after Ethan's money, so that anyone who wanted money from Ethan had to go through them first. These days, a recipient better have a damn good cause if they expect to get a dime out of the Hainstock Foundation."

The Foundation had given millions of dollars to a variety of charities and worthy causes over the years. Drew's parents and the rest of the board of directors were diligent in following up on their donations. They made sure the money went where the charity said it was going to go.

"I guess I can understand why you didn't trust me," Ryan said.

"I overreacted. I'm sorry, Ryan."

Ryan went silent. Drew held his breath, knowing his relationship with his sister hung on what Ryan said next.

"I accept your apology, Drew. I hope we can get to know each other better in the future."

Drew let out his breath. "Yeah. I hope so, too."

A GROUP OF TWENTY-FIVE Rotarians came for lunch, and the kitchen was slammed. Celeste was grateful the lunch rush left little time to worry about the written test for her learner's permit coming up that afternoon. Or the man who was going to drive her to Brainerd to take it. She'd only spoken to Drew in passing the last few days, waving to him if she happened to see him in the lodge. Mostly, she'd done her best to avoid him.

By one-thirty, the rush had slowed and she was able to take a breather as she cleaned her station and prepped for dinner.

"Maggie, I forgot to tell you. Cheryl's coming in an hour earlier today so I can leave to write my exam."

"Oh, my gosh, that's today? Do you need a ride? I could leave early, too. Hopefully things won't be too hectic for Cheryl."

"No, I've got it covered, but thanks."

"How are you getting there?" Maggie asked.

Celeste looked away, making a show of wiping down an already spotless stainless-steel counter. "Drew's taking me. He's been helping me study for the exam."

"Oh."

She heard both surprise and speculation in Maggie's one-word reply. She turned to Maggie and lowered her voice so the others in the kitchen couldn't hear. "Don't read anything into it. We're friends, that's all. I needed help and he offered it to me."

"That was very good of him."

"He's a good person." Celeste narrowed her eyes at Maggie, unsure why she was so annoyed. And why she felt the need to defend Drew. "He's promised to help me with learning to drive an actual car, too. I've seen a couple of used cars on the website of a car dealership in Brainerd that I'm considering buying. We're going to look at them this afternoon, after my exam."

"That's great, Celeste. If you need us to help you practice driving once Drew leaves, Luke and I will be happy to give you a hand."

The reminder that Drew's stay at the lodge came with an expiration date was sobering. She'd be smart to start distancing herself from him now.

She reached for Maggie's hand, her previous annoyance evaporating. "Thank you. I appreciate your offer. And Luke's too, even if he doesn't know about it yet."

"He's as keen to see you happy as I am. Do you think you'll be home by the time the school bus gets here? I could watch out for Hope."

"That would be great. If we look at cars, it could be late. I told her to wait for me in the restaurant."

"Send me a text. If you're running late, we can take Hope home with us to Minnewasta and give her supper. You can pick her up on your way by."

"Thanks. That would help a lot." Celeste didn't know what she'd do without help from friends like Maggie and Luke. And Drew.

"You never told me you wanted to get your driver's license, or a car," Maggie said. "I would have been happy to help, you know."

"I know. That's why I never told you."

Maggie shook her head. "That makes absolutely no sense. You're my friend, my *best* friend. Why wouldn't you tell me what you need?"

"Because I know you. You would have gone out of your way to help me, despite any disruption to your own life. And you've already done so much."

Maggie had hired her when she couldn't get a job in South Carolina, even though they'd only met over a video call. She paid for flights for her and Hope to come to Minnesota and had given her a wonderful apartment to live in. She gave her free reign creatively with their dessert menu and put her in charge of decorating wedding cakes whenever they hosted a wedding. But the best thing she'd given her was her unwavering friendship. Celeste didn't know how she'd ever begin to thank Maggie for everything she'd done for her. She couldn't ask for any more favors.

"I should have seen that you needed more independence, but somehow I missed it," Maggie said, squeezing Celeste's hand. "It was good of Drew to offer to help."

"Yes, it was."

"I always knew he was a nice guy, but honestly, he's surprising me," Maggie said. "He's turned into a special man."

Celeste couldn't disagree with that statement. Drew was very special.

Maggie gave her a soft smile. "I once told Drew that someday a very special girl was going to realize what a gem he was and never let him go. Maybe that girl is you."

Celeste backed away, blinking in alarm. "Don't go getting ideas, Maggie. We're friends. That's it. That's all we'll ever be."

Maggie's raised eyebrow and knowing smile told her she wasn't convinced.

DREW WAS CAREFUL TO keep his conversation with Celeste light as they drove to Brainerd. She was nervous about the exam, and most likely about being stuck in the car with him, so he did what he could to take her mind off everything on the half-hour drive. Even if it meant telling bad jokes.

"What did the left eye say to the right eye?"

"What?" Celeste asked, giving him a puzzled look.

"Between you and me, something smells."

Celeste's laugh was more of a groan. "That is so corny!"

"I've got a million of them. What's brown and sticky?"

"I don't know. What's brown and sticky?"

"A stick."

She groaned again and then laughed. "That one's even worse!"

If it diverted her thoughts from her upcoming exam, he'd tell her a million corny jokes. Besides, he loved her laugh, especially if he was the one making her laugh.

After a few more silly jokes, he steered the conversation to the Mistletoe Ball.

"I started making Christmas cookies," Celeste told him. "I can freeze them, then thaw and decorate them just before the party. I'm going to make and freeze the Christmas pudding, too. That way, I'll only have the trifle to make from scratch on the day of the party."

"I've been watching the budget and the number of tickets sold. Ticket sales are slow so far, but it's still early. A lot of people wait till the last minute before buying tickets for events, so I'm not worried. Yet."

Celeste smiled. "I have a good feeling about the Mistletoe Ball. I think it's going to be a big success, and even better next year."

"Way to be optimistic, Celeste." Her optimism was one of the things he liked best about her.

They lapsed into a comfortable silence. The snow that had fallen earlier in the week had melted off the highway and only remained in the ditches and on the trees. If she passed her test, and Drew was sure she would, could he convince her to drive for a few miles? With the highway dry, maybe she'd be willing to get behind the wheel of his car. He'd wait until after her exam to bring it up, perhaps on the way home. He didn't want to give her anything more to worry about.

He couldn't help thinking once again about their kiss last Friday night. In truth, he hadn't stopped thinking about it. He'd kissed a lot of girls, but there was something different about Celeste's kiss that he couldn't put his finger on. The way she'd felt in his arms in those few precious moments...

Drew swallowed hard to dispel the sensation. Celeste didn't want a relationship with him, or even a short-term affair. The best thing he could do for her would be to concentrate on being her friend.

They soon reached Brainerd and, using his GPS, Drew found the DMV and pulled into the parking lot. "Text me when you're done, and I'll come pick you up."

"What are you going to do while you're waiting for me?"

"I'll find a coffee shop somewhere close by and check my emails," he said. "Don't worry about me. Go in there and slay that exam."

She gave him a salute. "Okay coach. I'll try."

He caught her hand. "You're going to do great. You know the material backwards and forwards. Nothing is going to stop you."

"Thanks Drew. I appreciate the pep talk."

He squeezed her hand before letting go. "I'll see you soon. Good luck."

"Thank you." She opened the passenger door, then turned back to look at him. "I couldn't have gotten this far without you."

"It's been my pleasure."

With a smile, Celeste left the car. Drew waited until he saw her enter the building before pulling out of the parking lot.

As it turned out, there was a coffee shop around the corner from the DMV building. Drew parked and headed inside. The rich scent of freshly brewed coffee greeted him as he entered. They must have taken a fresh batch of donuts out of the oven because their sweet scent was unmistakable.

However good the donuts might be, he was sure they couldn't compete with Celeste's baking.

He got himself a cup of coffee and settled at a table near the window. He'd just begun scrolling through his unread emails when a call came through. "Hey, Harper. How are you doing?"

"Hanging in there. The babies are doing good, so I'm trying to concentrate on that, but I'm still bored. I've already knit six pairs of booties and two baby blankets."

Drew chuckled. "At least you've been productive."

"I try. I'm more interested in what's going on at the lodge. How are the plans for the Christmas dance coming along? Scarlet said she renamed it the Mistletoe Ball. Very fancy."

He gave her the latest updates along with the number of tickets sold so far.

"Not too bad," she said. "It's still early."

"Yeah, that's what I said. Scarlet has several radio interviews lined up in the next couple of weeks that we hope will move the needle. We had some snow the other day, too, so I'm hoping that puts people in a Christmas mood."

"No snow here in Minneapolis yet. Which is a good thing since Ethan would likely lose his mind if he thought we couldn't get to the hospital quickly."

Drew grinned to himself. His uncle was going to be a basket case by the time the twins were born.

"Did we get any hotel bookings that we can attribute to the Ball?" Harper asked.

"Just a couple, but I'm optimistic there's more to come. We've got everything in place—the food, the entertainment, the staff. As soon as people find out about the Ball, they'll jump on it."

At least he hoped that was the case. The slow start to ticket sales worried him, though he didn't want to share his concerns just yet.

"I should go," Harper said. "Ethan will be home any minute with my ice cream."

"Are you still sending him away to talk to me? He's not going to be happy with either of us when he finds out."

"Then we won't let him find out," Harper said. "Thanks for keeping me in the loop, Drew."

"My pleasure. Take care of yourself."

"I will. Bye."

He ended the call and started going through his email again, but this time his mind wandered. What would it be like to have a child? He loved hanging out with Hope, playing video games and board games. She was such a happy kid, a complete joy to be around. Celeste was a wonderful mother. It couldn't have been easy raising Hope alone after her husband's death. She'd taken a huge leap of faith in coming to Minnesota to work at the lodge. When she'd made her decision, the lodge was just reopening and there was no guarantee it would be successful. He wondered again why she'd left her family and everything familiar to her to come to a place she'd never been before. She must have had a compelling reason for her move. He was curious what that reason could be.

He was curious about every aspect of Celeste's life, he conceded. He also conceded that it likely wasn't healthy for him.

The ping of his phone indicated a text message. Celeste was finished. He thought it would take her much longer than this. She said nothing about how she'd done and he was afraid to ask in a text in case it hadn't gone the way either of them had expected. Instead, he texted that he'd be in the parking lot in a few minutes.

She was waiting outside near the exterior door of the DMV when he got there. He pulled into a nearby parking stall and Celeste slid into the passenger seat. She was almost expressionless and didn't speak.

"Are you okay?" Drew spoke carefully, unable to read her. Had nerves gotten the best of her? "I didn't expect you to be finished so quickly."

"Me neither." She pulled the seatbelt across her chest but instead of fastening it, she held it mid-air and stared off into space. She was starting to scare him.

He put his hand on her arm. "Celeste, whatever happened, it's going to be all right. I promise you."

She looked at him then, her eyes filling with tears. "I finished the exam before anyone else. I could see all the answers in my head like I was reading them from a screen. The person who gave the exam told me I got all the answers right, one hundred percent." Tears streamed down her face as she pulled a crumpled piece of paper from her pocket. "I got my permit."

The wonder in her eyes, the relief and joy, made him smile. Though he'd promised himself not to touch her today, he simply couldn't resist. He pulled off his glove and, leaning across the console, laid his hand on her soft cheek. Drew stared into her beautiful dark eyes. The intoxicating combination of her warm, welcoming scent and the silky feel of her skin made his heart soar and his body catch fire. The need to kiss her nearly overpowered him, but he held back, knowing it wasn't what she wanted.

She signaled her withdrawal with a soft sigh as she turned her head and leaned back against her seat, out of his reach. Drew let his hand drop and sat back in his seat as well. He stifled his own sigh as he pulled his glove back on.

Would she always be out of his reach?

"I'm sorry," she said before he had a chance to speak. "I don't know why I'm crying."

He made himself smile for her, knowing it was what she needed. "You got caught up in the excitement of crushing that exam. I knew you could do it."

"I couldn't have done it without you," she said, brushing away one last tear. "You gave me the confidence to go forward."

"You did it all yourself, Celeste. I merely provided the cheerleading." Drew tried to act like this brief moment of intimacy hadn't shaken him. "Are you ready to move forward some more? We've got that appointment at the car dealership. By the end of the day, you could be the proud owner of a brand-new used vehicle."

She gave him a tremulous smile. "I'm terrified, but yeah, let's go."

That's what he loved most about Celeste. Even though she was scared, she faced her fears and plunged ahead.

Loved? No, no, no, he couldn't be in love with her. Not when there wasn't a chance she'd ever feel the same way.

Drew had to stop himself from groaning. Instead, he gripped the steering wheel and drove to the car dealership.

BY THE TIME THEY NEARED the lodge, it was already dark, even though it was only six pm. Celeste's experience in Minnesota the last three years had taught her how short daylight hours were in the winter. Just one of the things she'd had to get used to.

Maggie texted that Luke got delayed by work and that they were still at the lodge with Hope. They were having dinner in the restaurant and would wait there for her. Celeste couldn't wait to tell them the news about her exam.

She dared a glimpse at Drew and saw the planes of his handsome face lit by the dashboard lights. She didn't know how she was ever going to thank him for everything he'd done. Apparently, he'd researched the two vehicles she'd told him about and discovered they both had decent safety ratings. Either would be suitable for her and Hope, but the SUV surprisingly had better gas mileage. He also learned the dealership was asking a premium price for the SUV and advised her not to pay a penny over the amount his research told him was the going rate for that model with that kind of mileage.

She made an offer on the SUV, refusing to go over Drew's number. She held firm on that number, trusting Drew's advice, and after some back and forth, the salesman agreed to sell the car to her for the price she wanted. They made a deal, signed a bunch of paperwork, and would pick up the car in a few days, after it had been detailed and a coat of rust proofing applied.

None of it would have been possible without Drew. He was such a good friend.

Celeste's face and body warmed at the thought of how close they'd come to kissing again. When she got into his car at the DMV, she was still shocked by getting a hundred percent on the exam. She never believed she'd get this far, but here she was, taking the first step on her road to independence. And then Drew touched her and for a moment, she wanted to let go and simply kiss him, enjoy him. She wanted to kiss him forever.

But then she remembered all the differences between them. In a few weeks, Drew would be gone and likely wouldn't give her a second thought ever again. He was a young man with his whole life ahead of him. He needed to explore the world and find out what was out there for him. She only wanted him to be happy.

So why did the thought of being parted from him make her so sad?

Celeste was pulled from her thoughts when Drew slowed the car, pulled to the side of the road and stopped. As he put the car into park, Celeste sat up straighter. "Why are we stopping? Is there something wrong with the car?"

"Nothing's wrong. We're a couple of miles from the lodge and I thought that since the highway is dry and there's practically no one else on the road, you'd like to get behind the wheel and drive the rest of the way."

Celeste blinked at him, her chest tightening with apprehension. "You want me to drive?"

"You just bought a SUV, Celeste. You're going to have to learn to drive. No time like the present."

In her head she knew he was right, but her heart screamed in terror at the thought.

"It's only a couple of miles, and we can go as slowly as you like. How about it?"

"What if I break your car or something?"

He smiled. "Not gonna happen. You'll be fine and so will my car."

His calm reassurance and his unwavering confidence in her were humbling. He always believed the best of her. She found herself nodding. "Okay. But if I drive into the ditch, it's on you."

"You won't drive into the ditch," he said with a chuckle. "Let's change places."

They got out of the car and passed each other in the headlights. In the driver's seat, Celeste fumbled to adjust the seat, finally finding the control that moved the seat forward.

She placed both hands on the wheel. "Now what?"

"Fasten your seatbelt."

Celeste couldn't believe she'd completely forgotten something so basic as the seatbelt. She fastened it and took a breath.

"Now press the brake with your right foot and slide the gearshift into drive."

She followed Drew's directions on autopilot, his calm voice soothing her.

"Check over your left shoulder to make sure no one is coming and then press slowly on the gas pedal with your right foot."

After shoulder checking, Celeste slowly made her way back onto the highway. She crawled down the road, both hands clutching the wheel, her back stiff and straight.

"You're doing great, Celeste. Try pressing a little more on the gas and see if you can increase the speed a little."

"Okay," she said breathlessly. Her heart pumped like she were running a hundred-yard dash. She slowly pressed the gas pedal and brought the speed up to thirty miles an hour.

"Try to relax. You've got the steering wheel in a death grip."

"Relax? Are you kidding me? I'm driving a freaking car for the first time in my life and you want me to relax?"

"My mistake."

She heard the chuckle in his voice and dared a quick glance at him. "Are you laughing at me?"

This time he couldn't hide his guffaw. "Of course not."

He *was* laughing at her. "You won't be laughing if I drive your expensive car into the ditch."

"You're not going in the ditch." Drew's voice was calm, as if he had no worries about putting his car in the hands of a rookie driver. "You're exactly between the lines. A snail could outrun you, but you're driving. I'm really proud of you."

Celeste laughed, suddenly amused at the idea of being behind the wheel of a car, a place she'd never thought she'd be. "I'm really proud of me, too."

"Good. Someday soon, when you actually learn to drive the speed limit, you'll be able to drive your own car. You got a lot accomplished today."

"Yeah, I did, didn't I?"

After crawling along the highway a bit longer, the sign for the lodge came into view.

"Get ready to make a right-hand turn," Drew said. "Don't forget to signal."

She turned the signal light on. "One good thing about driving this speed is that I don't have to slow down to make the turn."

Drew laughed. "Very true."

She managed a slow-motion right-hand turn, then made her way into the lodge's parking lot which was mostly full.

"Let's park over in the far corner where there's no cars," Drew said.

"Good idea. I'm not quite ready for a parking lesson."

Slowly, she crept into a parking spot farthest away from the lodge. Celeste braked and put the car into park.

She turned to Drew. "What do I do now?"

"Now you put your right foot back on the brake, turn the engine off and pull out the keys."

Again, she followed his directions and handed him the keys. The enormity of what she'd just done suddenly hit her. "Oh, my God! I did it!"

He accepted the keys with one hand and squeezed her shoulder with the other. "You sure did. You drove!"

"I drove!"

Celeste opened the door and jumped out. She squealed and launched into a happy dance beside the car. Euphoria overtook her. Learning to drive was going to change her life. And Hope's. They'd both be independent women.

Drew came around to her side of the car. "I'm really proud of you, Celeste."

On impulse, Celeste threw her arms around his neck. "Thank you, thank you! I couldn't have done any of this without you."

His arms tightened around her, pulling her close. It felt so good to be held in a man's arms. In *Drew's* arms.

She leaned back to look up at him. The amusement left his face, replaced by intensity in his dark eyes as he stared at her. Celeste cupped his cheek with her bare hand, needing to touch him, skin to skin. She couldn't think, or reason, or back away. She could only feel.

They came together in mutual need, their lips touching, questing, hands reaching, stroking. She met his lips with eagerness, opening her mouth to him. At her unspoken invitation, he plunged inside, sweeping her mouth with his tongue over and over until her knees weakened.

He trailed kisses across her throat. His breath was warm on her skin as he nuzzled behind her ear.

"Celeste." His voice was husky and low. "I need you."

She snapped to attention. What was she doing? She'd let herself get carried away. It was only the excitement of driving for the first time, nothing more.

Wasn't it?

"Drew, I can't."

Celeste pushed gently against his chest, and he immediately dropped his arms. She caught a fleeting look of hurt before he wiped his face of expression.

"I'm sorry," he said. "I promised I wouldn't do that again, and I blew it."

She couldn't let him take the blame. "No, I shouldn't have...I can't...I...I have to go."

He stepped back. Celeste wanted to go to him, to tell him she'd wanted to kiss him as much as he wanted to kiss her. That she loved kissing him, that she wanted to do it again and again.

Instead, she turned and ran all the way to the lodge, too frightened by her own thoughts to tell the truth.

Chapter Nine

THE NEXT MORNING, CELESTE was at work in the lodge's kitchen an hour before her shift was scheduled to start. She'd hustled Hope out of bed before six and helped her to dress, promising to make French toast at the lodge as a reward for getting up so early. Celeste wasn't even sure why she needed to get to the kitchen. She'd slept fitfully, finally abandoning all pretense of sleep around three in the morning when she got out of bed and paced the small apartment.

When they arrived at the lodge, no one was around, aside from a security guard and Mel, the new person at the front desk. Celeste whipped up the promised French toast for Hope but couldn't manage to choke down any herself, no matter how much maple syrup she poured on it. She put coffee on and then spent an hour cleaning the shelves in the commercial fridge and scrubbing down the already pristine stainless-steel counters. Hope sat on a stool at one corner of the counter and quietly drew pictures in her scrapbook, pausing every now and then to yawn. Celeste felt like the world's worst mother for forcing her to get out of bed before she needed to.

By the time Maggie arrived at seven, Celeste had almost convinced herself that her kiss with Drew was an aberration, a one-time thing brought on because of her excitement over passing her exam and driving for the first time. Though she had to admit it wasn't a one-time thing because she'd kissed him once before.

Her thoughts whirled in circles until she was dizzy. She did her best to put them aside and concentrate on the orders coming in from the restaurant. Aside from saying hello to Maggie, she was quiet. Since they were alone in the kitchen for half an hour until the rest of the kitchen staff arrived, the silence was deafening. She noticed Maggie giving her odd looks from time to time, but she kept her head down and continued to work.

Celeste kissed Hope goodbye when she left to catch the school bus around eight. As soon as she was gone, Maggie slapped down a spatula with a whack. "What's going on with you? Last night when you picked up Hope, you were all twitchy and nervous, and this morning you're the same? What happened?"

"Nothing." Celeste kept her voice low so the other kitchen staff couldn't hear their conversation. "I told you last night, I was nervous about driving for the first time."

"Maybe I bought it last night, but I'm not buying it now." Maggie scrambled a bowl of eggs with a whisk. "That was hours ago, and you're still acting weird."

"I'm just nervous, that's all. I made a deal to buy a used SUV off the lot at a dealership in Brainerd. What if I never get my driver's license? Then I'll be making payments on a car I can't drive. Or what if I do get my license, but I'm too scared to drive in the snow and ice?" There was a grain of truth in that, but it wasn't close to the whole story.

"The answer to the first question is if you don't get your license right away, you keep on practicing and working until you do. I know you well enough to say that's how you handle any obstacle in your life. And in answer to your second question, do what I do. Get winter tires. They're great on icy roads and give me a lot more confidence."

Celeste simply nodded. Maggie made everything sound so easy.

"Are you not getting along with Drew?" Maggie asked in a quiet voice. "Did you have an argument?"

Celeste's face heated, and she looked away. "No. We get along fine."

Maggie frowned. "I know something's not right between you. Has he harassed you, made you uncomfortable in any way? Because if he has—"

"No! Absolutely not! Drew's not like that. He'd never treat me that way."

"Ha." Maggie watched her closely. "Isn't that interesting?"

"What?"

"That you immediately came to Drew's defense."

"What's so interesting about that? We're friends." Celeste kept her head down, unable to meet Maggie's gaze.

"Are you sure that's all you are?" Maggie whispered. "Friends?"

Celeste blew out a breath. She desperately needed to talk to someone, to work out her confused feelings. She turned bacon on the griddle. "We kissed."

"Okay." Maggie didn't sound shocked or even mildly surprised. "How was it?"

"It was..." *Wonderful, amazing, mind-blowing, tempting.* "...nice."

"Nice? That's it? Nice?"

"Yes!" Celeste glanced over her shoulder to where Rocky, the dishwasher, was loading the commercial machine. She was grateful it made too much noise for him to hear their conversation. "We both got carried away by the excitement of me driving for the first time. I was so jazzed and so grateful to Drew for helping me. But it doesn't mean anything. Like I said, we're friends. He's been kind to me and Hope. I like him."

"But do you like him in a passionate kisses kind of way?" Maggie asked.

Celeste found that she couldn't lie to her friend or to herself. "I'll admit that I enjoyed kissing Drew. What woman wouldn't? He's a very attractive young man."

The truth was, she'd lost herself in Drew's kiss, in his scent, and in his strong arms. But it had been a long time since she'd been kissed and held and stroked by a man. Maybe it was the idea of being kissed she missed so much. Maybe she would have reacted the same way to a kiss from any man. "But we're totally wrong for each other. It won't happen again."

"Why not?" Maggie persisted. "You're two unattached adults who enjoy being together. Why can't something come of it?"

"The list of reasons we shouldn't be together is a mile long."

"Celeste, none of your reasons matter if you really care about each other. Those things can be overcome."

Celeste shook her head. "You don't know what it's like. I'm the product of a mixed-race marriage, and I saw firsthand that it didn't work in my family. I won't repeat that mistake, not when Hope's happiness and security is at stake."

Maggie cracked a couple of eggs onto her griddle. "I understand what you're saying. But you have to remember that I'm the product of two people who loved each other but never had the chance to be together. They were kept apart first by my grandparents and then by fear. Their story was tragic, and I don't want that for you. I don't want either one of you to be hurt."

The true story about Maggie's parents had unfolded around the same time Celeste had moved to the lodge. Learning the truth had been difficult, and painful, for all three Lindquist sisters, but especially for Maggie. The truth had changed her life.

"Nobody is going to get hurt because a couple of kisses is as far as I can let things go."

Standing there talking to Maggie, Celeste meant every word. But would she have the strength to resist Drew when they were alone together again? She honestly didn't know.

"You're not your parents, you know. You don't have to repeat their mistakes. You get to make your own way."

"You mean I get to make my own mistakes?" Celeste said with a smile.

Maggie returned her smile. "Definitely. But at least they'll be yours."

As the restaurant filled, servers put up a flurry of orders that kept them too busy to talk for the next hour. When the breakfast rush finally died down, Celeste prepped vegetables for a lunch salad while Maggie cleaned and scraped her griddle.

"You know, other than telling me that Easton was your first love, the love of your life, you've never talked to me about him."

Celeste's stomach knotted at the mention of his name. "There's not much to tell. We were young, we fell in love, we got married and had Hope. He was a good man and a wonderful father."

"It couldn't have been easy for you, losing him," Maggie said quietly.

"No, it wasn't."

For a long time, she'd wanted to die, too. If she hadn't had Hope to care for, she might have succeeded in that aim.

Maggie put an arm around her shoulders. "I'm sorry you lost him, Celeste."

Celeste caught her hand. "Yeah, me too."

CELESTE ADJUSTED HER seatbelt again, unable to stop fidgeting. Her unease had nothing to do with Maggie, who was an excellent driver, and everything to do with the passenger in the back seat.

Drew.

Here they were, stuck in Maggie's car together on the way to Brainerd to pick up her new-to-her SUV. Celeste had hoped the three of them could have driven there in Drew's car so that she and Maggie could drive home in her new vehicle. No such luck. Maggie planned to go on to Minneapolis to see Harper, so she was going to drop them off at the dealership. Celeste had had no choice but to ask Drew to drive the car home for her.

The memory of what happened the last time she and Drew were alone together in a vehicle kept her nervous and mostly silent all the way to Brainerd. Maggie maintained a steady stream of conversation with Drew, drawing her in on occasion. Celeste was grateful. Without her, the atmosphere inside the car would be unbearably tense.

How the hell was she supposed to get through the thirty-minute drive back to the lodge alone with Drew?

Though she'd done her best to avoid him the last few days, and they'd barely spoken, she'd missed him.

Celeste clutched her hands in her lap. Drew was a friend, nothing more. She had to remember that.

Maggie dropped them off at the dealership and, with a wave, was on her way. Celeste took a fortifying breath and entered the building with Drew.

An hour later, after dealing with insurance and license plates, one of the employees went through all the features of the vehicle with them. Then they were back on the road. Celeste stared straight ahead, her heart racing.

They drove in tense silence for about ten minutes before Drew cleared his throat. "You don't have to worry about any unwanted touches from me." Celeste turned to look at him but he never took his eyes off the road. "I promised you it wouldn't happen again, and I meant it. So please, don't be nervous."

Instead of being relieved, a sense of loss inundated Celeste. "It wasn't like you wrestled me to the ground and had your way with me. I was a willing participant in those kisses. Both times."

"Yeah, well, we both know those kisses won't lead anywhere. The best thing for us is to maintain a platonic relationship."

"Okay." *Maintain a platonic relationship?* His odd choice of words sounded rehearsed. And impersonal.

"I said I'd help you get your driver's license, and I won't go back on that promise. It's impossible to learn to drive without having another licensed driver in the car. It's important to me that you and Hope gain your independence."

"I appreciate that." Was teaching her to drive the only reason he'd have anything to do with her? Did that mean that once she got her license, she'd never see him again? The thought made her chest well with an emotion she couldn't put a name to.

For the next several miles, neither of them spoke. Finally, they reached Minnewasta and Drew took the turn that led to the lodge. After driving a short distance out of town, he pulled over to the side of the road.

He turned to look at her. "Would you like to drive from here? I know it's farther than the last time you drove, but I know you can do it."

Celeste stared back at him. No, she really didn't want to. It was nearly ten miles to the lodge from here. But she had to. If she didn't keep moving forward, she'd be stuck forever, and so would Hope. She'd come too far to quit now. "Yeah. Let's do this."

They got out of the SUV and exchanged seats. In the driver's seat, Celeste adjusted the seat to her height, trying to remember what the man at the dealership had told them about the controls. After some fiddling, she got the seat to a comfortable setting and buckled herself in.

"Do you remember what you have to do first?" Drew asked.

"Set my right foot on the brake, put the gearshift into drive." Celeste's hands sweated inside her leather gloves.

"Good. You're doing great. What do you have to do before pulling out on the road?"

"Signal that I'm making a left-hand turn and then shoulder check to make sure no one is coming."

"Yes, that's it. Now do exactly what you just told me."

"Okay."

Taking a deep breath, Celeste set her foot on the brake and changed gears from park to drive. Then she signaled and looked over her left shoulder, praying no one else was on the road.

"Good job, Celeste. Keep going." Drew's deep voice reassured her.

Cautiously, she pulled out onto the road, her hands shaking.

"I know you're nervous, but you're doing everything right. I couldn't be prouder of you."

His praise gave her much needed confidence. "Thank you."

"I mean it," Drew said. "If anyone can learn to be a good driver, it's you."

She relaxed in her seat at his words. "I appreciate you saying that."

"It's the truth. Now let's see if you can get the speed up a little."

"Okay."

Celeste pressed the gas pedal little by little until she was driving at forty miles per hour.

"Good. Now try turning on the cruise control. Do you remember how the technician told you to do it?"

Her mind went completely blank. "No, not at all."

"No worries. I'll talk you through it." Drew's tone never wavered. She could drive into the ditch and he'd still maintain his calm demeanor.

"Okay, first of all, do you remember where the cruise control buttons are?" he asked.

"Yes, they're on the steering wheel, on the lower right-hand side."

"Good. I want you to push the button that turns the cruise control on."

"Does that involve looking away from the road?"

He chuckled. "Probably, unless you've got another set of eyes you haven't told me about. Glance down quickly to see where the button is."

She took a quick glance. "Okay. Got it."

"Good. Glance down again and push the button."

First making sure there was no one behind them or heading toward them, Celeste glanced down and pushed the cruise button. "Now what?"

"Now you need to set the speed. Get the speed to where you'd like it and then hit the 'set' button."

The technician's instructions were coming back to her now and along with Drew's calm, step by step instructions, she set the cruise control. She took her foot off the gas pedal and marveled that the SUV retained its speed.

"You have remarkable patience," Celeste said. "If I was in your shoes, I'm not sure I'd be as cool."

"Then you're going to have to work on your patience," he said with a chuckle. "In a few years, Hope will want to learn to drive."

Celeste groaned at the thought. "Good grief. It'll be like the blind leading the blind."

"By the time Hope is ready to drive, you'll be an old pro."

"Or just old."

Drew laughed. "You? Never."

"Did your parents teach you to drive?"

"They did, but I didn't make it easy for them."

Curious, Celeste asked, "What do you mean?"

"My dad got so frustrated with me, he refused to take me out driving. I was a cocky teenage boy who thought he knew everything and didn't take driving seriously. Mom had to take over the job. I flunked the written learner's exam once and the driving exam twice. You're already ahead of me."

"No way! You flunked your learner's test?"

"I did. Unlike you, I didn't study the first time I wrote it. We'd covered some of the material in driver's ed in school, so I figured I knew everything. It was a rude awakening."

"I'll bet."

"My friends were getting their licenses and I didn't want to get left behind. So, I studied, at least enough to pass."

"Good for you." Celeste unclenched her hands to loosen her death grip on the steering wheel.

"Not so good. I flunked the driving test twice. My parents were fed up dealing with my attitude, so they hired a driving instructor who wouldn't take any crap from me. He was a former long-haul trucker."

"So, then you were able to get your driver's license? How old were you?"

"Seventeen. I got my license, but I didn't take safety seriously until I nearly had an accident."

"What happened?" Celeste asked.

"I was driving my sister to her soccer game, just outside of the city on a secondary highway. I had a heavy foot on the gas pedal and a nonchalant attitude. I got impatient with a slow driver in front of me and pulled out to pass, but I hadn't checked for oncoming traffic before committing to pass. Sure enough, there was a car rushing towards us in the other lane and I had no place to go. If that oncoming car hadn't pulled over onto the shoulder, we would have crashed."

"Oh, my God!" The Drew she knew today would never put anyone else in danger, especially someone he loved.

"The idea that I could have killed my sister rattled me. I drove a lot more carefully after that, especially when someone else was in the car." He laughed softly. "You know, I never told my parents what happened. I swore Carrie to secrecy, and remarkably, she never squealed on me."

"Doesn't surprise me. She loves you."

"Well, maybe she used to. I'm not so sure anymore."

Celeste heard the wistfulness in his voice. "She still loves you. You need to be patient with her."

"Yeah, well, when it comes to Carrie, I'm short on patience." She heard him sigh and blow out a breath. "What about you? Are you close to your sister?"

"Yeah, I am. When I was unemployed before we moved here, Gloria and her husband Marcus let Hope and me stay with them for a couple of months. I don't know what I would have done without them."

"So, things were pretty rough before you came here. What happened?"

Celeste didn't like talking about that time and had only told Maggie. The months before she moved to Minnesota had been scary and humiliating. But Drew had shared a harrowing experience with her, and she trusted him. She forced herself to relax her tight shoulders.

"I was working at a posh restaurant in Myrtle Beach. The head chef, Chef Andrew, knew I was a widow and a single mother. And he knew I was vulnerable.

"It started casually at first with an occasional touch that could have been accidental. I tried to ignore it, kept my head down, and continued working. But he grew bolder. Andrew went out of his way to be alone with me so that no one could see what was going on. His touches got bolder as well. One time he got me alone in a storage closet. He grabbed my breasts and tried to put his hand down my pants. If one of my co-workers hadn't opened the door..." She couldn't finish the sentence. "It was one of the most humiliating moments of my life."

Celeste adjusted the rearview mirror, even though it didn't need adjusting. "He was married, but that didn't stop him from demanding sex from me. I always refused. I only wanted to do my job. He began threatening me, telling me if I didn't have sex with him, I'd lose my job.

"I finally had enough. I went to the owners of the restaurant and told them what happened. I asked them to tell Chef Andrew to leave me alone. They called Andrew in and he denied everything. That wasn't a surprise, I suppose, but then he said I was the one who was harassing *him*. I couldn't believe it. None of my co-workers came to my defense. Most said they hadn't seen anything, but everyone knew Andrew had singled me out. They were all too afraid of losing their jobs or incurring Andrew's wrath. I suppose I can't really blame them."

Celeste forced her hands to relax on the steering wheel once more. It wasn't easy to speak about the harassment she'd suffered, but at the same time a weight lifted inside her. She'd kept her anger and shame and humiliation hidden inside for too long.

"The owners fired me. A sous chef is expendable, a world class chef is not. I suddenly found myself unemployed for the first time in my life."

"But why come all the way to Minnesota? Why not get a job closer to home?" Drew asked.

"Ah, that's the best part. Whenever I applied for another job, they checked my references and Andrew would be sure to tell them I was a troublemaker who had caused dissension in the kitchen and they'd had to fire me. No one would hire me. I even had trouble getting a job at a fast-food restaurant.

It wasn't enough for Andrew to get me fired. He wanted to destroy me because I had the audacity to refuse him and speak up against him. It makes me wonder how many other women he harassed over the years who felt they had no choice but to give in to him."

"My God." Drew's voice was incredulous. "I can't believe he did that to you. That he was *allowed* to do that to you."

"My situation is hardly unique. A lot of women get harassed at work. Maggie told me a similar thing happened to her."

"Are you kidding me?"

"I wish I was. A lot of men feel entitled to take whatever they want from a woman. It was because of her own experience that Maggie hired me. She knew what I was up against. And that's how I got to Minnesota and the lodge."

"Jesus, Celeste. I'm sorry."

"I didn't tell you this story so you'd feel sorry for me," Celeste snapped.

"Why *did* you tell me?" She felt him watching her as she drove.

"You wanted to know how I got to Minnesota."

"Yeah, I wanted to know. And for the record, I'm angry. I'm angry and I'm sorry you and Maggie and other women have to put up with crap like that."

Celeste risked a quick glance at him. He stared out the windshield, his face pensive. As she returned her attention to her driving, she wondered if she'd done the right thing in telling him her story. She didn't want him to feel awkward around her or treat her differently.

When Drew spoke again, his voice was soft. "I understand how it feels to be humiliated at work."

That was surprising. "What do you mean?"

"I graduated from the University of Minnesota with degrees in accounting and finance. School has always come easy for me and I graduated with honors. I was recruited to work at a prestigious investment firm in Minneapolis. They have offices around the world, and I had visions of living in exotic locations."

He went silent. Celeste gently asked, "Then what happened?"

"One day, after only working there for a few months, I got an email. I thought it was work related from someone I knew, so I clicked the attachment. Big mistake. It was malware, but with a twist. This hacker knew about Ethan's big lottery win and somehow he'd discovered that he was my uncle. He blackmailed me, saying that if I didn't give him five hundred thousand dollars in twenty-four hours, he'd unleash a ransomware virus on my employer and everyone would know it came from me. I panicked. I went to Ethan and begged for the money. He tried to tell me to come clean, to go straight to my bosses and tell them what happened so they could fight back or at least prepare in some way. But I was so afraid of losing this great job and all the prestige that went with it that I refused. I thought if I paid the hacker the money, the problem would go away." He gave a bitter laugh. "I should have known better."

"So the hacker didn't leave you alone?"

"No. Against his better judgment, Ethan gave me the money and I paid the hacker. And then he unleashed the virus on my company anyway. I don't know exactly how much they had to pay to get back their information, but it had to be in the millions. Like the hacker promised, my bosses knew exactly who to blame. They fired me. They said I could have been forgiven for clicking on an attachment without being sure it was safe, though that was bad enough. What they couldn't forgive was trying to cover it up and not give them any warning."

"Drew, I'm so sorry."

"They were right. I was trying to cover my ass, and I made a big mistake." She heard him blow out a long breath. "I can relate to you not being able to get another job. Word got around in the investment community. Everyone knew what happened. No one would hire me. In the end, my parents gave me a job at the Hainstock Foundation, but not in the investment end. As an admin assistant. Even my own parents no longer trusted me. That's been the worst part, the loss of my family's trust."

"I'm sure that's not true. Ethan wouldn't have left you in charge of the lodge's finances if he didn't trust you."

"I only pay the bills, Celeste. I'm not in charge of anything."

The defeat she heard in his voice saddened her. "How long have you been working at the Hainstock Foundation?"

"About a year and a half. Eventually I'm going to have to move on. I've been studying forensic accounting online. It started out as something to do while I was unemployed, but it's turned into a passion."

"What's forensic accounting?"

"It's a type of accounting that investigates financial information for potential evidence of crimes, like embezzlement or fraud. Eventually, I want to concentrate on online crimes. I don't want anyone to get burned the way I did."

Celeste nodded, keeping her eyes on the road. It didn't surprise her that he wanted to save others from the misery he'd gone through. He was a compassionate person. "I guess you really do understand the feeling that no one believes you, or believes *in* you."

"Yeah, I do."

"As someone who's been through unemployment hell, I can tell you that this is simply a bump in the road. You're going to come through this, Drew, and you're going to be stronger than ever. And some day you're going to get an even better job than the one you lost."

He chuckled. "Thanks for the pep talk."

"You're welcome."

"Here's a pep talk for you, Celeste. I believe you'll not only learn to drive and get your license, you're going to ace that road test. I believe you can do anything you set your mind to."

Celeste was humbled by his confidence in her. "It means a lot to me to hear you say that."

The sign for the lodge came into view.

"We're home." Drew leaned forward in his seat, all business once more. "To disengage the cruise control, tap lightly on the brake."

Celeste followed his directions, and the SUV gradually slowed. She made the turn into the lodge's parking lot and pulled into a vacant spot away from other cars. "Here we are. Safe and sound."

"You did great, Celeste."

"Thank you. And thank you for all your calm instructions. You made things much easier for me."

He smiled. "You're welcome. Thank you for telling me your story. I'm glad you felt you could trust me with it."

It was true. She *did* trust him. That was rare for her, especially since she'd only known Drew a short time. "Thank you for trusting me with *your* story."

"Yeah." He looked toward the lodge, not meeting her eyes.

"I should go. The school bus will be here soon."

Drew nodded. "How does your week look? Will you have time for some practice driving?"

"I think so. I'll check my work schedule and get back to you." Celeste summoned the courage to ask her next question. "You said you'd continue to help me get my license, but you didn't say whether we'd still be friends?" After the scorching kiss they'd shared, was it possible to be 'just friends'?

She held her breath as she waited for his answer. Finally, he spoke. "Of course we're friends."

"Good. I'm glad."

Drew sounded all right, but as she got out of the SUV she realized he hadn't looked her in the eye as he said the words.

Chapter Ten

DREW FOUND EIGHT ORANGE traffic cones in the lodge's utility garage and set them in a corner of the parking lot. Using the measurements he'd taken of his own car, he created a rectangle with four of the cones. Then he placed the other four behind the first set, leaving a space about the length of one and a half cars between them. He figured using the traffic cones was the safest way for Celeste to begin practicing parallel parking.

Celeste approached from the lodge, a bright red knitted hat covering her curls. She lifted her gloved hand in a wave, and he returned the gesture, his heart hammering in his chest. She was so damned beautiful. How was he supposed to keep his promise to only be her friend?

"Hey," she said when she reached him. "Don't tell me, let me guess. We're going to practice parallel parking today."

He made himself smile despite the turmoil inside his heart. "We are. How much time to you have?"

"I've got about an hour till my dinner shift."

"An hour should be enough time to get the feel for parallel parking, but it's something we'll need to practice over and over."

Celeste wrinkled her nose. "Wonderful. Everyone says parallel parking is the worst."

"Don't let other people's attitudes influence you before you even try. Maybe you'll be great at parking."

"And maybe pigs will fly."

Drew laughed. "That's the spirit. Come on, let's get your SUV and get started."

"Great." With a sigh of resignation, Celeste fell into step beside him.

"By the way, I talked to Ethan and told him about your new vehicle," Drew said. "You'll need somewhere to park it, and we both figured the best place would be in the utility garage. It's got plenty of space, and with the remote control for the overhead door, it'll be easy for you to get in and out."

Her eyes widened in surprise. "Oh. That would be wonderful. Thank you."

"The garage isn't far from your apartment. It'll keep the snow and ice off it and on the coldest days, you can plug it in," Drew said as he held open the door of the SUV for Celeste.

She looked up at him as she fastened her seat belt, her eyes wide. "Plug it in? Did I buy an electric car without knowing it?"

Drew grinned. "No, this baby is strictly gas-powered, but it's equipped with a block heater that you can plug into an electrical outlet. On the coldest days, the block heater warms the engine enough so the car will start. Have you learned nothing about Minnesota winters in the last three years?"

"Only that I don't like them much," she said with a chuckle. "In my defense, we didn't need these block heater thingies in South Carolina. But I did wonder why so many people here have electrical cords sticking out the front grills of their cars."

"Now you know. Come on, let's get started." He closed her door, then quickly made his way to the passenger side and hopped in the SUV.

She drove slowly to the spot where the cones were set up. "All right," Drew said. "Pretend the cones are two parked cars. The one in the front is Vehicle A and the one in the back is Vehicle B. The objective is to maneuver around Vehicle A and park between A and B without hitting either of them. Most of the time, you'll be parking on the right-hand side of the street so that's what we're going to practice. First thing, signal your intention to park by turning on your right signal light."

Celeste complied. "Okay, now what?"

"Now we want to pull in next to the first 'car', leaving a couple of feet between us."

"Okay."

Drew did his best to keep his voice calm and his instructions clear. If he kept his composure, Celeste would as well. But his entire body tensed with nerves, knowing how much she wanted to succeed. Parallel parking was difficult, and he didn't want her to get discouraged.

Celeste pulled the SUV beside the cones, but much closer than the two feet he'd recommended. She nudged one of the cones as she passed, and it fell over.

"Oh no!" She gave him a stricken look.

"It's okay. I'm sure it didn't feel a thing." He jumped out of the vehicle and righted the cone, then hopped back in. "Let's try again, but this time not so close."

She swallowed. "Okay. I can do this."

"Of course, you can."

Celeste circled the parking lot and came back to the plastic cones. This time when she pulled alongside the first set of cones, she was a comfortable distance away from them.

She turned on the right signal light. "What do I do now?"

"Put the SUV in reverse and then back up slowly until the back wheels of our vehicle align with the rear bumper of the front car. Or in this case, those cones out there which we've named Vehicle A. Then stop."

"All right."

Celeste slipped the SUV into reverse and ever so slowly began to back up.

"You're doing great, Celeste."

When she stopped, she'd backed too far and would have a hard time getting into the spot. But Drew said nothing, knowing she had to figure it out for herself. It wasn't like he'd be able to give her step-by-step instructions on the day she took the road test.

Celeste looked at him expectantly. "Okay. What's next?"

"Turn your steering wheel to the right as far as it goes and continue to back up. When your front right wheel aligns with the back left corner of Vehicle A, stop."

She took a deep breath. "Okay." She followed his instructions and then came to a stop.

"All right," Drew said. "Turn your steering wheel as far left as it can go. The car will straighten out. Just be careful not to go so far that you hit Vehicle B."

"Okay."

When she hit the curb and knocked over the cone representing Vehicle B, she let loose with an impressive string of expletives. Drew couldn't help laughing. "Wow! You kiss your mother with that mouth?"

Celeste rolled her eyes. "Very funny."

"So what do you think you did wrong?" he asked.

"I don't know! I thought you're supposed to be the expert."

"I'm no expert, but I've been parallel parking for several years. Plus, I found some YouTube videos. I'll send you the links."

"Terrific. So, tell me what I did wrong."

"When you came alongside Vehicle A, you backed up too far. It made it impossible to get into the parking spot without hitting Vehicle B. Let's try it again."

Celeste groaned. "Fine."

She attempted the maneuver three more times, ending up crooked or hitting one of the cones every time. After the third time knocking over a cone, she put the SUV into neutral and threw up her hands. "I give up! I'm never going to get this!"

"This is your first attempt at parallel parking, Celeste. Nobody gets it on their first try."

She frowned at him. "Not even you?"

"Especially not me. I told you what a jerk I was. It took me a long time before I was able to parallel park well enough to pass the exam." He reached over and squeezed her shoulder. "I know you're frustrated right now but remember that driving is a skill like anything else. You've got to put in the time. How many cakes and cookies do you think you baked and decorated before you got to be as amazing as you are now?"

A smile played on her lips. "Dozens. Possibly thousands."

"See? You can't expect to be perfect right out of the gate. You're going to have to put in the work."

Celeste rolled her eyes. "I suppose you're right."

"Of course, I'm right. I'm always right."

"Oh, please!" she said with a laugh. "Save me from insufferable men!"

Her comment made him think of her story about the harassment she'd endured. He'd thought of little else. The injustice of her experience infuriated him. Just give him five minutes alone with that bastard...

Drew forced himself to take a breath and smile. Celeste didn't need to know how deeply her story had affected him. "I may be insufferable, but I promise I won't let you down. We'll work on parallel parking and every other aspect of driving until you're comfortable. Okay?"

She looked into his eyes, all traces of laughter gone. "Thank you, Drew. I don't know why you're giving me so much of your time, but I appreciate it."

Drew simply nodded, unable to answer because he wasn't entirely sure himself. All he knew was that he wanted to make her life, and Hope's, easier. He wanted to be there for them.

Even if she didn't want him.

He didn't want to pursue that train of thought. "Let's try it one more time then call it quits for today. We both have to get back to work."

Celeste took a deep breath. "All right. One more time."

This time when Celeste attempted the maneuver, she managed to squeeze into the spot. She was crooked and too far away from the curb, but she hadn't hit any of the cones.

"I did it!"

"You sure did."

Celeste's smile was radiant. She leaned over the console and squeezed his shoulder. "Maybe I can do this."

Drew laid his hand over hers. "I know you can, sweetheart."

She saw him only as a friend, or God forbid, a little brother, but his feelings ran much deeper. He didn't know what he was supposed to do with those feelings. He couldn't stand to be rejected again.

"HI MAMA. I'M SO GLAD you called. It's good to hear your voice." Celeste put her phone on speaker while she folded laundry.

"It's good to hear your voice, too, CeCe."

Celeste couldn't put her finger on it, but her mother sounded...off. She wanted to ask if she was feeling okay, but then her mother began talking about one of her acquaintances from church who'd started seeing a widowed church deacon.

"Why on earth she'd want a man at her age I don't know."

"Maybe she wants companionship," Celeste said. She could understand the desire to have someone to share her life with. "Or maybe she's in love."

"In love?" Her mother made a scoffing sound. "She's too old to be in love."

"A person is never too old to be in love," Celeste countered.

"Are you speaking from experience, CeCe? Are you in love again?"

"No! I'm speaking metaphorically, that's all."

"You're still a young woman. If you wanted to, I'm sure you could have a man in your life again, and more children, too. You shouldn't be alone."

This was a talk she didn't want to have with her mother. "How did this conversation suddenly become about me? We were talking about your friend at church."

"Fine," Nora cleared her throat. "About coming to Minnesota. I thought about it, and I decided I can't come for Christmas. I committed to singing in the church choir on Christmas Eve way back in August, and I hate to go back on my word. And to be honest, I'd like to be home on Christmas day."

Celeste couldn't blame her mother for wanting to be home for Christmas. She preferred to be home in her cozy apartment in Minnesota for the holiday, too. The thought stopped her in her tracks. She hadn't consciously thought of Minnesota as home before, but looking back, she'd felt that way for a while now.

"I understand, Mama." A new idea occurred to her. "If it's the idea of being away at Christmas that bothers you, how about this. We're having a big dinner and dance here at the lodge a couple of weeks before Christmas. Why don't you come for that?" The more Celeste thought about it, the better she liked the idea. "I'll ask Gloria if she'd like to come, too, and I'll make all the arrangements. It'll be so much fun. What do you say, Mama?"

"Well, that sounds very nice." Her mother spoke slowly. "If Gloria says yes, I'll come, too."

"Really?" Celeste had almost given up hope her mother would ever come to Minnesota.

"Really. As long as Gloria comes. I don't want to travel alone."

"I'm going to hold you to that, Mama."

Her mother emitted a deep sigh. "Life's too short to be stubborn. If the only way I can see you and Hope is to come to you, then that's what I've got to do."

Celeste knew all about life being too short. But the note of sadness in her mother's voice alarmed her. "Mama, are you all right?"

"I'm fine, CeCe. Just feeling sentimental tonight, that's all. Why don't you call your sister and see if she can take a few days off for a visit?"

"I'll do that right now, Mama. I love you."

"I love you, too, CeCe girl."

As soon as Celeste ended the call with her mother, she called her sister.

Gloria answered right away. "Hi! How are you?"

"I'm great, Glory. Listen, I was just talking to Mama. Is she okay?"

"Did she tell you Martha died?"

Celeste gasped. "No! What happened?"

"She had a sudden fatal heart attack. No one knew she had a heart condition. I don't think Martha even knew."

Martha Brooks had been their mother's best friend since grade school. They were as close as sisters and had helped each other through many trials.

Celeste sat on the edge of her bed. "No wonder Mama sounded down. I wonder why she didn't tell me."

"She probably didn't want to burden you. You know how she is."

"Yeah." Ever since Easton's death, her mother tried to shield her from any unpleasantness. Maybe she was afraid bad news would send Celeste over the edge.

Perhaps, in the beginning, that had been true. Celeste was so overwhelmed by her grief there was no room for anyone else's problems. But after six years, she was much stronger and able to cope with whatever life threw at her. Maybe it was time to let her mother see that. All the more reason for Nora to visit.

She told her sister about the Mistletoe Ball and their mother's promise to visit if Gloria traveled with her. "What do you say, Glory? Can you get a few days off work? I'm paying your airfare as my Christmas gift to you and Mama. I'll arrange to pick you up at the airport in Minneapolis, too."

"I'd like to come, CeCe, and I think seeing you and Hope would be good for Mama. I'll speak to Marcus and then check at work. I'll get back to you as soon as I have an answer for you, okay?"

"Okay. Sounds good."

"I've been thinking about something," her sister began. "Have you thought about moving back to South Carolina? It would really help Mama if you were nearby."

Gloria wasn't trying to make her feel guilty but even so, guilt slapped her in the face. "No, I haven't thought about moving back for a long time. This is home now."

"I understand. I know how tough things were for you before you left. It's just that Mama misses you and Hope. So do I."

Guilt piled on top of guilt. "I know. I miss all of you, too."

Thankfully, Gloria changed the subject. "I'm optimistic about getting holiday time in mid- December. Most people would rather have time off during the holidays. I'll call as soon as I know for sure."

"That would be great, Glory. We'll talk soon."

Celeste ended the call and tossed her phone on the bed. She really should finish folding the laundry, and Hope's lunch for tomorrow still needed to be made. But she couldn't make herself get off the bed.

Should she start sending resumes to restaurants in Myrtle Beach? It might be pointless since Chef Andrew was still a powerful figure in the restaurant business there. But maybe she had no choice. Her mother needed her. And did she have any right to separate Hope from the family she had left?

Her thoughts flew immediately to Drew. Had he realized he called her sweetheart this afternoon? The words sounded so natural on his lips...

She loved her job and her friends at the lodge. The sorrow she felt at the thought of leaving made her heart ache. But what shocked her was the pang of loss at the idea of leaving Drew.

"CELESTE." MAGGIE HELD open the door of the commercial fridge. "Did you take the salmon out of the cooler? There should be four and I can only find two."

"No, I haven't touched it." Celeste glanced at Maggie over her shoulder as she diced a red onion. "Maybe it got put in the freezer by mistake."

Maggie walked into the freezer, then came out and shut the door. "It's not in there either. Damn it! How the hell do two whole salmons disappear?"

Celeste didn't have any answers for her. "You're sure there were four?"

"Yes! Absolutely! I bought them especially for tonight's dinner special, and they weren't cheap. I put all four of them in the cooler when they arrived late yesterday afternoon."

Celeste remembered. A delivery man had arrived in the middle of the dinner rush and she'd heard Maggie instruct him to put the salmon in the cooler, but Celeste had been too busy to actually see him do it.

Maggie glared around the kitchen at the rest of the staff. "Does anyone know what happened to the salmon?"

They all shook their heads. "No chef."

"Right," she said. "I'll figure out later how we're suddenly missing two entire salmon, but for now we have to figure out what to serve when we run out."

Luckily, there were several whitefish fillets in the freezer. It was less expensive and not as popular as fresh Pacific salmon, but a serviceable substitute. Once again, they had to scramble to prepare a new entrée for dinner on short notice.

What the hell was going on? It wasn't like the salmon had walked out of the kitchen on their own. Celeste couldn't help thinking about the beef strip loin that had disappeared. It gave her a sick feeling in her stomach.

She didn't have time to give it further thought. They did the best they could, but the servers reported that some dinner guests were disappointed when they ran out of salmon and were offered whitefish instead. Some had complained, and Maggie had had to go out to the dining room to try to smooth things over. She'd comped two dinners and several desserts.

Finally, the rush was over. After cleanup, the rest of the staff said goodnight, leaving only Maggie and Celeste in the kitchen.

Maggie straightened. "Something's not right, Celeste. I saw all four salmon in the cooler last night before I left."

"What do you think happened?"

"Sometime between close last night and dinner tonight, someone walked off with two salmon."

Celeste slumped against a stainless-steel counter and shook her head. It was hard to believe someone they worked with would steal from the lodge, but there didn't seem to be any other explanation. "I don't want to believe it."

"I know. I don't either, but we have to look at the facts. You remember the strip loin I thought I hadn't weighed properly?"

"Of course."

"Luke had our scales tested. There's nothing wrong with them. I couldn't figure out what I had done, but now, after this, I think the strip loin was also stolen."

"Who would do such a thing?"

"I'm not sure, but it had to be someone who knew the meat was in the cooler. Someone who could walk into the kitchen without causing suspicion."

"You're talking about a member of the kitchen staff." Celeste shook her head. "How could someone walk out of the kitchen with a whole salmon under their arm without anyone noticing?"

"I don't know, but somebody did."

Maggie was right. Theft was the only explanation. Celeste couldn't believe someone she knew was stealing from the restaurant. It was unimaginable. They were like a family in the kitchen.

And yet, it *had* happened.

Maggie wiped her hand over her eyes, looking exhausted. "When I get home, I'll talk to Luke and have him compile a list of kitchen staff who worked the breakfast and lunch shifts today, and on the day the beef went missing. Someone who worked both times could be our thief."

Celeste's stomach pitched. She was afraid to find out who was on that list.

AS SOON AS CELESTE joined Cheryl and Maggie in the restaurant for their weekly meeting, she could feel the tension in the air. Maggie brought out her notebook and set it on the table before turning her attention to her and Cheryl. "I'd like to finalize our entrée specials for the next week. I need to put in our food orders. We're going with chicken."

"Only chicken?" Cheryl asked. "We usually do a beef or fish special as well."

"We're not doing beef or fish." The hard look Maggie leveled at Cheryl made Celeste wince. "It's a cost cutting measure."

"Does this have anything to do with the salmon that went missing? It's all everybody's talking about in the kitchen." Cheryl shook her head. "I can't believe someone in our kitchen would do such a thing."

Maggie stared at Cheryl. "Neither can I."

The air bristled with mistrust. Celeste held her breath. Would Maggie accuse Cheryl of stealing? Did she have proof? She hoped that wasn't the case because Cheryl was a good friend. She couldn't believe she was capable of such deceit.

Finally, Maggie looked down at her notes. "Let's get this over with."

They decided on three chicken entrees—Chicken Marsala, Chicken Parmesan and Creamy Chicken Roulade with spinach and mushrooms—along with accompanying side dishes and appetizer specials for the week. Maggie wrote their choices in her notebook and then snapped it closed. She looked tired and stressed, Celeste thought, not her usual energetic and happy self. After what happened yesterday, it wasn't surprising.

Cheryl glanced nervously at Maggie, then checked her watch and got up from the table. "My shift is about to start. See you later."

"Bye, Cheryl. Have a good shift," Celeste said. Cheryl gave her a tense half smile, then turned to leave.

Once she was gone, Maggie slumped in her seat. "I hate that I suspect her."

"I don't believe Cheryl would steal from the kitchen."

"I don't want to believe it either, but she's on the list of people who worked both shifts when expensive food went missing. She has a key."

The kitchen was always locked overnight. Aside from Ethan, only Maggie, Luke, Celeste and Cheryl had keys. "I have a key, too. Do you suspect me?"

"No, of course not!"

"I could have snuck over here in the middle of the night and stolen the food."

"Don't be ridiculous, Celeste. All we know is that after Cheryl's shift, the salmon was gone."

"I can't help thinking something else is going on."

Maggie shook her head. "I don't want to think about it anymore. Let's talk about something else. How are your driving lessons going?"

"Well, I parallel parked for the first time the other day. Eventually, I might even graduate to parking between actual cars instead of traffic cones," Celeste replied.

"And Drew?"

Celeste hesitated, thinking about Drew's patience with her and the kindness he'd shown Hope. The thought made her...happy. "Drew and I are friends."

"You smiled when I said his name. Are you sure that's all you are?" Maggie asked. "Is something going on between you?"

Celeste carefully wiped all expression from her face. "There's nothing going on, not the way you mean, anyway. Like I said, we're friends."

"He's a very handsome young man."

"I'd have to be blind or dead not to notice how handsome he is. But like you said, he's young. Nine years younger than me to be exact." Celeste lowered her voice, hoping no one could hear their conversation. "I'm a mother, Maggie. I don't do casual sex."

"Does it have to be casual?" Maggie reached across the table and grasped Celeste's hand. "I've seen the way he looks at you. It doesn't appear to me that Drew is the least bit casual about you."

Celeste looked down at their joined hands. "The difference in our races is a consideration as well, at least for me."

Maggie let go of her hand, a look of surprise on her face. "Really? I know several interracial couples and it doesn't seem to be an issue for them."

"It is for me," Celeste confessed. "I told you before an interracial marriage didn't work for my parents."

"And I told you that you're not your parents. Maybe the two of you could make a relationship work. Drew is a good person."

"My father is a good person, too, but some in his family weren't happy when he eloped with my mother. They never accepted her, or me and my sister. The strain drove a wedge between my parents that they couldn't overcome, and they split for good when I was about ten. He eventually remarried, a white woman this time. I heard he had more children with her, but I've never met them."

"I'm sorry, Celeste," Maggie said."

"It's all right." It wasn't easy to talk about her father, even with Maggie. "I don't blame my father. I know he loved my mother, but the pressure from his family was too much for him."

"Are you still in touch with him?"

"I hear from him a few times a year, though I never tell my mom or my sister about it. They aren't quite so forgiving."

"Do you think your family would have a problem with Drew being white? Or are you worried his family would have a problem with you?"

"It doesn't matter because we're not headed in that direction." She had to nip Maggie's speculation in the bud. "We've only known each other a short time and soon Drew will be leaving to go back to the city. We're friends. That's all."

Maggie grasped Celeste's hand again. "Do you want something more than friendship?"

"No! Of course not."

She hadn't allowed herself to want 'something more' for a very long time. Just thinking about a real relationship with Drew, one with love and sex and commitment, made her heart pound with trepidation. Friendship was all she had to offer.

Chapter Eleven

IT WAS PAST MIDNIGHT when Drew entered the lodge through the service entrance. Luke was already waiting for him in the kitchen.

"You ready?"

"Yeah." Drew wiped his suddenly sweaty palms against his pant legs. "Did anyone see you?"

"Just the security guard on duty. I told him I had to change out the mixer before the early shift tomorrow. That's why I brought this box." Luke flipped on one of the overhead lights before opening the large cardboard box displaying the picture of the stand mixer it once held. From the interior, he pulled out three small boxes. "These hidden security cameras are small and magnetic. We can attach them to something metal, and they'll be practically undetectable."

"Maybe they'll give us some answers," Drew said.

"Maybe. Maggie says the kitchen staff is already talking about the thefts, so the thief may lay low for a while. But we've got to do something."

"Yeah." Anger burned in his gut at the thought that someone was stealing from his family. It brought back bad memories of the time shortly after Ethan's lottery win and the threats that were made, particularly against Carrie. They didn't get away with it then and they sure as hell wouldn't get away with it now.

Luke unboxed one of the cameras and showed it to Drew, holding it between his thumb and forefinger. The camera was about the size of a button on a man's shirt.

"We're only going to use one camera at a time. Because they're so small, they have a limited battery life and need to be recharged frequently. This one is charged and ready to go. Maggie will switch out the camera every day and give the used one to you. You'll recharge it and check the recording on the SD card."

"All right. Where should we put this?"

Luke pointed to a metal shelf directly across from the cooler and walk-in freezer. "Here." He attached the camera and it clung to the shelving. "No one will notice it and we should have a good view of the kitchen from here. Anybody who goes into the fridge or freezer after hours will be recorded."

He snapped a picture of the location of the camera with his phone so he could show Maggie where it was. Only the three of them knew of the hidden camera's existence.

"Hope this works," Drew said.

"So do I. Maggie is taking it hard. She's upset that someone in the kitchen could be behind the thefts."

Drew turned to him in alarm. "She doesn't suspect Celeste, does she?"

Luke hesitated. "I know she's your friend, but we can't rule anyone out. Neither Maggie nor I believe she would do such a thing, but we have to remember she has a key to the service entrance of the kitchen and because she lives nearby, she has easy access."

Drew gave Luke a hard stare. "There's no way Celeste is a thief."

Luke returned his scrutiny. "All the more reason to keep an eye on the kitchen. To rule her out."

Drew clenched his hands at his sides to keep from putting his fist through Luke's jaw. He nodded and made himself breathe.

Luke handed him the two remaining camera boxes. "Charge these in your office tomorrow, but don't let anyone see you. The day after tomorrow, Maggie will bring you the camera we just installed and you can check the footage. The instructions and power cords are inside the box."

"Fine."

The sooner the thief was caught, the sooner the cloud hanging over the lodge, and Celeste, would go away.

RYAN HIT A FEW KEYSTROKES and the new security system was activated on the lodge's computer network. "The previous security system was a good one, but we always need to keep one step ahead of the hackers. This system has some new features that will keep your information safer."

"I suppose that means in a few months we'll have to upgrade again," Drew replied.

"Possibly, but it'll still be cheaper than paying ransom to get your information back."

Drew grimaced. When it came to paying ransom, he had first-hand knowledge. He wondered if Carrie had told Ryan about the incident at his first job. "True enough."

Ryan cleared his throat. "While I'm here, could I have a private word with you?"

"Yes, of course." Drew had a feeling Ryan wanted to talk about Carrie, and he dreaded the conversation. "Let's go to my office."

Once they were inside the office, Drew shut the door behind them and Ryan turned his chair to face him. "I'm not going to beat around the bush. I love Carrie and she loves me. I want to ask her to marry me. The approval of her family is important to her, and to me, too, so I'm asking for your blessing to marry your sister."

"There's not many people I respect more than you, Ryan." Drew chose his next words carefully. "But I'm concerned about Carrie. She's very young, only eighteen."

"True, but she'll be nineteen in a couple of months. And she's mature beyond her years."

He wasn't wrong about that. Carrie had always been the responsible one, while he'd made more immature mistakes than he cared to admit, even though he was six years older. "What kind of life can you give her?"

"A good life," Ryan answered. "One filled with love and laughter and mutual respect."

"Marriage involves more than playing video games and being roommates. There's the physical aspect, the passion and the act of love."

"I'm well aware of what marriage involves," Ryan countered. "And I'm also well aware that Carrie deserves a good sex life. I admit to some limitations, but we love each other. We can make it work."

"I believe you when you say you love Carrie. I know you want her to be happy. So, don't you think she deserves more than something she has to 'make work'?"

For a moment, Ryan stared at him. Then his eyes darkened. "You don't believe she can be satisfied with me, sexually or otherwise."

It was a statement rather than a question, but Drew answered anyway. "That's not my call. It's Carrie's. I can see she loves you, but she's only eighteen. She doesn't know yet what she needs to make her happy."

Ryan stared at his hands in his lap. Then he lifted his head and straightened his upper body as he looked directly into Drew's eyes. "I only want what's best for Carrie. Thank you for your time."

Drew stepped out of Ryan's way and watched him open the door and maneuver out of the office. He closed the door and leaned heavily against it. He only wanted what was best for Carrie, too.

LATER, AS DREW HELPED Carrie cook pasta with vegetables and white beans, he couldn't help reflecting on his conversation with Ryan. Sex wasn't the only thing in a marriage, but it was a big thing. Had he made too much of it? He didn't even know exactly what Ryan was capable of, though he'd admitted to limitations.

Maybe he should have stayed out of it completely. It was none of his business.

They took their plates to the dining room. After taking a few mouthfuls, Carrie looked up at him with a smile that told him she was bursting with excitement. "Can you keep a secret?"

"Of course. What?"

"I think Ryan is going to ask me to marry him at the Mistletoe Ball."

Drew's heart fell into his stomach, but he kept his expression neutral. At least he hoped he did. "How do you know?"

"He's been dropping hints the past week." She squirmed in her chair, too excited to sit still. "It will be perfect. Mom and Dad will be there to meet Ryan. And I'm going to say yes!"

"You said you told Mom and Dad about Ryan's disability and the age gap between you, right? What was their reaction?"

"Yes, Ryan and I told them everything, and they seemed perfectly fine." She lifted her chin. "Have you told them about you and Celeste?"

He stuck a forkful of pasta in his mouth and answered around it. "There's nothing to tell."

"Please. It's obvious you're crazy about her, so don't insult my intelligence by trying to deny it." She pointed her finger at him. "Why are you so determined to dislike Ryan?"

"I don't dislike him. Not at all. I admire Ryan very much. But I don't know if he can make you happy."

Carrie put down her fork. "Ryan makes me very happy."

"Sure, when you're playing video games. But what happens when real life kicks in?" Drew couldn't believe he was going to have a conversation about his sister's sex life with her. "You have no idea what goes on in a real marriage."

She made a scoffing sound. "And you do? Ryan and I have talked about what every aspect of our lives together will be like, including our sex lives—if that's what you're getting at. He's explained what making love with him will be like, and the accommodations we'll need to make. But he's going to make sure it's a pleasurable experience for me, for both of us. I trust him. I'm prepared to do whatever Ryan needs because I love him."

"What happens when you discover that love isn't enough? What if you figure out you want a normal sex life?"

Carrie pushed away from the table and stood. "If you can't be happy for me, then I don't want to speak to you."

She stormed out of the dining room. Drew leaned back in his chair and closed his eyes. He was afraid she was about to make a big mistake, one that would change her life forever.

And he was afraid their relationship would change forever, too.

THE INTERCOM BUZZED at nine in the evening, signaling the arrival of a visitor at the bottom of the covered stairs leading to Celeste's apartment. She wasn't expecting visitors.

She pushed the intercom button and answered cautiously. "Yes?"

"Celeste, it's Drew. Can I come up?"

She hesitated for a split second. Why would Drew want to see her now? Was it wise to let him in?

Celeste pushed away the thought and hit the button that opened the door downstairs. This was Drew, and she trusted him.

When she opened the door, Drew stood on the other side, his mouth tight with tension.

"I'm sorry to disturb you," he said, before she was able to utter a word. "Is Hope asleep?"

"Yeah, she's in bed. What's wrong? Has something happened?" Celeste asked.

"Carrie and I had a fight about Ryan. We both said some things..."

He closed his eyes. Celeste touched his arm. "Come on inside and I'll make you some tea."

He tossed his jacket onto the back of a chair while she went into her kitchen and put the kettle on to boil. "Tell me what happened."

He recounted his argument with his sister as he paced back and forth in Celeste's compact living room. "I'm afraid she's headed into a disaster with Ryan. How can I stand by and do nothing?"

"Carrie's a smart girl, Drew. I'm sure she knows what she's getting into."

"She thinks she does, but imagination and reality are two different things." Drew stopped pacing. "It gets worse. Ryan came to see me today, asking for my blessing. He wants to ask Carrie to marry him."

Celeste knew they were serious, but she didn't realize they were talking about marriage. "What did you say?"

"That Carrie was too young to know what she wanted and what she needed to be happy. And that she deserved a normal sex life."

"Oh! You really went there?"

"I did. Damn it, I probably shouldn't have opened my big mouth. But I couldn't stand by and say nothing, either." He shook his head, his expression filled with confusion and regret. "Selfishly, what I'm most worried about is losing her. I hate the thought of Carrie no longer being in my life."

Celeste put the teapot and a couple of cups on a tray and carried it through to the living room. "You're not going to lose her. I know you love Carrie and want what's best for her."

He gave her a wry grin. "Thanks for not saying I'm a controlling jerk."

"You're not a jerk. You're a good brother." Celeste set the tray on the coffee table.

"I'm pretty sure Carrie doesn't think so right now."

"I know that whatever you said, you said out of love and concern." She didn't agree he had the right to get involved in his sister's relationship, but that wasn't what he needed to hear right now. "Carrie knows that, too."

"I hope that's why I did it." Drew bent his head and stared at the floor. "I hope I didn't discourage them because of Ryan's disability."

"You didn't," Celeste said. "You're not like that."

Drew lifted his head and looked directly into her eyes. "How can you possibly know that? I don't even know for sure."

"Because I know *you*."

Celeste hated that he questioned his motives, even his basic goodness. She couldn't let him believe the worst of himself. Without thinking, she stepped close and placed her hand on his cheek, the stubble of his beard tickling her palm. "You're the most kind, loving man. A man who goes out of his way to be kind to a little girl and to teach a hopeless driver like me how to parallel park. You're a good person, Drew Barnes. Don't ever forget it."

He stared at her, his eyes wide with surprise. Then he turned his head and kissed the palm of her hand. A jolt of electricity extended from her hand deep into her body.

"Celeste."

His voice was a whispered plea, and she found she couldn't ignore the attraction between them. She didn't want to, not anymore. He lowered his mouth to hers, but hesitated, waiting for a sign from her.

She was done waiting.

Celeste wrapped her arms around his neck and pulled him close. Their lips met in a hungry kiss, their bodies pressed together, arms tight around each other. When his tongue touched her lips, begging entry, she eagerly opened her mouth to him. Drew immediately swept her mouth with his tongue, the pleasure so intense her knees buckled. Over and over his tongue caressed hers. His hand snaked under her t-shirt to fondle her breast, his thumb and forefinger gently squeezing her nipple through the thin material of her bra. The delicious pleasure went straight to her core, dampening her panties. She wanted him *there*, now, touching her with his hands, his mouth. Filling her.

No! What am I thinking?

Terror filled her at her own thoughts. She couldn't do this.

She tore her mouth away from his. "Please, I have to stop. I'm sorry, Drew."

His hand stilled on her breast. Carefully, he withdrew his hand, then pulled down her t-shirt and stepped back. "I shouldn't have come here. I'm sorry. I should leave."

Celeste shook her head, her mind confused and her body burning. "Drew, I'm so sorry."

"It's okay." His gaze didn't meet hers. "I understand."

"Drew—"

"Shhh." He lightly kissed her forehead. "If we make love, I don't want you to have any regrets. I don't ever want you to be sorry."

He grabbed his jacket and left. The soft click of the door reverberated through the small apartment. For a few minutes she stared at the closed door, her heart pounding as her body gradually returned to normal.

Whatever the hell normal was.

What was the matter with her? A wonderful, handsome man wanted her, and judging by the state of her body, she wanted him, too. So, why did the thought of making love with Drew, of getting close to him, fill her with such overwhelming fear?

CELESTE WAS THANKFUL for the especially busy breakfast rush that kept her from reliving Drew's kiss. Mostly. She'd barely slept. She kept thinking about Drew's hand on her breast and how she'd nearly orgasmed, even though he hadn't touched her bare skin.

Good lord. What would she do if he actually touched her intimately? But that likely wouldn't happen if she kept running away.

She started on her hollandaise sauce for the Eggs Benedict. Sometime during the night, she'd come to the conclusion that she would have regretted making love with Drew. Not because it wouldn't have been wonderful, but because she wasn't ready. She needed more time.

Would she ever be ready? Celeste didn't have an answer to that question.

"Celeste, the hollandaise is burning!"

The alarm in Cheryl's voice brought her back to the present. Celeste pulled the pot off the burner and switched it off. A taste of the sauce told her it was scorched right through. She scraped the contents into the garbage, disgusted with herself. "Damn it, what's the matter with me? Why the hell didn't I use a double boiler?"

"It's not like you to lose focus," Cheryl said. "Are you okay?"

"I'm fine." Celeste brought four more eggs from the cooler and separated the yolks from the whites. "Just didn't sleep well last night."

"Is something bothering you?"

Celeste looked up into Cheryl's concerned eyes. "I'll be fine."

Cheryl lowered her voice. "Is it something to do with Drew? I know you've been spending a lot of time with him lately."

Celeste looked over her shoulder at the rest of the kitchen staff and to the spot in the corner where Hope was reading a book as she waited for the school bus. "Maybe we can talk later."

Cheryl nodded and went back to work. This time Celeste's hollandaise sauce was perfect, and she managed not to make any more mistakes during her shift.

When Hope left for school and things died down, Cheryl turned to her with a smile. "Let's take a break. How about I buy you a cup of coffee?"

They found a quiet corner in the almost empty restaurant to drink their coffee. Celeste stared into her mug. After several prolonged minutes of silence, Cheryl asked, "Was I right? Are you upset because of something Drew did?"

"He didn't do anything wrong." Celeste couldn't let her believe Drew was at fault. "He came over to my place last night. He had a fight with Carrie, and he was upset and needed to talk. I made tea." *Which we never got around to drinking.*

"Tea, huh?" Cheryl sipped her coffee. "When I see you together, I've noticed the way he looks at you."

"Why does everyone keep saying that? We're just friends."

"Maybe Drew doesn't feel the same way."

Celeste had no idea what the current status of their relationship was, but the thought of no longer spending time with Drew saddened her. "I don't know."

"Maybe he's looking for a romantic relationship with you," Cheryl said. "Why don't you ask him out on a date and find out?"

Celeste stared at Cheryl, her chest filling with anxiety. "A date? I can't date Drew!" Her voice rose higher than she'd intended.

"Whoa." Cheryl lifted both hands in surrender. "Take it easy, Celeste. I was talking about seeing a movie together, not going into combat."

"I'm sorry, Cheryl. It's just...I can't date Drew." She tried to think of a plausible reason. "Because we're too different."

"Tim and I are totally different, too. I was the cheerleader and he was the nerd. He's an introvert and I'm an extrovert. He considers things carefully before making a decision and I jump in with both feet. On paper, our relationship shouldn't work, but we've found that our differences are our greatest strengths."

Celeste was intrigued. "What do you mean?"

"He's strong where I'm weak, and vice versa. We agree on the really big issues like family and politics and our outlook on life, so everything else is just...fluff."

That made Celeste smile. "Fluff?"

"You know, superficial, meaningless. In the vast scheme of things, it doesn't matter that I'm indifferent about anime and he thinks it's the cat's pajamas. As long as we agree on the important things, nothing else matters."

"I'm glad you and Tim made things work."

"You don't think you and Drew could do that?"

Celeste shook her head. Drew deserved someone who could love him with her whole heart. He deserved everything good.

"That's too bad," Cheryl said. "If I'd said no to Tim, I would have missed out on finding the love of my life. Sometimes you gotta take a leap of faith, you know?"

Celeste smiled, but she knew she wasn't that brave.

Chapter Twelve

DREW POURED OVER THE monthly financial statements line by line, looking for figures that were out of whack with the previous month, or just seemed wrong. Before he presented these statements to Ethan he wanted to make sure he understood where every penny was coming from and where it was going. He wouldn't give Ethan any reason to regret putting him temporarily in charge of the lodge's finances.

His desk phone rang, breaking his concentration. "Hi Drew. This is Jeanette from the front desk. A woman from the accounting department at Stevenson Paper in Minneapolis is on line one. She was asking for Harper but I explained she's away. They want to speak to someone in our accounts payable department."

"That would be me." Right now, he was the entire accounting department. "I'll take it. Thanks, Jeanette."

He hit the line one button. "Hello? Drew Barnes here. How can I help you?"

"Hello. This is Susan Sinclair. I'm in accounts receivable at Stevenson Paper. I just want to remind you that your last invoice with us is overdue."

"Overdue?" That made no sense. All the lodge's bills were up to date. He'd paid them himself. "Let me check into that. What's the invoice number?"

Drew jotted down the number as Susan rattled it off, then searched for it in the accounting system. He found it immediately.

"Okay, here it is. Paper products for the hotel and restaurant. Napkins, tissues, and toilet paper in the amount of three thousand fifty-two dollars. Is that correct?"

"Yes, that's the one."

Drew dug deeper into the payment history. "According to our records, a check for that invoice was issued on October twenty-seventh. You should have received it shortly after that."

The check for Stevenson Paper was among the first batch of invoices he'd paid a couple of days after arriving at the lodge. He remembered putting the checks in the outgoing mail basket that Luke dropped off at the post office in Minnewasta every day.

"I'm sorry, but we have no record that any payment was received on that invoice," Susan said.

"Perhaps it got lost in the mail."

"That sounds like the most likely possibility," Susan said. "Why don't we double-check the address you have on file for us. Though I can't imagine there's a problem since this is the first time we've ever had an issue receiving your checks."

Drew looked up the address for Stevenson Paper that was stored in the accounting system. Anytime a payment was made to them, this address would be printed on the check.

He read the address out loud. "Stevenson Paper Inc., Box 26759, Minneapolis, Minnesota, 75247."

"Are you sure you have the right company?" Susan asked.

"What do you mean?"

"Our mailing address is the street address of our warehouse, not a post office box number. And we're Stevenson Paper Limited, not Incorporated."

Drew was starting to get a bad feeling in the pit of his stomach. "Let me double check. Maybe I've got the wrong Stevenson Paper."

But there was no mistake. There was only one Stevenson Paper in the system and apparently it had the wrong address.

How the hell had that happened?

"I'm going to need to look into this further and get back to you. Whatever's happened, we'll make good on the invoice."

"I was sure you would." Susan sounded relieved. "Solace Lake Lodge has been a valuable customer the last three years."

After taking Susan's contact information, Drew hung up the phone and immediately logged into the lodge's bank account. After a few moments of searching, he found the check in question. It had been withdrawn from the bank account on November second. But apparently the money hadn't gone to Susan's company.

He couldn't imagine that Harper would have changed the address or the vendor's name, and he certainly hadn't done it. Did that mean that someone had gained access to the accounting system and made adjustments? How many other vendors had been changed? The thought made him sweat.

It hadn't occurred to him to check the address in the accounting system against the one on Stevenson's invoice. He'd assumed it would be correct. He shouldn't have been so careless.

Drew sat back in his chair, his stomach pitching. It was happening again. Somehow, he found himself in the middle of another scam.

His first instinct was to run. Or to hide the mistake. *No.* He made himself calm down. This time he wouldn't try to hide what had happened. Last time, trying to cover up his mistake cost him his job. This time he was going to bring the scam to light. This time, he'd fight back.

With renewed purpose, Drew logged into the accounting program once more. He looked up every invoice he'd paid by check since arriving at the lodge. Then he dug out the paper copy of each invoice from the filing cabinet and checked the address in the accounting system against the address on the invoice.

The results were chilling. Drew found three more vendors whose addresses had been changed to a post office box number. The company names had been subtly changed, as well.

The original vendors had gone unpaid, and though Stevenson Paper had been the first looking for their money, they wouldn't be the last. Even though it was going to cost double, these vendors had to be paid. The lodge's reputation depended on it.

And so did his.

First, he changed the password to the accounting program once again to deny access to the intruder. Then, taking a deep breath, he picked up his cell phone and called Luke.

"Hello?"

Drew didn't beat around the bush. "We have a problem. A big one."

AFTER DREW SHOWED HIM the evidence, Luke sat back in his chair, a stunned look on his face. "My God! This is thousands of dollars. How the hell did this happen?"

"The only way possible is if someone gained access to our accounting program and changed the addresses. I can't tell you how that happened because Harper, Ethan and I are the only ones with the password. I keep my copy of the passwords with me at all times." He'd taken seriously Ethan's directive to guard the passwords with his life.

"So, what do we do?" Luke asked.

"I've changed the password on the accounting system again. Hopefully that will keep the criminal out. It looks like the changes to our vendor addresses were made between the time Harper left and when I changed the password the first time."

He wished he'd checked for anomalies as soon as he learned the invoice received for sugar and flour from the former vendor was bogus. But Luke had been convinced it was a random phishing scam, and he'd taken his word for it, probably because it was easier than believing there was a much bigger problem.

He couldn't blame Luke. He should have known better.

"I have to let Ethan and Harper know I've changed the password again. We might have to change the bank account as well. It's probably been compromised."

Luke nodded. "You're right. Let's call them."

Drew wasn't looking forward to speaking to Ethan. He'd trusted him to keep things running in his absence and he'd let him down.

Luke used his phone to call. "Ethan, hi. I'm here with Drew, and we've got some news. It's not good." He explained the situation.

For several moments there was silence on the line. Then Ethan swore. "Damm it, Drew. Did you leave the passwords lying around where anyone could find them?"

"No! Of course not!" He should have known Ethan would automatically assume he'd done something wrong.

"Then how the hell did someone gain access to our systems?"

"It's possible we were hacked," Luke said. "Though we haven't received any kind of ransom demand."

"I don't believe it's a ransomware situation," Drew said. "I think we should look closer to home. Theft from a business most often comes from an employee. Maybe we need to investigate whether the thefts from the kitchen are related to these thefts."

"What thefts from the kitchen?" Ethan's voice blasted from Luke's phone.

Luke brought him up to date with the issues in the kitchen. "We've beefed up security and installed hidden cameras in the kitchen. It's just a matter of time till we find out who's doing this."

Ethan swore again. "We leave for a few weeks and all hell breaks loose."

The comment hit Drew like a slap. Luke replied, his mouth tight with repressed anger as he spoke. "We don't know whether these incidents are related. And for all we know, they could have begun before you left."

"What do you mean?"

"Maybe *you* didn't guard *your* copy of the passwords as well as you should have."

Ethan was silent for a long moment. And then Drew heard him sigh. "You're right. We're going to get nowhere blaming each other."

It was probably the closest thing to an apology that Drew was going to get from Ethan. He'd nurse his bruised feelings later. Right now, they needed to act. "I think you should consider setting up a new bank account. The current one may have been compromised."

"I'll speak to the bank right away."

"You need to tell Harper what's going on. As part owner, she'll need to sign any documents for a new bank account," Drew said.

"No. Absolutely not. I won't upset Harper."

"You've already upset Harper. Keeping more secrets from her will make her even more anxious."

"What the hell are you talking about? How do you know anything about Harper?"

"Because she told me!" Drew was sick of the subterfuge. "She's called several times to find out what's going on at the lodge, but she kept it on the down low because she didn't want to upset *you*! Why do you think she's been eating so much ice cream from that shop on the other side of the city? She wanted to get you out of the house so she could call me."

"You had no right to interfere." There was a note of barely restrained anger in Ethan's voice.

"I didn't interfere. I was put in the middle. You and Harper are so worried about upsetting each other that you don't actually talk!"

Ethan didn't reply, and Drew didn't want to argue the point any further. His uncle likely wouldn't believe anything he said anyway.

Luke cleared his throat. "We'll keep you appraised of any developments here. In the meantime, I'm going to use my personal credit card to pay our vendors while you set up a new bank account."

"I'll transfer some money to you from my own bank account." Ethan's voice was clipped. "We'll talk soon."

The line went dead. Luke ended the call and set his phone on the desk. "I suppose that went about as well as we could have expected."

Drew choked out a bitter laugh. "Right."

"We'll figure this out," Luke said. "Honest to God, when I find out who's doing this..." He shook his head. "Maggie suspects Cheryl Johnson."

"Cheryl Johnson?" Drew shook his head. "If I'm right and both the theft from the kitchen and the theft from our vendors are related, it's hard to imagine how Cheryl could have gained access to the accounting system."

"We have no evidence they're related. Someone could have gained access to our systems from the outside. We could have been hacked."

"It's possible." They couldn't rule anything out at this point.

Luke picked up his phone and began texting. "I'm going to contact my dad and Ryan and have them check for any breaches."

"Luke, wait." Drew tapped his fingers against the desk. "Maybe for now, just speak to your dad."

"What are you saying?"

"Ryan could certainly get into our computer systems if he wanted to."

"That's crazy. There's no way Ryan would steal from us."

Drew refused to back down. He stared at Luke. "You're the one who said we can't rule anyone out. That includes Ryan."

Luke held his gaze for a long minute. Finally, he shook his head and looked away. "You're right. I don't like it, but for now, I'll talk to my dad. I'll ask him not to mention anything to Ryan."

Luke got to his feet and left the office. Drew slumped in his chair. They needed to do whatever they could to stop this thief. Or thieves. He'd misjudged scam artists and hackers once before, believing he could handle the problem himself. He wouldn't make that mistake again. But they had to be selective about who they trusted.

LESS THAN AN HOUR LATER, Luke returned. He sat across from Drew. "I just got off the phone with my father. I told him about what's happening here."

"What did he say?"

"That he'll be here shortly to check things out. Jerry also told me that Ryan will no longer be coming out to the lodge to do updates or fix problems. Ryan will do what he can remotely, but if something needs to be handled in person at the lodge, Jerry will do it. It was Ryan's request."

"Did he tell you why Ryan made the request?"

"No, and I asked. Jerry said he was pretty closed-mouthed about it. He's worried Ryan's getting ready to accept a job somewhere else."

Drew sat back in his chair, a sinking feeling in his gut. "I see." Ryan certainly had the skills to hack into their computer system and change information in their accounting system. Was that why he didn't want to come back out to the lodge? Was he getting ready to run?

"Did Ryan and Carrie have a falling out?" Luke asked.

"Not that I know of. Why?"

"Just a feeling my dad got. Ryan was subdued when he talked to him. Since he and Carrie have been together, he's been very happy. He said Ryan was much more outgoing than when he first arrived in Minnewasta, but he seems to be reverting to his old ways."

Or maybe he was simply becoming more secretive because he had something to hide. He had no proof that Ryan was behind any of the trouble at the lodge. But in his mind, Ryan was the most likely suspect.

There was no way he could have stolen from the kitchen. Unless he had help...

Carrie. What if Ryan convinced Carrie to steal from the kitchen?

A wave of nausea swept over Drew at the thought. He got to his feet. "Excuse me. I need to talk to Carrie."

Luke rose as well. "She's not in the kitchen. Maggie just told me she went home sick."

Drew felt sick, too. If Ryan was their hacker, it was going to kill Carrie. And if she was involved in the thefts, it was going to kill him. He had to find her. "Thanks for letting me know. I'll see you later."

"Whatever issue they have, I hope they can work it out. They're good people."

Drew swallowed hard. At least one of them was. "Yeah."

He grabbed his jacket from the back of the door and headed outside to his car. If Carrie was involved in the thefts from the kitchen...

Drew wasn't sure what his next move would be.

Chapter Thirteen

WHEN DREW OPENED THE unlocked front door, Carrie's winter boots were lying in the middle of the foyer. That was so unlike her. She liked order and neatness and had chastised him more than once about putting his things away. Drew picked up the boots and set them carefully in the closet.

Something was terribly wrong.

Drew walked through the living room, dining room and kitchen, but Carrie wasn't there. She had to be in her room. He took a deep breath and headed down the hall.

Carrie's bedroom door was shut. He knocked tentatively. "Carrie, are you in there?"

"Go away, Drew."

Her voice sounded muffled, like she'd been crying, and it gave him pause. Had she discovered that Ryan was the hacker or was it something else entirely? He suddenly felt less sure about his suspicions concerning Ryan. What if the conversation he'd had with Ryan about his limitations was the cause of Carrie's distress?

No. He'd spoken to him out of love for Carrie, for her own good. Ryan might not be the person everyone thought he was. Drew was only looking out for her.

But she likely wouldn't see it that way right now.

He turned the doorknob and discovered she hadn't locked it. Carrie was lying across the bed on her back, the covers rumpled and her long dark hair hanging over the side of the bed. She glanced at him before staring up at the ceiling once more.

"Didn't I tell you to go away?"

"Not happening." Drew moved a chair next to the bed. "Tell me what's going on."

"Nothing much. Only that the love of my life told me he doesn't want me anymore." Her words ended on a hiccupping sob, as tears streamed from her closed eyes.

"Did he say why?"

"He said..." She swallowed and tried again. "He said I was too young. He realized the age difference between us was too much."

"I'm sorry, Care Bear," he said, using her childhood nickname. "I'm sorry you're hurting."

Carrie turned her head and gave him a wry grin. "I forgot you have vast firsthand experience with rejection."

He grimaced, remembering his infatuation with Maggie and his current situation with Celeste. "Yeah, but it's the reason I can tell you you'll get over this. You won't feel this way forever, I promise. And someday, you'll find someone new and all the stars will align and nothing will stand in your way."

"Is that what happened to you? Are you and Celeste a couple now?"

He had no idea what he and Celeste were. "No, we're not a couple. We're friends. I was speaking hypothetically."

"Great." Fresh tears trickled down her temple and into her hair. "I have years of rejection to look forward to."

"Come on, Carrie." Drew grasped her hand. "Maybe it's for the best. You and Ryan are at different places in your life."

"It didn't seem to matter to him before. We had so many things in common that our age difference was irrelevant. Or at least I thought so." Carrie whispered, "I was going to make it work."

"You deserve more than something you have to make work."

Carrie sat up abruptly and stared at him. "What did you say?"

Her question, and the intensity in her eyes, caught him off guard. "I...I think a relationship shouldn't be like work. It should be natural, smooth. You shouldn't have to make things work."

She scooted to the edge of the bed and sat directly in front of Drew. "Ryan said those exact words to me: *You deserve more than something you have to 'make work'.*

"That's not fair."

She pulled the sweater over her head and pushed her arms through the sleeves. "At least I didn't go to Maggie and tell her what an immature dorkus you are. How could you do this to me, Drew?"

"I was trying to protect you. Do you have any idea what the reality of living with a paraplegic is like? What sex is like? Are you sure you want that for the rest of your life?"

Carrie gasped and dropped the sock she was trying to put on her foot. "Did you say that to Ryan? Oh my God, no wonder he broke up with me. Do you think it's easy for a proud man like Ryan to admit to the limitations in his life? I've liked him from the moment I met him. *I* was the one who pursued *him*. I convinced him we could have a good life together and then you go and remind him that he's not like all the normal men." She made air quotes around the word 'normal'.

"Carrie, what do you really know about Ryan? The lodge has been hacked and money stolen. Who is better placed than Ryan to do that?"

Carrie stared at him and shook her head. "I can't believe you just said that. Of all the ridiculous things you've said, that was the worst and the most insulting. I'm getting out of here."

She pulled her suitcase from the closet and began haphazardly throwing clothes into it.

"What are you doing?" A sense of dread tightened Drew's chest. "Where are you going?"

"I'm going to try to convince Ryan that you're wrong and you have no idea what you're talking about." She dragged her suitcase to the attached bathroom and tossed all her perfumes and shampoos inside.

"Carrie—"

"Don't say another word. You've said more than enough." She headed for the bedroom door, rolling the suitcase behind her. She turned to look at him. "For your information, relationships take real work. And sacrifice. Because you want to be with the person you love, you'll do whatever it takes, no matter how hard it is. Until you figure that out, you'll always be alone."

She turned and left the room. Drew followed her. "Carrie, wait. Let's talk."

She abruptly stopped and faced him. Her eyes flashed. "No! I don't know if I ever want to speak to you again."

His heart stopped at her words. "You don't mean that."

"I absolutely mean it. I'm not the dumb little sister you can boss around anymore. You interfered with my life, and with Ryan's. And now you're accusing him of stealing from the lodge? I'm not sure I can ever forgive you."

She turned and marched down the hall, not sparing another glance at him. A minute later he heard the front door slam shut. Drew stood completely still, his mind reeling.

What have I done?

"I HEARD HOPE'S HAVING another sleepover with Tessa tonight." Maggie balanced a cob of corn vertically on her cutting board and deftly sliced off the kernels with a sharp knife.

"Yeah, she was very excited. She just got off the school bus at Scarlet and Cam's house." Scarlet called to let Celeste know Hope had safely arrived. "As soon as I have a free weekend, we need to do a sleepover at our place. Hope's been at Tessa's house a couple of times, so it's our turn."

"We'll make sure to work a sleepover into your schedule." Maggie added the fresh corn to the sliced leeks she was sauteing. "How do reservations look for tonight?"

Celeste brought them up on the computer system. "Ten reservations for a total of forty people. Looks like it'll be a busy Friday night."

"Fantastic. I want to do something special with the corn and leek bisque. I think it would be fun to offer guests various garnishes that they can choose tableside and add to their soup. I'm thinking sliced jalapenos, micro greens, sliced grape tomatoes, avocado, and maybe cilantro if we have some. I've already spoken to our servers about it. Can you prep those items for tonight, Carrie?"

When Carrie didn't respond, Celeste glanced up from her work to see Carrie washing lettuce at the sink, her shoulders stiff with tension.

"Carrie? Did you hear me?" Maggie repeated.

Carrie lifted her head abruptly, her eyes blinking like she was emerging from a deep sleep. "Sorry, Chef. I missed what you said."

It wasn't like her to be inattentive. "That's okay," Maggie said gently. She repeated the instructions.

"Yes, Chef." Carrie's eyes were red-rimmed. "Is there anything else you need me to do?"

"Aside from getting the salad station ready, that's it, at least for now." Maggie tilted her head. "Are you okay, sweetie?"

As Carrie stared at Maggie, her chin began to tremble and her eyes filled with tears. She closed her eyes and shook her head. "No, not really."

Maggie and Celeste led her to a chair in the corner and made her sit down. Maggie sat beside her. "What's going on?"

"Ryan...he...broke up...with me."

Celeste knelt and clasped Carrie's hand. "I'm so sorry."

"I thought he was going to ask me to marry him, and then...and then Drew talked to him."

Oh dear. Celeste remembered her conversation with Drew. He was concerned about what he'd said to Ryan and whether it had been the right thing to do.

Looked like he'd been right to worry.

"Ryan doesn't want to speak to me anymore. I went to see him last night, and he said Drew was right when he said he could never make me happy. But he's wrong, they're both wrong!"

"You mean, he thinks he can't make you happy because of his disability?" Celeste asked carefully.

Carrie closed her eyes, tears streaming down her cheeks. "Yes. Ryan comes off as having his life together and coming to terms with his disability, but underneath there's a lot of uncertainty and fear. Drew set off all his insecurities and now, he doesn't want to see me anymore. He says it's for my own good."

"Oh, honey. I'm so sorry." Celeste wondered how Drew was taking this news.

"Why don't you go back to the house and rest for a bit," Maggie said. "You're too upset to work today."

"No! I'm never going back there! Not as long as Drew is there."

"Carrie, he made a mistake. He didn't mean to hurt you," Celeste said.

"I'm never speaking to him again. He's ruined my life." The words, spoken with absolute conviction, told Celeste this was no idle threat. Carrie took a deep breath and rose to her feet. "I'll be fine. I want to work."

"If you don't want to stay at the house, where will you go tonight?" Maggie asked.

"I don't know. I slept in my car last night. I suppose I can do it again."

Maggie shared a horrified look with Celeste. "Listen, why don't you come home with me to Luke's grandma's house tonight? We have a spare bedroom you can use." Luke and Maggie had lived with his grandmother, Phyllis Carlsson, since before they were married. It was an arrangement that suited all three of them.

"I don't want anyone to fuss."

Maggie laughed. "Are you kidding? Phyllis lives to fuss. She's not happy unless she's taking care of someone. If it makes you feel better, I'll call and check with her first, but I'm sure she'd be delighted to have you stay with us."

"Well, if you're sure, okay. Thank you. It was kind of cold in the car last night." Carrie straightened her spine and wiped her eyes. "I need to get back to work. That lettuce isn't going to wash itself."

They all went back to what they were doing, but Celeste couldn't stop thinking about Drew. What must he be going through? Blaming himself most likely. As far as she knew, he hadn't come to work today. He'd texted saying he wasn't able to give her another parallel parking lesson at noon the way they'd planned, but nothing more.

When the last of the diners left at ten o'clock and they closed the restaurant, Celeste hugged Carrie goodbye and watched her leave with Maggie, glad the girl wasn't sleeping in her car again. The last to leave, she shut off the lights, locked the kitchen and said goodnight to the security staff and Mel at the front desk before hurrying to her apartment.

Once inside, Celeste couldn't rest. She paced from the living room to the kitchen and back again several times, trying to figure out what to do. Finally, she picked up her phone and sent Drew a text, going for a friendly, I-have-no-idea-your-relationship-with-your-sister-is-falling-apart vibe.

Hey. How are you doing? Feel like watching a movie together tonight?

SHE WAITED FOR A REPLY, but none came. Ten minutes later she sent another text.

Drew, just let me know you're okay. Please.

STILL NO REPLY. NOW she was really starting to worry.

"Screw this."

She dressed in her warmest winter gear, grabbed a flashlight and her keys, and headed out. If he wouldn't respond to her texts, then he'd damn well have to respond to her in person.

Keeping to the shadows, Celeste made her way across the parking lot to the opening in the trees where the trail began. She'd only walked this path a few times but never at night. She hoped she didn't get lost in the bush and fall into a partially frozen lake.

Thankfully, the path was wide and well-used. A thick layer of wood chips, now partially covered in a dusting of snow, lined the path and made following easy, even though it was dark and illuminated only by her flashlight. After walking for about twenty minutes, the lights of Ethan and Harper's house came into view. She walked up the steps and knocked on the door. To her surprise, Drew answered almost immediately. Judging by the disappointment on his face, she wasn't the person he most wanted to see.

"Did you walk here in the dark?" he asked.

She held up her flashlight. "I was fine. I came prepared."

"Why did you come?"

His question made her doubt the wisdom of this venture. He wasn't exactly overjoyed to see her, but she wasn't going to leave until she made sure he was okay. "Because you didn't answer any of my texts."

"Sorry."

Drew ran his hand through his already messy hair. He wore a t-shirt and sweatpants, along with a day's growth of stubble. Celeste tried to ignore the fact that she found the scruffy version of Drew sexy as hell. She reminded herself that right now he needed a friend.

"Do you think I can come inside for a bit?" she said. "It's cold out here."

He moved aside. "Yeah, of course. Sorry."

Celeste stepped over the threshold, and he closed the door behind her.

He turned to her, unsmiling. "I don't feel much like talking."

She took off her mitts and stuck them in her coat pocket. She'd never seen Drew like this—stubborn, defensive, closed-off. But she couldn't get past the feeling that he needed her. "Then you can listen."

"I'm not in the mood for a lecture, either."

"You won't get one from me. In case you haven't already heard, I wanted to let you know that Carrie is staying at Luke's grandmother's house with him and Maggie."

Drew's expression immediately changed, his relief palpable. He bent over, his hands on his knees, his breathing labored. She resisted the urge to touch him, to rub his tense shoulders and give him some comfort.

Finally, he straightened and looked at her. "Thank God. I was worried about her. She wouldn't answer any of my texts or calls. Neither would Ryan. I was afraid something had happened to her."

"Why didn't you call me?" Celeste asked. "You know you can tell me anything. I won't judge you."

He shook his head and looked away. "I didn't want to get you tangled up in my mess. You didn't have to come here. You could have texted about Carrie."

"You didn't answer my texts, remember?" Celeste decided to go with honesty. "Besides, I wanted to make sure you were okay. Carrie told Maggie and me about your argument."

"Is she...is she upset?"

She wouldn't lie to him. "Yes. She went to Ryan, but he told her she was too young to know what she was getting into being with him. He admitted you'd spoken to him. She was devastated. Apparently, she spent last night in her car."

Drew closed his eyes, anguish written on his face. "She'd rather sleep in her car in the cold than be in the same house as me."

"She's safe now with Maggie and Luke. Phyllis will make sure she's well cared for."

He nodded, his Adam's apple moving as he swallowed. "That's good."

Celeste nodded as well, her hands clasped in front of her. Now that she'd delivered her news and seen that Drew was alive and well, she should probably leave. But it didn't feel right to leave him alone, at least not yet. "So, it's a long, cold walk back to the lodge. Maybe you could offer me a cup of hot chocolate before I go."

"What about Hope? Is she alone?"

"No, she's having a sleepover with Tessa." It warmed her heart that he was concerned about her daughter. Or maybe he was looking for an excuse to get her to leave.

He shook his head. "Sorry. I should have offered you something. Come on in."

Celeste shrugged out of her coat and hung it in the closet, then followed Drew into the kitchen. He rummaged in a drawer beneath the one-cup coffee maker.

"I think we've got some hot chocolate pods in here somewhere." He pulled out several different coffee and tea pods from the drawer, but no hot chocolate.

"I'm sorry. It doesn't look like there's any hot chocolate left. Carrie must have used the last one..." He averted his gaze.

Celeste picked up a pod of herbal tea. "That's okay. I'll have this instead. What would you like?"

He shook his head. "Nothing. I'm good."

He looked tired, and Celeste imagined he hadn't slept much last night. There weren't any dishes in the sink or any signs of cooking in the kitchen. "What did you have for dinner, Drew?"

He gave a negligent shrug. "I don't remember."

"Did you eat anything today?"

"I..." He shook his head. "I wasn't hungry."

She guided him to the kitchen island and made him sit on one of the stools. "Sit here and I'll find you something to eat."

"Celeste, you don't have to go to all that trouble. I'm fine."

She found a jug of orange juice in the fridge and poured a glass for him. "You're the one usually looking after me. Let me look after you for a change."

Drew stared at her without blinking. Finally, he gave her a hint of a smile. "Thank you."

"You're welcome."

She found eggs, a block of cheddar cheese, some deli ham and a loaf of bread in the fridge but not much else. "What would you rather have, an omelet with toast or a ham sandwich?"

"The eggs and toast might go down better."

"One omelet coming right up."

Celeste shredded cheese, then scrambled three of the eggs. While her pan heated, she put two slices of bread into the toaster.

"It's really nice watching you work," Drew said. "Kind of like a ballet."

"Really?" Celeste poured the eggs into the hot pan. "A ballet?"

"You look so comfortable in a kitchen, so graceful, like a dancer on a stage. I noticed it when you cooked here before." He didn't add it was the time she'd cooked for Ryan and Carrie, but he must have remembered because his shoulders slumped. He shook his head. "That probably sounds ridiculous."

"Actually, it sounds nice, very poetic." She sprinkled the cheese over the egg mixture and when it started to melt, she folded the omelet in half and turned off the heat. "I appreciate the comparison to ballet. Makes me feel very special."

"You're probably the most special person I know."

Celeste's heart lodged in her throat as they stared at each other.

The toaster made a popping sound, breaking the spell. She buttered the toast and placed it on a plate, then slid the omelet next to it. She set the plate in front of Drew. "There you go. *Bon appétit.*"

"Thanks, Celeste. This looks great."

He stared at the plate without eating. She refilled his orange juice. "You wouldn't want to upset me by not eating the food I went to all this trouble making for you, would you?"

He scowled at her. "Are you trying to guilt me into eating?"

"I'm a mother. I'm very good at using guilt. Eat."

"Fine." With a sigh he picked up his fork and took a bite of the omelet. "It's really good."

"Of course, it is. I made it, didn't I?"

He smiled as he took another bite. "Smart ass."

Satisfied that he was finally eating, she made herself the herbal tea and sat on the stool beside him. Celeste quietly sipped and watched. She was worried about him. He likely wouldn't have eaten anything if she hadn't shown up. What would happen if Carrie never forgave him?

For his sake, and for Carrie's, she hoped that scenario didn't come true.

Finally, Drew pushed his plate away. "I'm full. Thanks, Celeste. That was delicious."

"You're welcome."

She was pleased he'd eaten most of the omelet. She scraped what was left into the garbage and stuck the plate, her empty cup, and the pan she'd used into the dishwasher. After wiping the counters and the stove, there didn't seem to be a reason for her to stay any longer.

She dried her hands on a dish towel. "I guess I should go."

"You're not in a rush, are you?" Drew asked. "I mean, if Hope's away at a sleepover, you could stay for a while, couldn't you?"

Celeste searched his face. Though he appeared outwardly calm, something in his voice told her he didn't want to be alone.

Neither do I.

"I guess I could stay for a bit."

She was certain the smile he gave her was full of relief. "Great. You said you wanted to watch a movie, right?"

"So, you *did* read my text."

"Of course I did." He looked away and straightened the dish towel hanging over the handle of the stove. "Like I said, you don't need to get involved in my mess."

Oh, Drew. She wanted to hug him, or maybe shake him until his teeth rattled. Instead, she smiled. "We're friends, Drew. And friends take care of each other, even if it's messy. So get used to it."

He laughed, the first sound of genuine amusement she'd heard from him since she arrived. He lifted his hands in surrender. "Okay."

"Let's go find a movie to watch."

Drew touched her shoulder, all traces of laughter gone from his face. "Thank you."

"For what?"

"For coming here tonight, for being my friend, for not saying how wrong I am about Ryan. I'm sure everyone at the lodge thinks I am." He let his hand drop from her shoulder.

"Is that why you didn't go to work today?"

"That's part of the reason. But mainly to give Carrie space. I'm sure she didn't want to see me."

Celeste couldn't argue with him there. It would have been awkward for them both if he'd shown up at the lodge today, but they couldn't avoid each other forever.

"You and Carrie are family. She's hurting right now, but she's a smart girl. Eventually she'll figure out that what you did, you did out of love."

"Did I?" Drew shook his head and stared at the floor. "I don't know anymore. Maybe I was more concerned about having a brother-in-law in a wheelchair."

"That's not true. You're not like that. You would never intentionally hurt anyone. You're a good, loving person."

Drew stared at her. Then he pulled her into his arms, holding her tight. "Thank you," he murmured against her ear. "That's high praise, coming from the best person I know."

Celeste wrapped her arms around his waist. She tried to recall why it was so important to resist Drew. Nothing came to mind. All she could remember right now was the way she felt when she was in his arms.

Beautiful. Desired. Loved.

She leaned back to look at him at the same time he did. Celeste reached up to stroke his cheek, his stubble rough beneath her hand. When he lowered his head, his face close to hers, her heart rate spiked in anticipation. She wanted to kiss him. She wanted *him*.

Pushing away the frightened voice in her head that screamed at her to run away, she wound her arms around his neck and kissed him. When his soft lips met hers, everything faded away, until there was only the two of them. All she could do was feel.

Yes, this is what I want. This man. He's everything I need.

Her body hummed with pleasure as he pulled her against him, letting her feel the strength of his desire. Drew pulled his mouth from hers and looked into her face, his dark eyes boring into hers.

"I want to make love with you, Celeste, but only if you want it, too."

"Yes." She answered quickly before she could overthink her decision. "Yes."

A grin flashed across his face before he gave her a quick, hard kiss. Then he lifted her into his arms and carried her out of the kitchen. Celeste wrapped her arms around his neck and hung on, her heart beating fast. Though her head still whirled with doubts and fears, the demands of her body overrode them all. More than anything, she needed to feel alive again.

In the bedroom, Drew carefully set her on her feet and kissed her again. Kissing Drew was magical. Celeste felt light, her spirit lifting, floating, soaring.

Drew dragged his mouth away from hers and trailed kisses down her neck. "You're so beautiful, Celeste. So damn beautiful."

Celeste braced her hands against his chest, loving the solid, strong feel of him. It made her believe he would always hold her like this, always be there for her. "So are you."

"Will you let me undress you?"

Her breath hitched, but then she pushed the doubts away. Why shouldn't she be with Drew? Why shouldn't she be allowed one moment of joy, of happiness?

"Yes," she breathed. "Yes, please."

Drew wasted no time. Grabbing the hem of her sweater, he pulled it over her head and dropped it to the floor. Celeste fought the urge to fold her arms over her chest to cover herself. But this was Drew, and she trusted him.

"God," he whispered as he kissed the swell of her breasts above the silky material of her bra. "So damn beautiful."

In one deft move, he unfastened her bra and tossed it aside. Then he unzipped her jeans and, kneeling in front of her, pushed both jeans and panties slowly down her legs. Celeste's breaths came in short pants, and her body trembled in anticipation. When he looked up at her and she saw the hunger in his eyes, her embarrassment and apprehension disappeared. All she felt was desire.

He kissed his way up her legs, pausing briefly to kiss the triangle of hair at the apex of her thighs. She forgot to breathe. Before she could recover, he moved his explorations upward, trailing kisses across her lower abdomen and stomach. When he kissed the underside of her left breast, Celeste shivered.

"Do you like that?" he whispered.

"Yes."

His tongue made wet, lazy circles around the areole that had her alternately shivering with cold and burning with heat. He licked her distended, hard nipple and her knees buckled. Moisture pooled between her legs. She only remained standing by hanging on to Drew's shoulders.

Drew pulled her nipple into his mouth and sucked, the pleasure so intense it hovered on the edge of pain. He moved his exploration to her other breast and lavished it with the same attention. Tension built inside her body. When he nudged a finger inside her wet, throbbing channel, her orgasm exploded from her. A thousand colorful lights erupted into a starburst of fireworks behind her closed eyes. She shouted her release, holding Drew's head to her breast as she came over and over again.

Slowly, the spasms lessened, leaving her boneless. Drew rose to his full height and put his arms around her, holding her up. Celeste pressed her face against his chest.

"I didn't expect..." Emotion made it difficult to speak. She couldn't remember ever coming that fast or that hard. "Drew."

He tenderly kissed her hair. "I know, baby. I know."

He seemed to understand what she couldn't put in words. After kissing her once again, he stepped away to throw back the covers, then lifted her easily and laid her carefully on the bed, her head on the pillow. Celeste's eyes locked on his as he quickly shed his clothes. In seconds he was naked and her breath caught.

Drew was absolutely beautiful. Broad shoulders, flat stomach, narrow hips, powerful thighs. And an engorged penis that told her he wanted her as much as she wanted him.

He reached into a drawer in the nightstand and pulled out his wallet, producing a couple of condom packages from inside. "You caught me by surprise. These are all I have."

Celeste blinked. She hadn't even considered birth control. She definitely wasn't thinking clearly.

But right now, she didn't care.

Drew broke open one of the packages and quickly rolled the condom over his penis. Then he came to the bed and settled between her thighs. He lowered his forehead to hers.

"Baby, I can't wait. I need to be inside you now."

Celeste reached for him and spread her legs wider. "I want you inside me, too."

Drew entered her with one thrust. As her body stretched to accommodate him, one short phrase played over and over in her brain.

At last.

She didn't have time to analyze her thoughts. Drew's thrusts quickened, over and over. She lifted her hips to meet him. The feel of him in her arms, inside her, was exquisite.

It feels like home.

She closed her eyes at the thought, turning her head to the side. What did that even mean?

"Baby, open your eyes," Drew commanded. "Look at me, Celeste."

She turned to face him, forcing her eyes open. Drew's gaze met hers. "I'm here with you now. I want you to see *me*. Only me."

With one last thrust, Drew orgasmed. His body went still, the muscles in his shoulders bunching and tensing. But he kept his eyes open and his gaze locked on hers.

Finally, he collapsed on top of her, their bodies still joined. Celeste held him and rubbed his back in gentle circles, her mind racing. Did Drew care for her or was this just sex? Was his desire to be with her simply a reaction to his fight with Carrie? If he asked to sleep with her again, what should she do?

"I can practically hear the wheels in your brain turning," Drew mumbled against her shoulder. "Relax, Celeste."

She tried to unclench her tense muscles. "Sorry."

Drew lifted his head to look at her. "I don't want you to be sorry. I want you to be happy."

"I *am* happy." She heard the defensiveness in her voice and tried to soften it. "I'm happy, Drew. Really."

"I hope so." His frown told her he wasn't totally convinced. But then he gave her a wicked grin. "I know what will make you happy."

"You do?"

"Yeah." He slid off her, pulling out of her body, and Celeste experienced a momentary feeling of loss. But then he settled beside her and propped his head up with his hand. With his free hand, he fondled her breast, rubbing the nipple gently between his thumb and index finger. Her breath caught at the sensation.

"You like that don't you?"

Celeste closed her eyes. "Yes."

"And you like this, too." He leaned over and took her nipple in his mouth, teasing, tugging, licking. Celeste groaned and once more moisture pooled between her legs. She felt herself reaching once more, her body on the edge of pleasure.

Drew touched her between her legs, inserting a finger, and she cried out at the sensation. His mouth left her breast, and she whimpered in protest. He kissed his way down her body and when his mouth replaced his hand between her legs, she could barely breathe.

"Drew! Oh God, Drew!"

He suckled and licked, thrusting his tongue inside to touch sensitive nerves. She lifted her hips, desperate to get closer. Her climax built and rose until Drew once more inserted a finger deep inside her. Her orgasm again exploded without warning. "Drew!"

He wrung every last ounce of pleasure from her until she was boneless, sated, and exhausted.

Drew kissed her cheek as he settled beside her. "Are you happy now?"

She smiled, her eyes still closed. "Ecstatic."

"Good."

He rolled her onto her side, and curled in behind her, wrapping a protective arm around her waist. "Sleep well, sweetheart."

Chapter Fourteen

CELESTE WOKE WITH A start in the unfamiliar room. Then she felt the weight of Drew's arm around her waist and the events of the previous evening rushed back. She remembered kissing Drew, making love with him. It had been wonderful, magical even.

Dear God, dear God, dear God.

She was scared as hell. Had she made love with him because he was in pain and she wanted to comfort him or were her feelings deeper, stronger?

No, no, no. She couldn't have feelings for Drew. She just couldn't.

Drew stirred and when she turned her head to face him, his eyes opened. He gave her a sleepy, sexy smile. "Good morning, beautiful."

"Good morning." Celeste leaned over his shoulder to look at the clock on the night table. "It's only five am. Go back to sleep."

His hand tightened at her waist. "Are you leaving?"

"Yes. Before people start coming to work. They might wonder what I've been doing if they see me walking out of the woods so early in the morning."

She kept her tone light, but her attempt at humor fell flat. Drew stared at her, and even in the dim light she could see the hurt in his eyes.

He removed his arm from around her waist and sat up. "Yeah, you wouldn't want anyone to think you were here with me."

"Drew, I just meant—"

"It's all right." He moved to the opposite edge of the bed, his back to her. "I understand you have to go."

He lowered his head, his elbows braced on his knees. The dejection in his pose tore at her heart. She couldn't leave him like this. She crawled across the bed to him and pressed against his back, wrapping her arms around his neck and resting her head on his shoulder.

"Drew, last night was amazing, truly. Please believe me when I say making love with you was very special. But it can never happen again. I'm not who you need. You deserve someone wonderful. I know that's not me because I'll never feel more than friendship for you. I'm sorry, but I don't feel the way someone should feel going into a relationship. I don't think I ever will."

Her voice hitched on her last words. She buried her face into the crook of his neck.

God help her, she never wanted to let him go.

Fear made her tighten her hold. She'd been in love before but, in the end, it had brought such pain. He deserved someone who loved him with everything she had, her whole heart. Celeste had nothing left to give him.

She kissed Drew's neck one last time. "I should go."

He grasped her arms, preventing her from leaving but then with a sigh, he dropped his hands. Her heart filled with regret as she left the bed.

Neither of them spoke as they picked up their clothes from the floor and slipped them on.

Drew followed her to the front door. "I'll give you a ride."

"There's no need. I can walk."

"It's dark and cold. I'm not letting you walk alone."

"Drew—"

"Can't you let me do this one small thing for you?"

Though she wanted to get out of the house as quickly as possible, the pain in his voice stopped her. Celeste swallowed. "All right. Thank you."

They drove the short distance to the lodge in silence. Drew pulled up to the entrance to her apartment and put his car into neutral. He turned to look at her. "Thank you for letting me know Carrie was safe."

"I thought you'd want to know. Are you going to work today?"

"Yeah. I can't hide forever."

"Good. I guess I'll see you later then." She set her hand on the door handle.

"When should we schedule your next driving lesson?" Drew asked.

She turned to look at him. "You're sure you still want to do that?"

"Yes, I'm sure." He reached for her gloved hand. "We're friends, and I promised my friend I'd help her learn to drive."

He squeezed her hand before letting go, the expression in his dark eyes unreadable. "At least, I hope we're still friends."

A strange combination of relief and loss swirled in Celeste's gut. "Of course, we're still friends. Always."

THE NEXT DAY, MAGGIE popped into Drew's office right after the lunch rush. "Ethan called to ask if we can do some work on the babies' room. Harper's stressed about getting the room ready, so he was hoping we could paint and set up the cribs. Can you help?"

"Yeah, sure. When?"

"Later this afternoon, if that's okay. It'll be me and Luke and Scarlet and Cam, and you, of course. Scarlet and I are pretty good with the paint brushes, so I figured we could handle that while you boys put together the cribs and the mobiles and haul in the other stuff that Ethan had shipped to the lodge."

"How much stuff is there?"

"Boxes and boxes of it. We've been putting it in the event center as it arrives, but we've got to get it cleared out so we can get ready for the Mistletoe Ball."

"Boxes and boxes? How much stuff do two little babies need?"

Maggie laughed. "A lot, apparently. Harper's been shopping up a storm online. Her way of nesting, I guess."

"Have you got the paint and supplies you'll need? I don't know if there's any brushes or rollers at the house."

"Yeah. Luke went into Brainerd yesterday and got the paint color Harper wanted along with drop cloths and brushes and a few other things. I think we're ready."

"What time will Luke and Cam be at the event center to load up?"

"Luke figured about three."

"Okay. I'll meet them there."

"Great. I'll let Luke know." Maggie got up to leave. "Have you spoken to Carrie?"

"No." He'd tried to approach her in the lobby, but she'd walked away without speaking to him.

"I know she's angry right now, and sad, but she'll come around. I'm certain of it."

Drew wished he could be as sure. Maggie hadn't seen the coldness in Carrie's eyes. It hurt to know his sister despised him so much. He nodded for Maggie's sake, and she left his office.

He had to come to terms with the possibility that Carrie might never forgive him, that they could be estranged forever.

And he had to come to terms with the fact that Celeste would never feel the same way he did. She saw him as her friend, nothing more.

She said they could never make love again. For him, their lovemaking had been breathtaking, life-changing. It was far more than sex. It was the melding of two souls.

But Celeste didn't feel the same way. Somehow, he had to live with that.

MAGGIE HADN'T BEEN kidding about the number of boxes stored in the event center. One whole corner was piled high with boxes. Drew stared at them. "Seriously, all this stuff is for the babies?"

Cam grinned. "You'd be astonished by the amount of paraphernalia a baby comes with. And when you multiply it by two, this is what you get."

"Good thing we brought two trucks." Luke rubbed his hands together. "Let's get it loaded."

They managed to load everything in the truck beds of both Luke and Cam's trucks, with some overflow in the back seats. They made the short drive to Ethan and Harper's house and backed up to the front door. Maggie met them on the porch.

"For now, put everything in the living room. As soon as Scarlet and I are finished painting you can start setting up the cribs, and she and I will go through the rest of the boxes."

Drew walked into the house carrying two boxes. He came to a complete stop when he saw Carrie glaring at him.

"Maggie, I thought you said Drew wouldn't be here," she said.

"I'm sorry I lied to you, but the two of you need to talk," Maggie said. "You can't let this animosity continue to fester, Carrie."

Carrie moved toward the door. "I won't stay with him here."

Drew set his boxes on the floor. "Carrie, come on. We need to talk."

As she attempted to pass, he grasped her arm. "Please, don't leave. Talk to me."

Carrie shook off his hand with a forceful shrug. "Fine, I'll talk. How would you like it if I told you, or better yet, if I told Celeste, that you couldn't be together because of the color of her skin?"

Anger instantly filled Drew. "That's a goddamn awful thing to say. You're being offensive."

"Yeah, I am. The same way you were offensive to Ryan. There's no difference in the treatment except that for some reason, it's still acceptable to discriminate against disabled people, whether it's the lack of services for them or the way we underestimate their capabilities." Carrie's dark eyes blazed with anger. "Ryan won't talk to me because of you. He says he doesn't want to come between me and my family, but it's too late for that. The damage is done. I'm only glad he doesn't know you accused him of stealing from the lodge."

She turned to Maggie. "Consider this my notice. I'll be leaving the lodge right after the Mistletoe Ball." She gave Maggie a quick hug. "I want to thank you for the opportunities you've given me. I'll see you later at Phyllis' house."

She stormed past Drew without looking at him and left through the front door. All the oxygen in the room seemed to leave with her, making it hard for him to breathe.

No one said anything, and the silence stretched to an uncomfortable length. Finally, Drew cleared his throat. "We still have a lot of work to do. We'd better get back to it."

Maggie and Scarlet went back to their painting and the men brought the rest of the boxes into the house. Drew did his best to put one foot in front of the other.

THE NEXT DAY, DREW wasn't surprised when his uncle Cam knocked on his open office door.

"Do you have a minute?" he asked.

"Sure."

Cam stepped inside, closing the door behind him.

"If you're here to tell me I need to fix things with Carrie, you're talking to the wrong person. Carrie's the one who won't talk to me."

Drew didn't know if she'd ever talk to him again. In her opinion, he'd not only discriminated against Ryan because of his disability, he brought his integrity and honesty into question. It was beginning to look less likely that Ryan was their thief. Luke told him Jerry Fields didn't find any evidence that Ryan hacked into the system and changed accounting records.

He really hoped that was true because if Ryan was innocent, so was Carrie.

Cam sat in one of the chairs in front of Drew's desk and stretched out his long legs. "Yeah, I saw yesterday she wasn't in the mood to talk to you. She was pretty upset."

"Yeah." Drew could barely get the word past the lump in his throat. Carrie continued to avoid him at work and at home. She'd sent Luke and his grandmother Phyllis to pick up the rest of her clothes from the house the previous evening.

She hated him so much she wouldn't even let him pack for her and touch her things. Somehow that hurt most of all.

"Ethan told Scarlet and me about the thefts here at the lodge and that you discovered someone hacked into the accounting system. I'm glad you didn't try to cover it up this time."

Drew fought to keep his expression neutral. The last thing he wanted was to rehash his previous mistakes. "We'll find out who's behind the trouble and make them pay."

"Good. I'd hate for all the work that everyone has put into this place to be put in jeopardy by some greedy hacker."

"We'll figure it out."

"Good, good." Cam intertwined his fingers. "What Carrie said about you and Celeste, was that true? Are you together?"

Cam's question caught him off guard. Drew sat up straighter. "Would you have a problem if we were?"

"No, of course not. Celeste is a great person, and I have nothing but respect for her. I trust her with my daughter, so that says a lot."

"So, what *are* you saying?"

"I'm saying that Celeste is a package deal. She comes with a ready-made family, just as I did with Tessa. It's a big responsibility. Can you handle that?"

The question incensed him. "Contrary to popular belief in this family, I'm an adult and I can handle adult situations."

"This can't be some casual affair, Drew. Celeste is a mother. You can't pop in and out of her life, and Hope's, whenever you feel like it. She's not some young college girl."

"Wow." Drew sat back in his seat and gave a mirthless laugh. "Your confidence in my integrity is truly underwhelming."

"This is serious, Drew. You can't play around with Celeste."

Drew slapped his hand on the desk. "You think I don't know that? I would never treat Celeste with disrespect. In fact, I've never treated any woman with disrespect, but I don't expect you to believe it." He took a deep breath to calm himself. "Hope deserves love and stability in her life, and I would never do anything to jeopardize that."

"I'm glad to hear you say that," Cam said.

A new thought occurred to Drew and his jaw clenched. "Are you sure you're not asking if I'm ready to be in a relationship with a black woman?"

"You know you're going to be asked that question," Cam said quietly. "Not by me, but by some people. I want you to understand what you're getting into, on every level, if you take your relationship with Celeste any further."

Drew's gut burned. "Well, you're in luck. Celeste has made it clear that we're friends and nothing more. So, you have nothing to be concerned about."

They stared across the desk at each other. Drew held his uncle's gaze defiantly, even though he had the feeling Cam could see right through the thin, protective façade he'd erected.

Finally, Cam spoke. "I'm sorry. It's obvious your feelings for Celeste run much deeper."

Drew gave a curt nod and looked away. He didn't want to talk about it anymore.

But Cam wasn't finished. "And it's also obvious you've got a chip on your shoulder. We all know what happened with your previous job wasn't your fault. You were the victim of a crime. But somehow you've got it in your head that the whole family is against you."

"Aren't you? You and everyone else has treated me like an immature kid for as long as I can remember, but since I lost my job, it's off the charts."

"I won't deny I was disappointed when you tried to cover up your mistake, but you paid the price. I think you were so angry at yourself for what happened that you're seeing judgment where it doesn't exist. Do you honestly think Ethan would have asked you to come to the lodge if he didn't have full confidence in you?"

"He was desperate. That's the only reason I'm here."

"You're here because you're family and because we trust you. You're the one who doesn't trust yourself."

With that, Cam rose to his feet. "You know where I am if you need me." He left the office and closed the door behind him.

Drew stared at the closed door, his emotions in turmoil. Was Cam right? Was he still so angry and disappointed in himself that it skewed the way he believed his family looked at him?

And was he right about any potential relationship with Celeste? In this day and age, were there still people who would discriminate against an interracial couple?

Perhaps he was naïve, but he didn't want to believe it. When he looked at Celeste, he only saw beauty and light and everything good.

Something Carrie said came back to him. *"Because when we're together, we're not two people with a big difference in age. We're just Carrie and Ryan."*

Another of Carrie's comments swirled in his memory. She'd said he'd discriminated against Ryan because of his disability the same way some people discriminated against Celeste because of the color of her skin. Had he done that? *No.* He wouldn't do that. He was only concerned about his sister.

The idea of anyone treating Celeste and Hope disrespectfully made his gut burn. He hated confrontations and usually went out of his way to avoid them. But he'd go to war with anyone who hurt them.

Because I'm in love with Celeste.

Drew hung his head. He'd been trying to avoid the truth, to save himself some pain and probably some embarrassment. But he might as well admit it, at least to himself. He was in love with Celeste. It had happened so quickly, maybe soon after he arrived at the lodge, but he hadn't wanted to acknowledge it because she didn't feel the same way. The last thing he needed was another one-sided love affair.

He'd been infatuated with Maggie, he realized now. When she'd told him she was in love with Luke, not him, his pride had been more bruised than his heart. But what he felt for Celeste was the real thing. His heart was taking a beating he wasn't sure it could ever recover from.

Maybe he was doomed to always want a woman he couldn't have. He groaned out loud at that depressing thought and forced himself to go back to work.

AT THE VIBRATION OF her phone in her back pocket, Celeste turned off the vacuum cleaner and checked the screen. Her mother. She hesitated and considered letting the call go to voice mail, but Nora always seemed to recognize when she was avoiding her. With a sigh, she accepted the call. "Hi, Mama."

"Hey baby girl. How are you?"

She had no idea how to answer. Since the night she'd spent with Drew, she'd been unsettled, even weepy at times. As promised, he'd given her another parallel parking lesson. He'd been kind, respectful, patient. And distant. He was putting space between them, and she couldn't blame him. She was the one who told him they couldn't be together again.

"I'm great, Mama." She injected a cheery note into her voice and hoped her mother couldn't see through it. Best to steer away from her feelings. "What's up?"

"Gloria is able to get a few days off work so we plan to fly up to Minnesota for your big Christmas Ball."

"Oh!" Celeste fought to keep her emotions under control. She hadn't really expected her mother and sister to come since they'd both made plenty of excuses not to in the past. Tears pricked her eyes. "That's wonderful."

"CeCe, are you all right?"

The concern in her mother's voice undid her. Sobs burst from her mouth and tears streamed down her cheeks. What on Earth was the matter with her?

"CeCe, baby, tell me what's wrong."

Celeste grabbed a tissue and blew her nose, taking deep breaths to get herself under control. Finally, she spoke into the phone. "Sorry about that. I'm just happy you and Gloria are coming. I've missed you."

"I've missed you, too. But I think there's more going on with you than missing your mama."

Her mother had always been her rock. She'd supported her through her darkest days, and she'd never asked for anything in return. Celeste was suddenly curious. "Mama, when we were kids, after Daddy left us, did you ever think about bringing another man into our lives? Did you ever want another relationship?"

After a short silence, Nora spoke. "I thought about it. There was a man I cared about. We went out several times, but I never brought him home to meet you and Gloria."

"Why not?"

"At the time, I told myself I didn't want to disrupt your lives."

When she didn't elaborate further, Celeste asked, "What do you tell yourself now?"

Nora sighed. "That I was afraid. I'd been so hurt when your daddy left me. I couldn't go through that again."

Celeste's heart ached for her mother. "Do you have any regrets?"

"Sometimes. I'll never know if we could have had something good together. You and Gloria were my first responsibility. I did what I thought was best for you girls." Nora hesitated before speaking again. "Is there someone you're considering bringing into your life?"

"Yes," she admitted. "But we're so different. I don't know how I could make it work. He's nine years younger than me and he's white."

"Oh."

Celeste waited for her mother to say something more, to offer a word of encouragement or advice. But Nora said nothing. Which spoke volumes. An interracial relationship hadn't worked for her, and it wouldn't work for Celeste.

Disappointment and despair swamped her. She changed the subject. "When will you be able to come here? I need to know what dates to book your airline tickets for."

If Nora was startled at the abrupt change, she didn't let on. "We'll arrive on Monday and leave the following Monday. I've taken myself off the substitute teaching list for that week and Gloria has taken holidays."

"Sounds good. I'll make sure to bring warm winter coats to the airport when we pick you up."

"Makes me shiver to think of the cold, but I can't wait to see you and Hope."

"I can't wait to see you, too."

Celeste was about to sign off when her mother spoke again. "CeCe, if you're seriously considering a new relationship, you need to be careful. You've got to consider Hope's future."

"I know, Mama."

"Will we meet this young man?"

"Yes, probably."

"All right. Bye, CeCe baby."

"Bye, Mama."

She stuck her phone in her back pocket once again and resumed vacuuming. Her mother had been divorced for over twenty years. She'd never given any indication before that she was lonely and until now, Celeste hadn't given it much thought.

Celeste had been a widow for six years. Though she'd been busy raising her daughter and trying to earn a living during that time, she'd often felt the weight of loneliness. It wasn't easy being alone, having no one to share her life with. She couldn't imagine what it would be like when Hope finished school and left home. She'd be truly alone then.

Drew's face floated into her thoughts the way it had so often since their night together. She could almost feel his touch as his hands skimmed over her body, caressing, stroking, loving.

She couldn't shake the feeling that if she pursued a relationship with Drew, it would end in disaster. Telling him they could only be friends had been for the best. She pushed the image of his beautiful face away.

ON WEDNESDAY MORNING, Drew made the call he'd been dreading for almost a week. "Hi, Mom."

"Drew, hi!" Lydia Barnes sounded excited to hear from him. "Are you and Carrie on the road already?"

"You haven't spoken to Carrie?"

"No, I haven't heard from her since she told me you two would be driving home together today. What's going on?"

Drew hated that he had to upset her with his news. "I'm sorry, but I won't be coming home for Thanksgiving after all. But as far as I know, Carrie still plans to come."

"As far as you know? Aren't you under the same roof? How come you don't know? What the hell is going on?"

Drew told her everything, from his reservations about Carrie's future with Ryan, Ryan's subsequent breakup with her, and Carrie blaming Drew for it. "I've never seen Carrie so angry. She hasn't spoken to me in days. That's why I think it's best if I don't show up at the house while she's there. It would ruin Thanksgiving for everyone."

Lydia sighed. "Carrie and Ryan video chatted with us and they told us about his disability. I admit I have concerns, but Carrie loves him."

"Carrie's too young, Mom. You can't possibly support a marriage between them. She doesn't know what she's getting into. She's going to ruin her life!"

His final conversation with Carrie haunted him. Had she been right? Had he been discriminating against Ryan? If it were true, what kind of person did that make him? What kind of brother?

Lydia went silent. He was about to ask if she was still there when she finally spoke again. Her voice held a note of concern. "What's really going on here, Drew?"

"I told you, Carrie's too young to get married. Even if she's angry with me forever, it'll be worth it if I stop her from making a huge mistake."

"Carrie knows her own mind. Ever since she was a child, I could depend on her to think through her decisions carefully before she acted. So, if she tells me that Ryan is the one, I have to believe her."

"It doesn't really matter what Carrie wants because Ryan has backed out on her."

"Because of what you said to him," Lydia said.

"If he really loved her, he wouldn't have let anything I said stop him from being with her," Drew said stubbornly.

"What's really bothering you, Drew?"

"My sister won't speak to me, and lots of things are happening at the lodge." He didn't want to get into a discussion about the thefts with her. "Isn't that enough?"

"Ordinarily I would say it is, but I have a feeling something else is going on."

Celeste's voice telling him they could never be anything more than friends drifted through his memory. "Nothing else is going on, Mom. Nothing at all."

DREW POINTED AHEAD. "Let's make a right-hand turn at the next corner. But first move into the right-hand lane." Minnewasta was small, but it gave Celeste the opportunity to practice skills like changing lanes and parking without having to worry about traffic.

Celeste signaled and checked over her right shoulder before moving the car into the lane. "I feel a little silly signaling to change lanes when there really aren't any lanes."

With the exception of the business district, no lines were painted on Minnewasta's streets. But they were wide enough that Celeste could pretend to change lanes and get a feel for how it should be done. Drew knew from experience that changing lanes properly was one of the things she'd be marked on in the driving test.

After she practiced pulling into and backing out of an angle parking spot a few times, Drew called it a day. "We should get back to the lodge. Hope will be home from school soon."

"Right."

Celeste headed toward the intersection with the highway that took them to the lodge. "You haven't told me how your Thanksgiving went."

He didn't want to talk about it. "It was quiet."

"What do you mean? Didn't you go home to your parents' house?"

"No."

"What did you do?" she asked.

"I caught up on work at the lodge, hung around the house. Nothing much."

She glanced at him, her expression stricken. "You mean you were by yourself the whole holiday?"

"It wasn't a big deal, Celeste."

It was probably the loneliest day of his life. Luke and Maggie had closed the restaurant on Thursday, giving the kitchen and wait staff the day off for the holiday. Carrie caught a ride with Cam and Scarlet and the kids to Minneapolis, where they stayed with Drew's parents. They took food over to Ethan and Harper's condo and celebrated the holiday with them.

He was the only one alone. He spent most of Thursday in his office at the lodge, getting caught up on work he'd put off for a while. When he finished that, he started doing busy work, like making new labels for files in the filing cabinet and polishing furniture. When he couldn't find anything else to do, he walked back to the house and made himself a sandwich. Then, he'd cleaned and vacuumed and dusted until he fell into bed exhausted at midnight.

Some holiday. But it was better than fighting with Carrie and ruining everyone's Thanksgiving.

"Why didn't you tell me you weren't going to Minneapolis? I would have cooked something for the three of us instead of going to Cheryl's."

"I wasn't going to do that, Celeste."

"Why not?"

Anxiety built in Drew's chest. "Because Thanksgiving is for families."

"That's not true. Hope and I spent the day at Cheryl's house and we're not family. No one should be alone on Thanksgiving. If you'd said something, I'm sure Cheryl would have invited you, too."

"I didn't want a pity invite from Cheryl, and I sure as hell didn't want one from you."

Drew stared out the windshield, not wanting to talk about it anymore. Then he glanced over at her, feeling terrible for being so short with her. "I'm sorry, Celeste. That was uncalled for."

She kept her eyes on the road. "It's okay."

They drove the rest of the way in complete silence. Though Celeste said she forgave him, the tension inside the SUV was oppressive. Trying to simply be Celeste's friend wasn't possible.

Drew came to a decision. He had to leave as soon as possible.

Because it was becoming increasingly clear that staying at the lodge was slowly killing him.

Chapter Fifteen

DREW KNOCKED ON LUKE'S open office door. "Have you got a minute?"

Luke put down his pen. "Sure. What's up?"

Drew entered and closed the door behind him before taking a seat. "I'd like you to begin looking for my replacement. It should be someone who could take over full-time while Harper is on maternity leave, and when she returns, the new hire should be willing to work part-time."

"Ethan's already told me that Harper doesn't feel she can come back full-time. She's afraid she won't be able to give her best to her kids or to the lodge. I've written a job description but haven't posted it anywhere yet. I was waiting to see how long you were able to stay."

"It's time for me to go."

"Do your parents need you back at the Foundation?"

"Not really." Drew cleared his throat. "They've hired a temporary admin assistant and my mother tells me she's working out very well."

"Then what's the rush?"

Drew ignored the question. "I won't leave immediately. I want to see things through with the Mistletoe Ball and make sure my replacement is fully trained before I go." And he couldn't in good conscience leave before the person responsible for the thefts and upheaval at the lodge was apprehended.

Luke gave him a long stare before finally nodding. "All right. I'll submit our ad to online job sites and the local papers. Hopefully, we'll generate some interest."

"Can I ask a favor?"

"Sure. What is it?"

"When I leave, can you help Celeste with her driving lessons? It's really important that she gain her independence and she won't be able to do that until she learns to drive."

"Of course I will. I want Celeste to be happy." Luke paused and gave Drew a considering look. "Are you sure you want to leave? You and Celeste have become very close. Maybe—"

"No." He didn't want to get into it with Luke. "I have to go. It's best for both of us."

"Are you sure about that?"

The morning after he and Celeste made love and the things she'd said to him were seared into his memory. She made it perfectly clear she didn't want him. He gave Luke a firm nod. "Yeah, I'm sure."

"All right. Are you going to work at the Foundation again?"

"I don't know. They don't seem to need me there anymore. To be honest, it's not the job I want to do for the rest of my life."

"What would you like to do?"

Drew contemplated the man across the desk and decided to trust him. "I'm sure you heard about how I lost the job I had at an investment firm."

"Yeah. Ethan told me. Is that what you want to do, investments?"

"I thought so at one time. But after I got fired, I had some time on my hands. Because of what happened to me, I became interested in investigating and exposing financial crimes, especially cybercrimes. I started taking online classes in forensic accounting. I already had a degree in accounting so it was a natural fit. I completed my forensic accounting degree a couple of months ago."

Drew had worked hard on the classes, sometimes taking two classes at a time while still working full-time. It hadn't been a hardship since he'd found most of the classes fascinating.

"Have you looked for work in this field?" Luke asked.

"No, I haven't." To make forensic accounting his career, he needed to become accredited and to do that, he needed work experience.

"Why not?"

A good question, one he'd been asking himself for some time. Before he'd earned his degree, he would tell himself he needed to finish his classes before looking for a new job. But he no longer had that excuse. He was certain it was work he'd enjoy and be good at. But he hadn't been able to make himself leave the safety of the Foundation.

"Maybe it was easier to stay where I was, doing a job I knew I wouldn't mess up."

"Eventually you have to forgive yourself for what happened at your previous job. You made a mistake, sure. But don't let one bad decision hold you back for the rest of your life."

Luke was right. It was time to forgive himself. But after the complete shattering of his confidence, self-forgiveness was hard to find.

"Yeah. I know you're right. When I get back to Minneapolis, I'll start sending out resumes." His stomach hitched at the mere thought of putting himself in the job market.

"You've got a lot to offer a prospective employer, Drew. You're smart, loyal, hardworking. I think what happened to you makes you even more valuable."

That surprised Drew. "How do you figure that?"

"You have first-hand knowledge of what cybercrime can do to a victim, and how it can up-end their lives. You know what's at stake, and you've armed yourself with education so you can fight back. Don't sell yourself short. Any employer would be lucky to have you."

Luke's assessment rendered Drew momentarily speechless. He stared at him silently before finally nodding. "I appreciate you saying that. Of all the things the cyber criminals took away from me, my confidence has been the most difficult to get back."

"I understand," Luke said. "Don't let the bastards win."

Drew chuckled. "I'll do my best."

"Good. Now, if we're done here, I've got a job to post."

Drew got to his feet. "Thanks for the pep talk, Luke. I appreciate it."

"Any time."

Drew made his way back to his office. He'd been prepared to dislike Luke because of Maggie. He hadn't expected him to become an ally. They still had differences in opinion and clashed over tactics, but Luke Carlsson had definitely become a friend.

LATER, BACK IN HIS office, Drew turned his attention to the security footage from the hidden cameras in the kitchen. Every day, Maggie brought him a camera from the kitchen. He gave her a freshly charged one, then carefully reviewed the recording. So far, all he'd seen were hours of footage of the cooler and freezer doors. It was tedious work, but important. He only wished it would give them some answers.

His desk phone rang, breaking into his thoughts. "Hello? Drew here."

"Drew, it's Jeanette. I have someone on line one who wants to speak to a manager, and Luke's line is busy. This gentleman insists on speaking to someone in charge and won't wait until Luke can call him back. Can you talk to him?"

"Do you know what he wants?"

"No, he won't tell me, but he sounds annoyed. All he's told me is that he and his wife stayed at the lodge last month."

Drew bit back his frustration. The last thing he needed was a confrontation with an irate customer. But he couldn't let Jeanette deal with the man on her own.

"Okay. I'll talk to him."

"Thanks so much, Drew. Line one." She sounded relieved.

He pressed the line one button. "Drew Barnes here. How can I help you?"

"Are you a manager?"

Good question. He wasn't exactly sure what his title was, so he made one up. "Yes, I'm manager of accounting. Jeanette said you and your wife stayed with us last month. Was there a problem with your stay?"

"The stay was fine, but while we were there, our credit card was compromised."

That was a surprise. "What do you mean by compromised?"

"I mean that charges not made by us appeared on our credit card statement. I've since cancelled the card."

"That sounds like a good idea, and I'm truly sorry, but what makes you think it had anything to do with Solace Lake Lodge?"

"Because the bogus charges started racking up right after we used the credit card to pay for the room. The only time I used that card in October was when we stayed at Solace Lake Lodge. Unfortunately, I didn't notice anything was wrong until we got our statement in the mail a few days ago and saw all the items that had been charged to it. Someone at the lodge stole our information."

Drew didn't know what to say. Was this another scam? Was a member of the staff skimming credit card numbers?

Finally, he cleared his throat. "Sir, can I get your name?"

"It's James Murphy."

Drew wrote down the information. "Can you tell me the exact dates you stayed at the lodge?"

"Of course. I have the receipt right in front of me. My wife and I stayed from October 20 to 23."

"Do you remember where you used your credit card? Was it in the restaurant or bar, or maybe to rent sports equipment?"

"We only used the card once. We charged all our meals to our room, so we only made one payment at the front desk."

The front desk? "So, you made this payment when you checked out in the morning, correct?"

"No. We had to get an early start in the morning, so I settled our bill at the front desk the evening before. It was past nine, I believe."

He'd have to double check last month's schedule to see who was working that evening. Both Jeannette and Dave had been with the lodge since the reopening, and there had never been any question about their honesty. And it was inconceivable that Mel had stolen a credit card number, given the glowing recommendation her previous employer had given her and how long she worked for them.

"Mr. Murphy, I promise you we're going to get to the bottom of this, and we're going to make this right."

"I'm holding you to it. I'm currently in negotiations with our credit card company to have those bogus charges made null and void. If Solace Lake Lodge acknowledges what happened, it'll go a long way to making that happen. What was your name again?"

"Drew Barnes."

After getting Mr. Murphy's contact information, he hung up and immediately opened last month's employee schedule. Mel was on duty at the front desk on the date Mr. Murphy said he used his credit card.

He tried Luke's office phone and was relieved that he was available. He told him about his conversation with Mr. Murphy.

"I can't believe Mel has anything to do with credit card theft," Luke said. "But we have to look into it. Too many crazy things have been happening lately."

"Agreed. What are you going to do?"

Drew heard Luke blow out a breath. "I guess I'll start by going back to the hotel in Minneapolis where Mel worked. I'll speak to the manager again and see if there were any problems when she was there. But I doubt it. The manager was surprised she'd come out of retirement to work at the lodge, but he couldn't praise her highly enough."

"In the meantime, I'll keep watching the videos. No luck so far."

"Okay. I'll let you know if I find anything," Luke said.

They said goodbye and Drew went back to the tedious work of watching the hidden camera videos. He'd do whatever it took to get to the bottom of this mystery.

AS THEY WERE PREPPING for the lunch crowd, Celeste turned to Maggie. "Can I ask you for a favor?"

"Of course. What do you need?"

Celeste cleared her throat. "I was wondering if you could drive with me to Minneapolis to pick up my mom and sister. They're coming for the Mistletoe Ball."

"That's great news, Celeste! I know how much you've wanted them to visit. When are they coming?"

"Next Monday. Their plane arrives at four-forty-five."

"Oh, I'm sorry, Celeste. I gave Cheryl next Monday off to attend her husband's Christmas concert at the high school, so I'm working that night. And Luke isn't available, either. He has to go to Bemidji. You know the band we hired to play at the Mistletoe Ball? Their van broke down, and he has to haul their equipment here in his truck. It was the only day he could go."

Celeste's heart fell, but she kept her tone light. "Oh, don't worry about it. I'm sure someone else will help me."

"Yes, of course. Have you talked to Drew? I'm sure he'd help you out."

Celeste swallowed. She couldn't imagine being trapped in a car for two hours with Drew. It would be excruciating to be that close to him and not be able to touch—

No! That's not what she meant! After the tense confrontation the other day, she couldn't imagine subjecting him to hours alone in the car with her. It was obvious he didn't want to be with her.

She shouldn't have questioned him about Thanksgiving. He'd been upset about it, yet she continued to pick at him until he exploded. It was becoming clear they could no longer spend time together.

She missed him.

Dear God. She was losing her mind.

"Oh, hey. Just the guy we wanted to see," Maggie said.

Celeste turned to see Drew enter the kitchen. As he approached Maggie, his dark gaze collided with hers for a brief moment. The dark circles under his eyes mirrored the ones she'd seen on her own face. Maybe he wasn't sleeping any better than she was.

"Sorry to bother you, Maggie. I wanted to double check this invoice with you." He handed her a piece of paper. "I know you okayed the purchase order, but is this the price you were quoted for t-bone steaks? I checked our last invoice and the price was lower."

Maggie examined the invoice. "It's legit. The price has gone up quite a bit."

"Okay. I'll go ahead and pay it." He met Celeste's gaze again, but then he quickly turned away, ready to make a fast getaway. A short, sharp pain struck her at his dismissal.

"Drew, wait." Maggie put her hand on his arm. "Can you help us?"

Damn it, why couldn't Maggie have left it alone? Celeste tried to catch Maggie's eye, but her friend didn't see the shake of her head. Or if she did, she ignored it.

"Celeste's family is flying in from South Carolina next Monday and neither Luke nor I can drive to Minneapolis with her to pick them up at the airport. Would you be able to do it?"

"Yes, of course." He turned to Celeste, his expression not giving away his thoughts. "What time do they arrive?"

"At four forty-five. But if you're busy, I can ask someone else."

"No, it's fine. We'll leave here about two. Good practice for driving on the highway."

"Oh, sure, okay. Thanks."

He gave her a brief smile, but she detected something in his face, a hint of despondency. Or maybe disappointment.

Or maybe she was projecting her own feelings onto Drew.

When he left the kitchen, Maggie turned to her with a smile. "There. That's settled. I'm glad we were able to arrange transportation for your family."

Celeste resumed deveining shrimp for the shrimp cocktail special that evening. "Yes, me too."

"It was good of Drew to offer to help, wasn't it?"

She ripped the vein out of a shrimp, tearing it in half. "You asked, so of course he was going to say yes."

"Are you mad at me for asking him?"

Celeste glanced away from the confused look on Maggie's face. "No, of course not." Although a heads-up before she asked a favor of Drew on her behalf might have been nice.

"You could have fooled me. You sound pissed."

Celeste squeezed her eyes shut. It wasn't fair to take her frustration out on Maggie. Maggie was her friend, probably the best friend she'd ever had. She wasn't even sure why she was frustrated. "I'm sorry. You're right. I've got transportation arranged for my mom and sister and that's the most important thing."

Maggie leaned closer, lowering her voice. "What's going on? I thought you and Drew were friends?"

"We were. *We are.*" She hoped it was still true. But she was no longer certain. Everything changed after they had sex. Being with Drew had been magical. Celeste didn't know if either of them could go back to friendship.

"Did you have an argument?"

Celeste shook her head. She wished Maggie would give up this line of questioning.

"Well, if you didn't argue, then what's the prob—Oh!"

Celeste could practically hear bells going off in Maggie's head. Her face heated.

"You slept with him!" Maggie put her arm around her shoulder and whispered. "Was it awful?"

"No!" Tears pricked behind Celeste's eyes as she shook her head. "God, no! Just the opposite."

"Then why are you crying? What's wrong?"

"I can't be with him, Maggie. It wouldn't work."

"How do you know if you never try?"

She couldn't control her tears. "I just know!"

"Oh, sweetie. Come sit down for a minute."

Maggie handed her a towel to wipe her hands and then led her out of the kitchen to a quiet corner of the restaurant. After they sat, she said, "If you ever want to talk, I'm here for you."

Fresh tears threatened to fall but she held them back. "Thank you, but it's not necessary."

Maggie looked like she wanted to argue, but in the end she simply nodded. "Okay. I'm sorry."

Celeste blew her nose. "For what?"

"I'm sorry you're so unhappy. I know how gut-wrenching it is when you want something, or someone, that you believe you can never have. But I discovered that what was holding me back from having the relationship I wanted was me. I hope you figure that out, too." She squeezed Celeste's shoulder and went back to the kitchen.

Maggie had told her about her relationship with Luke, which had begun when she was fourteen and he was eighteen. Maggie's grandparents, who raised her, were afraid their relationship was far too serious for a girl that young, so they bribed Luke to go away and start a new life in California. Maggie had been devastated by his desertion. After he returned to Minnewasta three years ago, it had taken her a long time to forgive him. But once she did, they formed a tight, loving bond that Celeste was certain would weather any storms.

She and Drew didn't have that kind of history. Though they'd met briefly three years ago, they'd really only known each other a few weeks. And Drew would likely be leaving the lodge after Christmas...

She didn't want to think about it. She took several calming breaths before rejoining Maggie in the kitchen.

It was best to keep things simple until then. And to keep her distance.

THE FOLLOWING MONDAY afternoon, they left the lodge's parking lot at two with Celeste behind the wheel. Drew knew she was nervous, but whether it was about driving on the highway or being in the car alone with him for two hours, he wasn't certain.

"Like I said, you don't have to drive all the way to Minneapolis. You can pull over any time," Drew said.

Celeste signaled and looked both ways before turning onto the highway. "My goal is to get to the outskirts of Minneapolis. I don't think I'm ready for city driving."

"I recommend we change places before we get on Interstate 94. Traffic can be crazy heading into the city."

"Good idea."

Drew reminded Celeste how to operate the cruise control and pointed out things to watch for on the road but aside from that, they said little.

He studied her while she was occupied with driving. She was so beautiful. She had a perfect profile, with high cheekbones, a straight nose, and full, delectable lips. He remembered well the feel of those lips, the taste of her mouth—

Don't go there.

She'd made it clear there was no room in her life for him as anything other than a friend. He had to stop fantasizing about being with her.

Halfway to Minneapolis Celeste said, "I know you didn't want to drive with me today. Maggie kind of pressured you into it."

"I never said I didn't want to drive with you."

Celeste gave him a quick glance before turning her attention back to the road. "It's got to be awkward for you. After what I said...about not being together anymore."

He heard the stress in her voice, and something else. Regret? "Celeste, I'm fine. You know I wish we could have taken our relationship farther, but it's not in the cards. Whatever happens, I'll always be your friend. Okay?"

Her throat worked as she nodded, her eyes glued to the road in front of her. "Okay."

He wished he could tell her how he really felt, how much he loved her and wished they could be together. How he wanted to spend his life with her. But that would only upset her, and he didn't want to cause her any distress. Especially now when she was about to see her family.

They drove a few more miles before she spoke again. "I want to give you a heads-up. I...I mentioned you to my mother. So, don't be shocked if she says something to you."

"Ahh...I see." Had she told her mother they'd slept together?

She must have read his thoughts. "I didn't tell her we've been intimate. That's no one's business but ours. I only said we were friends, and that I...I cared for you."

Drew stared at her. It was the first time she'd admitted to having feelings for him that extended beyond friendship. He wondered if she realized that.

"My mother is a direct person, and she's very protective of my sister and me. I don't want you to be blindsided by any comment she may make."

"Should I be afraid?"

She chuckled. "Maybe."

"That doesn't exactly ease my mind."

Celeste gave him a quick smile. "Don't worry. She hardly ever bites."

"Very funny."

She laughed again, and Drew laughed with her. He was relieved that they seemed to be back on a more friendly footing.

If only it could be more.

A few more miles down the road, Drew instructed Celeste to take an off-ramp leading to a service road. They found a gas station and filled up. In a short time, they were back on the road with Drew driving.

"Maybe I should drive home, too. You've only driven that one time in the dark, and only a short distance. You don't have to get all your highway driving experience in one day."

"Yeah, that's a good idea." Celeste sounded relieved.

The heavy late afternoon traffic meant Drew was too busy concentrating on driving to continue a conversation with Celeste. By the time they reached the airport, the wind had picked up and fingers of snow drifted across the road leading to the parking garage. Once parked, Celeste pulled the two parkas she brought with her from the back seat, and they headed to the terminal. The parking garage was attached to the airport terminal by a skywalk which protected them from the weather.

"As soon as we find your mother and sister's luggage, we'll take off. I heard a storm's moving in, so we want to get home before it hits."

Celeste gave a rueful smile. "Of course we'd have to have a storm the day my family arrives."

"Welcome to Minnesota."

The arrivals board in the terminal showed that the flight had just landed.

"Perfect timing," Celeste said.

They waited by the door where arrivals entered the terminal. Celeste stepped anxiously from one foot to the other, peering over the head of the man in front of them.

"Are you nervous?"

"I guess I am," she said. "I want them to love the lodge as much as I do. I want them to understand why I want to stay."

"They want you to move back to South Carolina?" It was the first time she'd mentioned moving and his heart did a little stutter step at the thought.

"They'd like us to live nearby again. My mother's getting older..." She didn't finish her thought.

Of course her family would want her and Hope to live closer to them. How long would it be before Celeste decided it was time to move back home?

"Have you looked for work there?" he asked.

"No. Not yet." She didn't look at him as she spoke, but her tone implied it was only a matter of time until she began her search.

People started to emerge through the double doors. "There they are!" Celeste handed him the jackets.

She pushed her way through the crowd to embrace a grey-haired woman and the younger woman with her. They greeted each other with joy.

Finally, Celeste took her mother's hand and led her to where Drew was waiting. Nerves danced in his stomach as her mother approached. He had the feeling she was sizing him up.

"Mama, this is my friend Drew Barnes. He drove with me since I only have a learner's permit. Drew this is my mother, Nora Emerson, and my sister, Gloria Evans."

He extended his hand. "It's good to meet you, Mrs. Emerson, Mrs. Evans. Celeste's been very excited about your visit. We hope you enjoy your stay at the lodge."

"Mama and Gloria will be staying with Hope and me in our apartment. It'll be nice to be together." She took her mother's hand. "Drew's uncle and aunt own the lodge."

"I've been filling in for my aunt in the office. She's about to have twins any day now."

"Good for you for helping out your family," Celeste's mother said with a nod.

He wasn't sure what to make of her compliment, if it was one. "Well, my uncle Ethan has always been very generous to me, so it's the least I can do." He handed the jackets to Celeste. "A storm's coming, so we need to get back on the road as soon as possible. Let's go find your luggage."

Luck was with them as their luggage was among the first to appear on the baggage carousel. After they identified the bags, Drew grabbed them and they headed out of the terminal and back to the parking garage.

"Oh, my goodness! I've never felt anything so cold!" Gloria said as they left the warmth of the skywalk and headed into the unheated parking garage.

Drew wasn't about to mention that it was only the start of winter and would likely get much colder. The last thing he wanted was to give Celeste's family more reasons to convince her to move.

They left the garage and in a short time were back on the highway, with Drew behind the wheel.

"Where's my sweet granddaughter? I was hoping she'd be at the airport," Nora asked.

"She was still at school when we left. She's hanging out in the kitchen with Maggie until we get home."

"I can't wait to see her. It's been too long."

Drew's heart ached. Would her mother be able to convince Celeste to leave? He couldn't blame her for wanting to see her granddaughter more often. But the idea of losing them was hard to take.

His logic was skewed. Celeste and Hope didn't belong to him. And he'd soon be leaving the lodge himself. One way or another, he'd be separated from Celeste.

For the rest of the drive, he listened as Celeste caught up with her mother and sister. From the way the three of them laughed and teased each other, Drew could tell they had strong, tight bonds. The snow held off until they were within ten miles of the lodge, and they made it home without any problems. After parking in front of the event center, Drew unpacked the luggage from the back of the SUV and carried it up the stairs.

Celeste opened the apartment door and he deposited the suitcases inside. He turned to her mother and sister. "It was a pleasure meeting you. I hope you enjoy your stay."

Gloria extended her hand to him. "Thank you so much for picking us up and getting us here safely."

"I was happy to help." He turned his attention to Celeste. "I'll park the SUV in the garage and leave the keys with Maggie in the kitchen."

"Great. Thanks for everything, Drew."

"You're welcome."

He was about to make his escape when Hope burst through the door, her face wreathed in smiles and her body vibrating with excitement.

"Grandma! Auntie Gloria!" She ran straight into her grandmother's open arms. "I missed you so much!"

Nora bent over her, holding her tight. "I missed you, too, baby girl."

Drew's heart constricted. Hope shouldn't be deprived of being with her grandmother. He cleared his throat as Hope hugged her aunt. "I'd better be going."

"Drew! Wait!" Hope dragged herself away from her aunt and came to him. "Aren't you coming for dinner? Auntie Maggie said everyone should come to the restaurant for a special dinner tonight because they flew all the way from South Carolina and they'd be hungry."

"You should visit with your grandma and auntie. You don't get to see them very often."

"But I want you to come, too." There was a note of distress in Hope's voice that Drew couldn't ignore.

He got down on one knee in front of her. "Tonight is for being with your family, but how about you come to my office after school tomorrow? We can play video games and maybe I can finally beat you." He'd brought his gaming system to his office at the lodge and added games appropriate for a child Hope's age.

"You promise?"

"I pinkie swear promise." He held up his right hand with his pinkie finger extended.

Hope looped her much smaller finger around his. "I pinkie swear, too."

"Okay. See you tomorrow."

Hope wrapped her arms around his neck. "See you."

She surprised him by kissing his cheek before letting go. With one last squeeze, he got to his feet. He saw the startled expressions on Celeste's mother's and sister's faces and wondered what they would make of that exchange.

He needed to leave.

"Goodnight, everyone."

"Goodnight, Drew," Celeste said. "And thanks again."

Drew acknowledged her thanks with a nod and left. After parking the SUV in the garage and leaving the key in the kitchen as promised, Drew walked briskly across the parking lot and entered the trail leading to the house. He stopped, giving his eyes a moment to adjust to the darkness of the forest. The wind howled through the trees, making the branches sway above him.

He'd never been more confused in his life. Crazy things were happening at the lodge that threatened its credibility and reputation. He was estranged from his only sibling over her choice of a partner while at the same time, in love with a woman who only saw him as a friend.

He wished the cold wind could tell him what he was supposed to do.

MAGGIE HAD INDEED PREPARED a special dinner for them. After Celeste introduced her mother and sister to everyone in the kitchen, Maggie led Celeste and her family to a table in a cozy alcove of the restaurant. Soon after, she and Janelle, one of the servers, returned with a bowl of salad and a platter of egg noodles covered with a creamy sauce. Fragrant steam rose from the platter.

"I hope you don't mind," Maggie said. "I thought a family dinner deserved family-style service. Celeste told me that beef stroganoff is one of your favorites, Mrs. Emerson."

"Please, call me Nora. And yes, I love beef stroganoff. This looks delicious. Thank you."

"Thank you for the warm welcome," Gloria said.

"You're very welcome. We're all so pleased you were able to come." Maggie tugged gently on one of Hope's pigtails. "This little one was hungry as a bear when she came home from school so she had a bowl of vegetable soup with crackers. She may not have such a big appetite."

"I have a big appetite for dessert!" Hope announced. She turned to her grandmother. "Auntie Maggie made chocolate pie! It's my favorite."

"It's my favorite, too. I wonder how she knew?" Nora said with a laugh.

"A little birdie told me," Maggie replied with a wink in Celeste's direction. "I'd better get back to the kitchen. Enjoy your meal, ladies."

Celeste sent her friend a grateful smile. "Thanks for everything, Maggie."

With a wave and a smile she left. Celeste's mother helped herself to salad and stroganoff. "It was very kind of her to go to all this trouble for us. The restaurant is busy. I'm sure she had enough to do."

"Maggie and her sisters have treated us like family since we arrived. We've been very happy here."

Nora simply nodded, a thoughtful expression on her face. Celeste wanted her mother to understand that she and Hope had a good life here, that they considered Solace Lake their home now. Aside from her family, there was nothing for them in South Carolina any longer.

"Auntie Maggie says I can do my homework in the kitchen when I come home from school and Mama is working," Hope said.

"Is that right?" Gloria said.

"Ah huh. I like being in the kitchen. It smells good, and I always get a snack after school."

Gloria laughed. "You're a lucky girl, Hope. If your snacks are as good as this meal, you've got it made!"

Celeste was well aware that allowing the child of one of the staff to hang out in a restaurant's kitchen was highly unusual. But Maggie and Luke and the rest of the Hainstocks had created a workplace that was supportive and fun, and they treated staff like valued members of the family. In return, staff were loyal to the lodge.

At least most were. It still struck her as unbelievable that a member of the staff would steal from the lodge.

They spent the rest of the meal laughing and catching up with each other's lives. After years of renting, Gloria and her husband and two kids were about to move into their own home after Christmas. Nora was active in her church, especially the choir, and most of her friends were there.

"I am going to miss Gloria and Marcus and the kids," Nora said. "It's been so nice having them right next door all these years."

"It's been great for all of us, Mama," Gloria said. "But we're only moving a few blocks away. This house is so much bigger and gives the kids a chance to have their own rooms.

You know we've wanted to buy our own place for a long time."

Nora's shoulders slumped. "Yes, I know. Forgive an old Mother Hen for wanting to keep her chicks close. I know my babies have to fly free but knowing doesn't make it any easier."

She changed the subject and talked about the antics of her choir mates and soon had them all laughing. But underneath it, Celeste detected an air of loneliness in her mother. She felt torn. Did she do what was right for her mother and go back to South Carolina, or did she please herself and stay at the best job she'd ever had with her best friends?

Near the best man she'd ever known?

Whenever she thought of leaving, Drew entered her thoughts. The idea of not seeing him again caused her heart to thump with anxiety. He'd made it clear he wanted to take their relationship to the next level, and she felt terrible for causing him pain. At the same time, she felt disloyal to Easton's memory for even thinking about another man. He'd been a wonderful husband, father and friend. How could she forget him? How could she let another man replace him?

Celeste felt pulled in a dozen directions. Each choice she made would mean losing something, or someone, she loved.

Later, in her apartment, she made tea and relaxed with her mother and sister while Hope had a bath and prepared for bed. As soon as Hope kissed her grandmother and aunt goodnight and Celeste returned from tucking her into bed, her sister pounced on her.

"So, what's really going on with you and Drew?"

She should have known it was coming, but still it took her by surprise. "We're friends. Like we said, he's been teaching me how to drive."

"Seems like Hope is very attached to him," her mother said.

"Yes." That fact had been made abundantly clear to her tonight. She knew Hope liked Drew, but she hadn't realized the depth of her affection. Or Drew's to her. With him leaving soon, it probably wasn't good for either one of them.

Or me. Her heart pinged at the idea of Drew's departure.

"I think there's more going on than simple friendship," Gloria said. "There's a definite vibe between the two of you."

Celeste sank into a chair in the living room. There was no point denying their relationship since they'd already figured it out. "We...care for each other."

"Are you sleeping together?"

Her sister was nothing if not direct. Celeste let out a breath, her shoulders slumping. "Once. But I told him it couldn't happen again."

"Why not?" her mother asked.

Celeste blinked at her, shocked she was the one asking the question. "Because he's younger than me. Because of Hope."

"Looks like Hope has already made her decision," Gloria said. "What's really going on with you, CeCe?"

Celeste shook her head, unable to answer. All she knew was that every time she thought about giving her heart away again, she was filled with apprehension.

"Baby, nobody knows better than me how tough an interracial relationship can be," Nora said. "If you're going to risk a relationship like that, you have to be sure, for your sake and for Hope's."

Celeste nodded. Whatever she did, she was going to lose.

Chapter Sixteen

MAGGIE SET THE HIDDEN camera on his desk, then closed his office door. "It happened again."

"Another theft?" When she nodded, Drew groaned. "What was it this time?"

She dropped into a chair. "An assortment of tinned goods—smoked oysters, mussels and crabmeat. I planned to use them to make appetizers for a couple of Christmas parties we're hosting next week. Luckily, they're not expensive items, but still, it adds up. Good thing I didn't store the caviar in the kitchen."

"Caviar?"

"The bank in Minnewasta is having their Christmas party here and the manager asked if we could make a caviar canape as a special treat for the staff. Even a small tin of caviar is expensive, so I'm guarding it at home."

"Good idea. When did the canned goods go missing?"

"It must have been last night. They were still there when I left yesterday afternoon. I haven't told anyone other than Luke, and now you. If anyone in the kitchen notices and asks where these canned goods are, I'll tell them I returned them to our distributer."

The fewer people who knew about this latest theft, the better. The kitchen staff were already on edge, pointing fingers at each other. "When the other items disappeared, we didn't have the hidden camera set up." Drew picked up the camera and held it between two fingers. "With any luck, all the evidence we need is right here."

Maggie let out a tired sigh. "I really hope so. I can't take much more of this."

"I know." The thefts at the lodge had been stressful on all of them, but Maggie had taken them particularly hard. She couldn't get her head around the idea that a member of her kitchen staff, a person she treated like family, could do this to her.

Drew handed her a recharged camera. "This will be over soon. I feel like we're nearly there."

Maggie got to her feet and put the camera in the pocket of her chef's whites. "I just want to go back to normal."

She left the office and went back to the kitchen. Drew began watching the video footage from the latest camera.

He wished he had a normal to go back to. But after his stay at Solace Lake Lodge nothing would be the same.

A SHORT TIME LATER, Drew saw the school bus pull into the parking lot through the window in his office. He turned off the hidden camera footage, locked the camera in his desk, and opened the video games. As far as he knew, Hope was still coming to his office after school. Unless Celeste had instructed her to go straight home to spend time with her grandmother and aunt.

He was relieved to see her when she arrived at his door. But the minute Hope stepped inside and tossed her backpack carelessly into a corner of the room, he could tell something was wrong. "Hey, what's going on? You look upset."

Hope stared at the floor. "I'm fine."

Drew lifted her chin gently with one finger so he could look into her eyes. "You don't look fine. You know you can tell me anything, don't you?"

"Yeah, I know."

He closed the office door, then sat in his chair and faced her. "It's just you and me here. What's going on?"

Hope looked up at him, her chin trembling. "There's this boy. He says mean things to me."

Drew struggled to keep his anger in check. How dare anyone make Hope cry. "What kind of mean things did he say?"

"He said my skin was an ugly color and that my hair was weird. He said I was weird looking because I'm black. He said it in front of all the other kids when my teacher wasn't there. Some of the other kids laughed, too."

Shock rendered Drew speechless. He pulled Hope onto his lap and held her tight. When he was sure he could speak without cursing, he took a deep breath. "That boy is an idiot. No one has the right to say things like that to you, Hope. No one. You are as beautiful and perfect as your mom. Don't believe anything else."

She snuggled against his chest. "You think so?"

"Of course, I do, sweetheart. You are a beautiful little girl. No doubt about it." He held her closer. "When someone says mean things like that, it says more about them than it does about you. It means his thinking is all messed up. He's the one who's wrong."

"I thought he was wrong, but I wasn't sure," Hope said.

"Well, I'm sure. Don't ever believe anyone who says there's something wrong with you because of the color of your skin. Okay?"

She looked up at him and nodded solemnly. "Okay."

"Has this happened before?"

Hoped nodded and lowered her gaze.

"Have you told your mom what this boy said?"

She shook her head. "No. She gets sad when bad things happen."

Had Hope always been so protective of Celeste? "You have to tell her. She should know."

Hope looked up at him. "Will you come with me when I tell her?"

"Of course I will. Do you want me to come with you now?"

"No." She shook her head vigorously. "After Grandma and Auntie leave."

It was probably for the best. They wouldn't be happy to know Hope was being harassed at her nearly all-white school. "Okay. We'll talk to your mom then. Hope, what's this boy's name?"

"Jacob Mains. He lives in Minnewasta."

Drew kissed her forehead. "You want to play some video games till you have to go home?"

"Okay."

Drew played, though his mind was on the visit he was going to pay this Jacob Mains and his parents.

AFTER A DISCREET CONVERSATION with the restaurant's head server, Drew learned the address of Jacob Mains and his mother. According to Lorraine, Jacob's mother Sally was separated from his father and had moved Jacob and his sister into a trailer on the outskirts of town.

Now, as he sat in his car in front of the trailer with the windshield wipers slapping away the falling snow, Drew wondered if he was doing the right thing. Celeste might not like him interfering. But then he remembered Hope's sad face and her insistence on not immediately telling her mother what had happened. He couldn't idly stand by and do nothing. With that thought firmly in mind, he turned off the ignition and left his car.

He knocked on the trailer door. A moment later a woman opened it, a little girl with curly hair balanced on her hip. Both were wearing heavy woolen sweaters and socks.

"Yes?"

"Are you Sally Mains? Jacob Mains' mother?" Drew asked.

She eyed him suspiciously. "Why? What do you want?"

"Jacob is in the same classroom as the daughter of a friend of mine. He subjected her to some harassment that I want to speak to you about?"

"What kind of harassment?"

"Racial slurs. Hope is black and your son made some racist comments about her appearance. She was very hurt and upset by them."

Sally's shoulders sagged. "You'd better come in. Close the door before what little heat we have left is gone." She stepped aside to let him in, and he closed the door quickly behind him.

Drew slipped off his wet shoes at the door and walked on the cold linoleum floor to the chair at the kitchen table that Sally directed him to. Sally sat across from him with the toddler on her lap.

"Would it be possible for me to speak to Jacob?"

Her chin came up. "Not if you're going to yell at him or call him names. We've got enough troubles."

It was obvious from the look of the trailer and the lack of heat that the family was going through some hard times. "I wouldn't do that. But I want him to know that his words were hurtful. He needs to learn that racist comments like that are not okay."

"My husband—soon to be ex-husband—talks like that. That's likely where Jacob heard it."

Drew chose his words carefully. "Maybe if we show him now, while he's young, that discriminating against people who don't look like him is wrong, he won't grow up to be like his father."

Sally stared at him across the table. Finally, she said, "That's what I want for my boy."

She rose to her feet, taking her daughter with her, and moved to the end of the hallway, just beyond the kitchen. "Jacob! Can you come here, please? I need to talk to you."

A few moments later, a skinny red headed kid wearing faded jeans and a worn-out green sweatshirt made his way into the kitchen. He eyed Drew suspiciously as he leaned against his mother's side.

Sally put her hand on his shoulder. "This man says you said some bad things to the little black girl in your class. Is that true?"

Jacob stared at the floor and said nothing, his mouth twisting in a frown.

Sally tried again. "Jacob, I asked you a question and I need an answer."

Still nothing. Drew could barely contain his impatience. Maybe the kid figured if he said nothing, he could get away with being a racist little shit.

Not on his watch.

"Jacob, my name is Drew and Hope is a friend of mine. Do you remember what you said to her?"

The kid gave a negligent shrug of his shoulder. Drew wanted to shake him until his teeth rattled. Instead, he rose and stood over Jacob.

"You told her that her skin was ugly and that her hair was weird. Do you remember now?"

Jacob must have heard the anger in his voice. He cowered at his mother's side, and for the first time he looked directly at Drew. "Are you going to hit me?"

His words shocked Drew, and he stepped back. "No, of course not. I would never hit a kid."

Sally smoothed her son's hair. "His father sometimes...disciplined him."

Good God. Drew sat in his chair once more and tried to figure out what to do, what to say. "Jacob, how would it make you feel if I said your red hair was weird, that it was unnatural? Especially if I said it in front of a bunch of kids in your class?"

Again, the kid shrugged and stared at the floor. Now that he knew Drew wasn't going to hit him, he didn't care what he had to say.

He was going to have to make him care.

"You are one ugly kid, Jacob Mains. I mean, those freckles." Drew laughed derisively. "They're ridiculous. You look like somebody painted spots on your face and did a really bad job of it."

"Hey!" Sally said. "What do you think you're doing?"

Drew held up his hand to stop her. "You're nothing but a scrawny little shit. You're not worth anything. You're stupid and you're ugly."

"I'm not ugly!" the boy yelled. "You can't say that!"

He'd obviously hit on a sore point. "How does it make you feel when I tell you you're ugly?"

"It makes me mad!"

"I can understand that. What else does it make you feel?"

The boy's lower lip trembled. "It makes me sad. I hate it when Daddy says my red hair is ugly."

Sally pulled him to her side. "Oh, Jacob. I'm so sorry." She turned to Drew. "His daddy is actually his stepfather. He's my second husband."

It was beginning to make sense. The stepfather picked on Jacob and he, in turn, took out his frustration and anger on Hope.

"Before you say ugly words to someone else, remember how it makes you feel when someone says them to you. It's not a good feeling, is it?"

"No."

"Please don't say ugly things to Hope again. Or to any kid. If you do, you and I will have to have another talk."

Jacob turned to his mother. "Can I go back to my room now?"

She smoothed his hair from his forehead. "Yeah, you can go."

"One more thing, Jacob," Drew said. "You're not the least bit ugly or stupid and you should feel proud of your red hair and freckles. Anyone who tells you otherwise is ugly in their heart, and you shouldn't believe them."

Jacob stood completely still as he stared at Drew. Then he hurried down the hallway. Drew watched his retreating back. Only time would tell if he'd gotten through to the kid. He stood. "I'd better go."

Drew went to the door and slipped on his shoes. They were cold inside, and he shivered involuntarily. "Is your furnace not working?"

"It doesn't throw much heat. I'm looking for something better, but without a job...I'm sorry. You don't want to hear my problems."

"What kind of work are you looking for?"

Sally moved her daughter to her other hip. "Whatever I can find. I've applied at the restaurants in town but none of them are hiring. I don't have training for anything else."

Drew pulled on his gloves, wondering if what he was about to say next was a mistake. But he had a feeling Sally Mains was a decent person who needed someone to give her a break. "I work at Solace Lake Lodge. We're always looking for good people to work with us."

Her eyes widened in surprise. "I would love to work there!"

"We're having an event on the weekend. You could work with the catering team. If that works out, we could see about something more permanent. Come out to the lodge tomorrow afternoon and I'll introduce you to our head server. She can show you the ropes."

Sally's enthusiasm faded. "I don't have a car. I have no way of getting to the lodge. It's far from town, isn't it?"

"Ten miles. Most of our staff live in Minnewasta. Maybe it would be possible to carpool."

"That would be incredible," Sally whispered.

"I can't make any promises, but I'll talk to our head server and see if we can arrange a ride."

After adding her number to his contact list on his phone, Drew left. He hoped he'd done the right thing. And he hoped he'd gotten through to Jacob.

He needed to let Luke know what he'd done so he wasn't blindsided when Sally showed up to work. He pulled his car into an angle parking spot on Lakeside Drive and made the call. "Hi Luke. Just wanted to let you know I offered someone a job." He told him Sally Mains' situation.

"We can always use more people. I'll have her fill out some paperwork when she arrives. We'll see how she works out."

"Good. All I'm asking is to give her a chance."

"I was about to call you," Luke said. "I talked to the manager at the hotel again. I mentioned that Mel told us she came out of retirement and moved to Minnewasta because her husband recently died and she needed a fresh start. The manager was confused by that because he was under the impression Mel had been a widow for many years."

"I suppose he could be wrong."

"True. He said he was going to talk to a friend of hers who still works at the hotel and find out for sure. He'll get back to me."

"Let me know what you find out."

"I will. Talk to you later."

Drew set his phone in the cup holder in the console and pulled out of his parking space. He hoped Sally would fit in at the lodge. A decent job could change her life, and the lives of her children. She just needed a chance to prove herself.

If the family was more stable, maybe Jacob would stop tormenting Hope.

WHEN DREW RETURNED to the lodge and made his way across the lobby to his office, he gave a quick wave to Mel at the front desk.

"Hey, what are you doing here so early?"

"Early?" Mel laughed. "It's after six. My evening shift begins at four, remember?"

Drew shook his head. He'd been so consumed by events of the afternoon that he'd completely lost track of time. "Right. Ignore me. I can't tell time."

Mel laughed again as he hurried to the office. Once inside, he began watching the kitchen videos again, determined to find something that would provide some answers. His mind wandered as he fast-forwarded through the recording and he had to keep reminding himself to stay alert. So far, all he'd seen was people working hard and doing their jobs, followed by hours of an empty, darkened kitchen at night.

Just when he thought the hidden cameras weren't ever going to provide any useful information, someone walked into the kitchen. The time stamp on the video said it was two in the morning. Drew sat up straighter and stopped the fast-forward motion, making the video play at regular speed. Though it was dark in the kitchen, the shape of the person was definitely female. He tried to identify the person but he couldn't see her face clearly.

The woman entered the walk-in pantry. Exactly three minutes later, according to the time count on the video, she came out carrying a bag that, from its appearance, was loaded with something heavy.

Who the hell was this?

His question was answered a moment later. Before leaving the kitchen, the woman turned her head just enough for the camera to get a shot of her face. Drew stopped the video.

Mel White.

He sat back in shock, not sure he could believe his eyes. But there was no doubt. Mel was walking out of the kitchen in the middle of the night with something that didn't belong to her.

His attention was diverted when Luke entered his office and quickly closed the door behind him.

"I was just about to call you," Drew said.

"I have to tell you something first." Luke sat in the chair in front of the desk. "I just got off the phone with the hotel manager. He talked to Mel's friend at the hotel. They're still in touch and very close. The manager was right. Mel's been a widow for over ten years."

"Why would she lie to us about that?"

Luke held up a hand. "It gets worse. The friend said Mel recently discovered that her identity had been stolen. It started with someone using her credit card and then escalated to this woman impersonating her at different businesses. It's been a nightmare for her."

"Wait." Drew stared at him, stunned. "Are you saying that's not the real Mel White currently at our front desk?"

"That's exactly what I'm saying. The real Mel White is retired and living in a condo in Minneapolis. The manager gave me a glowing account of her work because she'd been excellent at her job. He had no idea someone was impersonating her."

"There's something you have to see," Drew said. "Look at this. I just found it."

He turned the monitor so Luke could see the still shot of Mel, or whoever she was, in the kitchen. "Getting into the locked kitchen wouldn't be a problem for her since there's a key at the front desk."

Luke swore. "I can't believe I didn't see through her. Damn it, I'm the one who hired her. I brought her here!"

"Don't beat yourself up. This person is an accomplished liar. I doubt it's the first time she's done something like this." Drew leaned forward in his chair, his nerves on edge. "What do we do now?"

Luke pulled out his phone. "We call the police. And we keep an eye on her till they get here."

They waited in nervous anticipation in Drew's office with the door open so they could see Mel at the front desk. When they saw a police car pull into the parking lot about a half hour later, they quietly headed into the lobby. As soon as the police entered the lodge, 'Mel' hurried out from behind the front desk and headed toward a back exit.

"Going somewhere?" Drew stepped directly in front of her, preventing her escape. When she tried to go around him, Luke blocked her.

Her gaze darted between them, her expression resembling that of a trapped animal's. "Excuse me. I need to use the washroom."

"You can use the washroom at the police station," Drew said. "Mel, or whatever the hell your name is, consider yourself fired."

LUKE STAYED AT THE hotel and manned the front desk while Drew followed the police to Brainerd. He took the evidence they'd gathered with him. The video from the hidden camera, the bogus invoice, the changes to vendors names and addresses in the accounting system. He also provided the police with Mr. Murphy's contact information. There was no telling how many other customer credit card numbers this woman had stolen, or perhaps sold on the dark web. They would have to contact every guest who'd paid with a credit card during Mel's time there and tell them what happened. They'd have to provide these guests with credit monitoring so they could guard against identity theft. It was going to cost the lodge a lot of money.

The police managed to identify the woman as Rebecca Shore. She was a notorious grifter and con artist who went by many names and had swindled dozens of businesses in the past with her knowledge of accounting and banking and computer systems. Her *modus operandi* was to steal a legitimate person's identity and use their good name and references to convince an unsuspecting business to give her a job. Then, she'd pilfer as much as she could as fast as she could before disappearing. When police searched her rented house in Minnewasta, her bags were already packed for her escape.

Rebecca Shore confessed that she targeted the lodge when she learned that Harper, the person in charge of finances, was about to have a baby and would be away from the lodge for an extended period. She knew from experience that the person replacing her wouldn't have the knowledge to spot any subtle changes in the accounting system and likely wouldn't care as much, either. So, she bided her time, on the lookout for information. She regularly picked the lock on Harper's office door during her overnight shifts.

Her patience was rewarded when, on one of her regular forays into the office, she discovered that Harper had left the notebook containing all the passwords for the lodge in her desk. Rebecca photographed every page with her phone and using the information she found, was able to open Harper's work email account. After that, it was relatively simple to gain access to the accounting system. If it asked for a code number before it would let her in, she directed it to the compromised email address. Once in the accounting system, she used the name of a former vendor to create a fake invoice and changed the addresses of other vendors to a mailbox that she controlled.

She'd placed the fake invoice in Harper's file, hoping that Drew would go ahead and pay it. That hadn't worked, but she'd collected on the vendor addresses she'd changed. The police discovered she'd set up bank accounts for these four businesses with their altered names so she could deposit the checks. The police also believed she was about to empty the lodge's bank account when she was caught.

Rebecca Shore exhibited no signs of remorse. Her only regret, she admitted to police, was that she'd stolen from the kitchen. She usually stuck to financial crimes, but a large gambling debt and a collector on her tail meant she was forced to resort to other kinds of theft. In the end, the kitchen theft had been her undoing. She denied any wrongdoing until confronted with the hidden camera footage. But there was no refuting what was right there in black and white.

The lodge would likely take a hit to its reputation with vendors and guests. Drew hoped it didn't affect attendance at the Mistletoe Ball. Everything had already been purchased—the food, the band, the decorations. If they had to cancel, it would be a big financial hit on top of the hits they'd already taken.

But what infuriated him even more was the distrust this woman had sown. Maggie had suspected Cheryl, a loyal employee and one of her good friends. And it shamed him now that he'd suspected Ryan. Perhaps he'd *wanted* Ryan to be guilty so that Carrie would drop him and no longer be angry with Drew.

As he drove back to the lodge, Carrie's words came back to him as they had so many times. *You're discriminating against Ryan the same way some people would discriminate against Celeste.*

She was right. It had nearly killed him when Hope told him what Jacob Mains had said. He'd done the same thing to Ryan. He'd been focused on the things Ryan couldn't do instead of celebrating what he *could* do.

He needed to fix what he'd broken. And there was no time like the present.

Drew drove through Minnewasta until he found Ryan's house. He pulled up in front and turned off the engine. For a moment, he stared at the ramp leading to the front door of the neat bungalow. Ryan had worked hard to come back from a devastating injury and in the process, created a new career and a new life for himself.

And with just a few words, Drew had negated everything Ryan had accomplished. How could he have been so callous?

He left the car and walked up the ramp to the front door. Ryan answered his knock after a short wait. His expression told Drew that he was the last person he expected to see.

Or wanted to see.

"Can I come in? We need to talk," Drew said.

Ryan gave a brief nod and wheeled out of the way while Drew stepped inside and took off his shoes at the door. The house was small and uncluttered, with a minimum amount of furniture in the living room. Aside from a rug at the entrance, the hardwood floors were bare. As he followed Ryan through the living room and into the kitchen, he realized it wasn't a decorating decision. It was so Ryan could wheel freely around his house. Drew chastised himself for being so dense.

"Can I get you coffee, tea?" Ryan asked.

"No, thank you. I won't take up much of your time. I want to apologize." Drew pulled off his gloves and stuffed them in his pockets. "I'm sorry I came between you and Carrie. I discriminated against you because of your disability, and that was completely wrong."

Ryan looked taken aback by his apology. "You were trying to protect your sister."

"Was I? Maybe I was trying to impose on her my idea of who she should be with. But she loves you. You're the one she wants."

Ryan hung his head. "But you were right. Carrie is young. She doesn't understand what marrying me will mean."

"You're wrong. I'm the one who didn't understand. Carrie understands the challenges, and she loves you enough to face them. Would you talk to her? She's hurting."

"The last thing I want to do is hurt Carrie." Ryan's voice was rough with emotion. "But she deserves so much more than I can give her."

"She deserves *you*, Ryan." Drew sat at one of the kitchen chairs and scrubbed his hand across his face. "I'm not going to lie. Part of the reason I'm here is so that I can salvage my relationship with my sister. She won't even stay in the same house with me."

"Yeah. Luke told me."

"Carrie's always known what she wanted. Somehow, she always understood what was right for her, no matter what anyone else said." Drew laughed softly. "When she was about ten and in a gymnastics class, she wanted a trampoline for the backyard. My parents weren't keen on it, but she persevered. She researched online and found the best price in the city for the model she wanted. Then, she wrote an essay about the health benefits of exercise for kids. She also argued that she'd have better balance and coordination if she had access to a trampoline. My parents decided that if she wanted the damn thing that badly, they should probably get it for her."

Ryan smiled, but there was a touch of sadness in it. "That sounds exactly like Carrie."

"There's something else. Our front desk clerk was arrested today. We discovered she was the one who stole from the lodge."

Ryan's eyes widened. "Wow. Really?"

Drew told him about Rebecca Shore's crimes and how she'd managed to escape detection for so long. He swallowed before continuing, looking briefly at his clasped hands before lifting his gaze back to Ryan. "I suspected you. I believed that with your knowledge, you could have easily entered our accounting program. When I told Carrie what I thought, she blew up. She said you were honest, a person of honor, and you would never steal from anyone. I'm sorry I suspected you and called your integrity into question."

Ryan gave him a hard stare. "If we're playing true confessions, I suspected you, too. You had the means and the opportunity. But I couldn't figure out your motive. Why would you steal fish from the kitchen?"

At first, Drew was stunned by Ryan's admission, but then he laughed. "If you ask my family, they'd probably tell you my motive is being an immature jerk." He sobered. "Come to the Mistletoe Ball on Saturday. Meet our parents and talk to Carrie. I know she wants to see you."

Ryan shook his head. "I don't know."

"At least consider it. I'll leave a ticket for you at the door. It would mean everything to Carrie." He rose. "I hope I see you on Saturday."

Ryan followed him to the front door. "Thanks for coming, Drew."

"Thanks for listening. If I was in your position, I'm not sure I'd be as generous."

"I only want what's best for Carrie."

"I can see that now. I came because I believe you're important to Carrie's happiness, now and in the future. Take care of yourself."

With that, he opened the door and left. Drew hoped he'd gotten through to him.

Just as Ryan was important to Carrie's happiness, Celeste was important to his. Maybe it was time to find out if she felt the same way.

THE MORNING AFTER THE arrest, the kitchen buzzed with the news. Celeste hadn't known the woman who called herself Mel White very well, but even so, the news was shocking. She was relieved the real thief had been caught. Maggie had tearfully apologized to Cheryl for suspecting her. Cheryl had accepted her apology, but Celeste wondered if their relationship would ever be quite the same.

She couldn't stop thinking about how all this had affected Drew. He'd likely be feeling betrayed, or perhaps he somehow blamed himself. He tended to do that.

Celeste took a break from the kitchen, telling Maggie she needed to check on something. In a way, it was true. She needed to check on Drew. She hadn't seen him since he'd dropped her mother and sister at her apartment three days ago. A feeling in her gut told her he was avoiding her.

He had every right to do so. And hadn't she told herself to keep her distance as well? It wasn't smart to spend time with Drew.

Because when she was with him, he made her want things. Things she couldn't have.

The way she'd left him so abruptly after they made love, and the things she'd said, must have hurt him, and she regretted it. But if she'd stayed, she would have made love with him again. It would have been even harder to walk away then.

Why do I have to walk away from Drew? She couldn't answer her own question.

Celeste headed to his office and knocked on the open door. "Hi. Have you got a minute?"

Drew set his pen on the desk. "Sure. Come in."

She sat in one of the chairs in front of his desk. "I heard what happened with Mel. Are you okay?"

"I'm fine. It's been a crazy couple of days. I apologized to Ryan, though I'm not sure it did any good."

She was proud of him for admitting he'd been wrong. "You don't think he'll make up with Carrie?"

Drew shrugged. "I hope so. I asked him to come to the Mistletoe Ball to meet our parents, but I don't know if he will." He shifted in his seat. "What can I do for you?"

His formal tone gave her pause. "I was wondering if you were busy this evening. We're decorating our tree after dinner and Hope and I would like you to come over. We're having hot chocolate and gingerbread cookies."

He didn't answer right away. His hesitation made Celeste squirm uncomfortably. A bubble of panic began to grow in her chest at the idea of Drew pulling away from her. "Hope really wants you to come."

"And you, Celeste? What do you want?" His eyes bored into hers, his voice lowering to a whisper. "If I come to your apartment tonight, what will you tell your mother and sister? That I'm a friend? Or will you tell them that when we touch, we can't get enough of each other? That when I'm inside you, you scream my name?"

She shook her head. "Don't." The memory of making love with him was already seared into her brain. Thinking about what could never happen again was too painful. "Please don't."

His smile was sad. "Okay. I thought so. Thank you for the invitation, but I think it's best if I don't accept."

"Why not?"

Drew went to the door and softly closed it. Then he sat in the chair next to her. "I love you, Celeste. Being with you these last few weeks has been the most special time of my life."

She stared at him, his *I love you* reverberating in her head. Fear swirled in her gut and she couldn't respond, could barely breathe.

"It's okay, sweetheart. I don't expect you to say the words back. I know you can't. But I needed to say them to you, at least this one time." He paused and looked down at his hands in his lap. When he lifted his gaze to hers once more, his eyes were filled with resignation. "I can't pretend I don't care and you can't pretend you do, so maybe it's best if for my remaining time here at the lodge we don't see each other. It hurts too much. I've asked Luke to help you with your driving lessons after I go."

She tried to make sense of what he was saying, but his "after I go" drowned out everything else. "You're leaving? You mean soon?"

"Yes. As soon as I can arrange it. Luke is looking for someone to replace me."

Celeste touched her forehead, a headache beginning to pound. It didn't make sense. He loved her, but he was leaving her?

Dear God, it was happening again. Her worst nightmare was happening again and once more, she was going to be alone.

"Maybe I'm being a coward, but I need to protect myself. Being with you, knowing I'll never have your heart, it'll break me. For my own sanity, I have to go."

She managed a nod as she got to her feet, her knees shaking. She had to get out of this room before she splintered into a thousand shards.

Drew rose as well. "Celeste—"

"I have to go."

She wrenched open the door and ran.

CELESTE RAN TO A STAFF washroom and cried. The washroom was a single small room with no other cubicles so no one could hear her, but to be sure, she muffled her cries with her hand over her mouth. She cried so hard she made herself sick to her stomach.

Finally, her tears subsided. She washed her face in the sink and patted it dry with a paper towel. She needed to get herself together and go back to work. She'd already been away too long.

When she returned to the kitchen, Maggie examined her face. "Are you okay? You don't look well."

"I'm—" Celeste tried to say she was fine, but tears clogged her throat once more and all she could do was to shake her head.

Maggie placed her cool hand on Celeste's hot forehead. "Maybe you're coming down with something. Go home and lie down for a while. Let your mom look after you."

"Maggie—"

"Go." Maggie put an arm around her and accompanied her out of the kitchen. "We can take it from here. We need you to get some rest so you're feeling better for the big event on Saturday. We'll see you tomorrow but only if you're feeling up to it."

In the staff room, Celeste put on her coat and then trudged the short distance to her apartment. When she walked inside, her mother and sister put down their teacups.

"Celeste? We didn't expect you home so early," her mother said.

Celeste hung her coat in the closet. "Maggie sent me home."

"Are you sick?" Gloria asked.

She shook her head, and the tears started again. "No. Yes. Drew told me he loves me."

Through her tears she saw them exchange a look. Her mother led her to the couch and then sat beside her. "Why does that make you so sad, baby?"

"Because in the same breath that he says he loves me, he told me he's leaving the lodge! He's leaving me! Why does everyone always leave me?"

Nora put her arms around her. "Oh, baby girl. I'm so sorry."

Celeste sank into her mother's arms. She cried for the loss of a love that could never be, and she cried for the love she'd shared, and lost, with Easton.

Finally, the tears subsided. Celeste was exhausted, spent. She barely had the energy to blow her nose when Gloria handed her a couple of tissues.

Her sister set a steaming cup of tea on the table beside her. "Here. Drink this."

Gloria refilled her teacup and her mother's and for a few moments they sat quietly sipping.

Finally, Nora broke the silence. "CeCe, can you tell us what happened?"

Celeste repeated the story. "He said being with me would break him and for his own sanity, he had to leave."

"What did he mean by that?" Gloria asked.

Drew's words were burned into her memory. *Being with you, knowing I'll never have your heart, it'll break me. For my own sanity, I can't stay.*

"He said he knows he'll never have my heart."

"If that's true, if you don't care for him as much as he cares for you, then why are you so upset?"

Celeste stared at her sister. Suddenly, the fog that had been clouding her thinking for so long lifted. "Because I love him, too."

The knowledge left her breathless. And afraid. What did she do now?

It was there all along. In the way she sought out his company, in her desire to console him when his relationship with Carrie went wrong. In the way she'd felt when they made love.

"It's my fault," her mother said. "I've been going on and on for years about how interracial marriages don't work. It didn't work for me, but that doesn't mean it can't work for you and Drew."

"It's not your fault, Mama. It's no one's fault. It just is." She tried to put her thoughts into words. "It has more to do with protecting myself." Her mother's attitudes about interracial relationships had indeed been burned into her brain but being with Drew had blown those ideas away. It no longer mattered to her, if it ever did. But she'd used the difference in their races, as well as the difference in their ages, as an excuse.

"Protecting yourself?" Celeste heard the alarm in Gloria's voice. "Has Drew hurt you in any way?"

"No, no. That's not what I mean." She took a deep breath. "Drew is the first man I've wanted to be with since Easton. And I can't go through that loss again."

"What happened with Easton was tragic, but that doesn't mean it will happen again," Gloria said.

"It already has!" Celeste shouted. She jumped to her feet and started pacing. "Drew's leaving me!"

"Maybe he doesn't love you as much as he says he does," her mother said.

Celeste stopped her pacing to look at her. "No, he means it. I know he does. I'm the one who said..." She hung her head, unable to continue.

"What did you say, CeCe?" Gloria asked.

She gathered her courage and faced them. "After the night we spent together, I told him it could never happen again because I didn't feel the same way about him. I lied to him. I hurt him."

Shame rained down on her. She'd lied to Drew and hurt him. No wonder he was pulling away. But what else could she have done? The fear of once more losing someone she loved was too great.

"Maybe if you talked to him, told him how you feel, he'd stay."

Celeste shook her head. Even though she loved Drew, the fear of being hurt again stopped her. It was best to let him go now. While she still could.

Chapter Seventeen

THE DAY BEFORE THE Mistletoe Ball, Drew's parents arrived at the lodge. He met them at the entrance and after hugging them, grabbed their luggage and took them to the front desk to check in.

"Where's Carrie?" Lydia asked when they finished checking in. "I'd hoped to see her when we arrived."

"She's probably working in the kitchen right now."

"Probably? Does that mean you two haven't patched up your differences?"

Drew knew the rift between him and Carrie was deeply upsetting to his mother. "No. Carrie is still staying with Maggie and Luke at his grandmother's house."

"How long are you going to let this go on, Drew?" Graham Barnes demanded.

Drew lowered his voice. "Let's talk in your room."

As they turned to leave, Celeste entered through the front doors. She hesitated a split second when she saw him, but then smiled politely at Drew's parents and walked toward them.

Lydia lifted her hand in greeting. "Hi, Celeste. How are you?"

She glanced quickly at Drew before answering his mother with a smile. "I'm well. Are you here for the Mistletoe Ball?"

Though she gave the appearance of outward calm, Drew noted the way her hands clenched and unclenched and the tight line of her smile.

"We are. It gives us the opportunity to see family, especially our children. Carrie tells us she loves working in the kitchen."

"Carrie is doing great. She's a very talented chef."

Drew was grateful Celeste didn't mention that Carrie had given her notice and planned to leave after the Ball. Apparently, his sister hadn't told their parents she was quitting.

"That's good to hear. We're very proud of her." Lydia threaded her arm through Drew's. "We're proud of both of our children."

Celeste's gaze skittered briefly to his. "You have every reason to be proud of your children. They're both wonderful people."

"Thank you. I appreciate that," Lydia said.

Celeste offered his mother another polite smile. "I'd better get to work. Enjoy your weekend."

"Good seeing you, Celeste." Lydia and Graham shook her hand before she left.

Drew watched her go, his heart breaking a little more with every step she took. Had he been wrong to back away from her?

No. It was time. Luke would soon have someone in place to take over his duties and there would be no reason for him to stay.

"Drew?"

His mother's voice brought him back to the present. He forced himself to smile as he grabbed the handle of her suitcase. "I'll show you to your room."

After Graham used the keycard to open the door, Lydia pushed their suitcase into a closet. "Have you tried to talk to Carrie?"

"I've tried to apologize. She won't listen."

"You've really made a mess of things." Drew could always count on his mother to be direct. "What are you doing to fix things with your sister?"

"I went to see Ryan, to apologize. I hope he knew I was sincere. I asked him to come to the Mistletoe Ball tomorrow, to talk to Carrie."

"Do you think he will?" Lydia asked.

"I don't know."

His mother hugged him. "Carrie will come around. She's probably angry right now, but she's got to know you meant well."

He wrapped his arms around his mom. He couldn't stand the idea of being estranged from his sister long term. "I hope you're right."

Lydia leaned back to look at him. "I noticed something between you and Celeste just now. You couldn't stop staring at her."

"Have you been seeing each other?" Graham asked.

The last thing he wanted to discuss with his parents was Celeste. He stepped out of his mom's embrace. "We're friends. I'm teaching her to drive." He told them how he'd helped her study for her learner's permit and was now acting as her driving instructor.

"You didn't look at each other like you were simply her driving instructor." Lydia tilted her head and watched him carefully, a sure sign she wasn't about to give up. "What's the real story, Drew?"

He let out a breath. He might as well come clean because once his mother got wind of a problem, she wouldn't let it go until she'd dealt with it. But there was nothing she could do about this. "I care about Celeste, very much, and her daughter Hope. But she doesn't feel the same way. She only thinks of me as a friend."

Graham leaned his hip against the dresser and folded his arms across his chest. "She's got to be older than you, isn't she?"

"Yes. Nine years older." There was no point denying it. "You didn't seem concerned about the ten-year gap between Ryan and Carrie. Why is this any different?"

"We didn't say we weren't concerned about the age difference between them. Carrie is very young and Ryan is her first serious boyfriend. But Celeste has a child, Drew." Graham said.

"I love Hope. She's a great kid."

"It's one thing to hang out with a kid occasionally and quite another to be a parent," Graham said. "Are you prepared for that?"

In his heart he knew he was totally prepared, but there was no point debating with his father. "It doesn't matter, Dad. Like I said, Celeste doesn't have the same feelings for me that I have for her."

"I'm sorry, honey," Lydia said.

"Apparently, she feels the same way about the difference in our ages as you do. And the difference in our races."

"That's an issue for her?"

"Her father is white. Her parents' marriage was turbulent, mainly because his family didn't accept her mother. So yeah, she has an issue."

Lydia put her arm around his shoulders. "I hate that you're hurting."

"I'll be okay, Mom."

"Celeste is divorced, isn't she?" Graham asked.

"Widowed. Her husband died in a car crash when Hope was three."

"That must have been awful for her," Lydia said.

"Yeah." Celeste had told him very little about her husband. Was she still mourning him?

Maybe that explained her withdrawal the morning after they'd made love. He wasn't who she wanted.

Maybe he'd never had a chance with Celeste from the very beginning.

CELESTE ARRIVED AT her apartment after work on Friday night just in time to tuck Hope into bed. She kissed her daughter goodnight, grabbed her pajamas and robe, and closed her bedroom door. In the living room, she tossed her night clothes over a stool at the island and sank into a chair in the living room.

"You look done in, CeCe," her mother said.

"It was a busy day. We're making last minute preparations for the big Christmas dinner tomorrow." It *had* been a busy day, but Celeste's exhaustion was likely due to not being able to sleep last night. Her mind had raced, her thoughts of Drew not letting her rest. Part of her wanted to throw caution to the wind and tell him she loved him. But whenever she considered doing that, her heart pounded in fear.

Seeing him with his parents today had been difficult. He'd tried to cover it, but the hurt on his face was hard to witness. She hated that she was the cause of his pain.

Gloria set a cup of chamomile tea on the table beside her. "Maybe this will relax you."

Celeste smiled her thanks. "It's really nice having you both here. For me and for Hope. A little pampering feels good, even if it's just having someone bring me tea."

"Marcus and I have a nightly ritual. He brings me tea, and I rub his feet. It helps both of us relax after a hectic day."

She and Easton had done little things like that for each other, too. Backrubs, running bubble baths, even breakfast in bed occasionally. Easton had been such a loving husband.

And then suddenly he was gone, and she was alone. She couldn't go through that again. She might not survive this time.

Her mother cleared her throat. "I think I've done you a disservice all these years, CeCe."

"A disservice?" Celeste couldn't imagine having a better mother.

"Ever since your father left us, I went on and on about how interracial marriages don't work. But the truth is our marriage didn't work for *us*. Our marriage likely wouldn't have survived even if we had been of the same race."

"What do you mean?"

"We had different outlooks on life. I was career driven, and he was more laid back. He had four different jobs in the nine years we were married. We fought over his lack of ambition all the time. At least, that's what I thought it was. I didn't take the time to ask him what he really wanted or whether he was happy. Turns out he wasn't."

Nora paused to drink her tea. "There were a few people in his family who had a problem with your father marrying a black woman, but if we'd been a stronger couple, it wouldn't have mattered. We could have weathered those storms together. Built something lasting. But I was stuck on what I thought our marriage should look like and what your dad should be. When he left me, he said he couldn't pretend to be something he wasn't anymore."

After he left their family, Celeste's father opened a small studio where he created stained glass art. Eventually, he married another artist and from what Celeste could tell, they'd been happy together for a lot of years.

"I was angry when he left us, and I didn't want to accept the blame, so I told you and everyone else it was because he was white and I was black." She stared into her teacup as if she were looking at old memories.

Celeste glanced at her sister and from the look of shock on Gloria's face, it was evident she hadn't heard this story before either.

"And then I did you a further disservice when you were older. I had the chance to marry again, to give you a loving stepfather, but I was afraid it would end the same way, with me alone and broken again. So, I said no. Because I was too afraid to take a chance, I ended up alone anyway. I can tell you, those chances for love don't come along very often."

"Mama, don't blame yourself like this."

"It's high time I took responsibility." She clutched her hands together. "The man I'd almost married died a couple of years ago. Maybe if I'd taken that second chance, it wouldn't have worked out. But maybe it would have. We could have had a lot of good years together. I'll always wonder what might have been. Don't wonder, CeCe. Don't let life and love pass you by because you're afraid."

"Oh, Mama."

Celeste got up from her chair to sit beside Nora on the sofa. Gloria sat on the other side.

"Thank you for telling us. That must have been hard for you."

"I should have told you a long time ago. You two girls deserved the truth from me." Nora dabbed at her eyes with a tissue. "CeCe, I don't want you to get to be my age and have regrets."

"I'm scared, Mama," Celeste confessed. It wasn't easy to speak of her fears. "Losing Easton was the hardest thing I've ever gone through. It nearly destroyed me. I can't do it again."

"Nothing bad is going to happen if you let yourself love again," Gloria said.

Celeste shook her head. "You don't know that for sure."

"You're right. I can't guarantee something bad won't happen. Nobody can," Gloria said. "A meteor could fall from the sky and wipe us out like the dinosaurs."

Celeste let out a choked laugh at her sister's attempt at a joke. "There's a comforting thought."

"My point is, we deserve to grab every ounce of happiness while we can. If Drew makes you happy, CeCe, if you love him and he loves you, don't let him slip away."

Gloria and her mother were right. There was something special between her and Drew. But was she brave enough to fight for it?

"THE LIGHTS LOOK REALLY good, Drew," Scarlet said. "I think you've got a future in decorating."

Drew balanced on the stepladder and stretched to attach a section of mini string lights to the next hook. "No, thank you. You're not going to convince me to risk life and limb on top of a rickety ladder again."

Scarlet chuckled. "Quit trying to pretend you don't love doing this stuff as much as I do."

"I think you're confusing me with some other nephew of yours."

"Nope, no confusion here. You're the only nephew I've got."

Drew laughed and shook his head. It was good working with Scarlet today. She was one of his favorite people, and he could always count on having a laugh with her. Besides, the work kept him too busy to think about Celeste.

At least some of the time. In reality, she was never far from his thoughts.

He tried to think about something else. Like how tickets to the Mistletoe Ball had sold out in the last day and a half. The lodge was completely booked, too. As predicted, people waited until the last minute to purchase their tickets. Drew was relieved they finally made up their minds and that news about the thefts at the lodge hadn't deterred people from attending.

Drew finished attaching the mini lights to small, unobtrusive hooks around the perimeter of the event center. The place looked beautiful. Four live Christmas trees decorated with red and green lights and red and green ornaments stood majestically in each corner of the room and filled the event center with their fresh pine scent. Dozens of potted red poinsettias in various sizes were placed strategically to lend a Christmasy air.

He only wished his heart was in the Christmas spirit.

He climbed down the ladder and made himself smile for Scarlet. "I've got to admit, the place looks good. You really know your stuff."

"Why thank you. Just wait till we set up the tables. We have gold tablecloths and mistletoe centerpieces with glass bowls that each hold a flameless candle. When we have the house lights down and the candles and mini lights on, it's going to be magical." Scarlet smiled. "It kind of reminds me of my wedding. Maggie and Harper went all out with the Christmas theme then, too."

Drew remembered. His uncle Cam had married Scarlet in a Christmas wedding in the main lodge three years previously. "Remember Harper and Ethan's outdoor wedding? We had that tent looking like a castle."

Scarlet chuckled. "We did, and we had a lot of fun, too. You and I were just getting to know each other then."

"Yeah, and you were just getting to know Cam."

She smiled and her eyes shone with happiness. "Yeah, I was. It was the first time I realized what an artist he was. It took me a while to get past his prickliness, but once I found the beautiful man underneath that thorny exterior, I was hooked."

"What made you hang in there?" The words were out of Drew's mouth before he could take them back. But he had always been curious. "Most women would take a hard pass on a man who's both a single father and a recovering alcoholic. Why did you stay?"

"Loving Tessa was easy. Cameron, however, was a much tougher nut to crack. As much as I loved him, we couldn't be together until he got over his fears."

"His fears? What do you mean?"

"Cameron was so afraid of falling back into alcoholism, of being a failure as a husband and a parent. He was afraid he was just like his father. He didn't believe he deserved happiness, or to have love in his life."

Drew remembered a little about his grandfather. Mostly he remembered a bitter, sick old man full of anger and resentment. His mother did her best to look after him in his final days, but nothing she did was ever good enough for him. No wonder Cam was afraid of following in his footsteps.

"It wasn't until Cameron realized there are no guarantees about anything in life that he was finally able to let go and commit to love." Scarlet placed her hand on Drew's arm. "Cameron told me that you care for Celeste, but she doesn't feel the same way. I'm sorry, Drew."

He looked away, the lump in his throat preventing him from answering.

"Celeste is a wonderful person. She's devoted herself to her job, and especially to Hope. In the three years she's been here, I've never known her to go out with another man and from what I hear, several have been interested. It makes me wonder if she's afraid the way Cameron was."

"What do you mean?"

Scarlet shrugged. "Cameron was afraid of failing. Maybe Celeste is afraid to love again. If something happened to Cameron..." She shook her head, as if the idea was too horrible to even think about. "I can't imagine how awful it must have been for her to lose her husband. If I'd been through what she has, I think I might be afraid to love again, too."

Drew stared at her. Was she right? Was Celeste still so in love with Easton Bishop that she couldn't imagine herself with anyone else?

If that was the case, what hope did he have? He couldn't compete with a ghost.

Over Scarlet's shoulder, he spotted Jerry Fields at the entrance to the room. When he saw Drew, he raised his hand in a wave and walked toward him.

"Drew, hi. Luke told me you'd be here. Do you have a few minutes to speak with me? I promise I won't take up too much of your time."

Scarlet touched his arm. "You go ahead. I'm going to recruit some staff members to help me set up tables. I'll catch up with you later."

With a smile she walked away, leaving him standing in the middle of the room with Jerry. Drew cleared his throat. "What can I do for you?"

"I know you're busy, so I'll get straight to the point," Jerry said. "Luke mentioned you may be looking for a new job. I'm expanding my business, and someone with your background in finance and accounting would be an asset to my company."

Drew blinked at him. "You're offering me a job?"

"I am. Are you interested?"

"I'm not sure. What does this job entail?"

"Victims of cybercrime have come to me seeking help, and I haven't been able to offer them much assistance. I'm planning to assemble a team who can fight back."

"I have no practical experience in fighting cybercrime."

"I know, but Luke told me you studied forensic accounting. He highly recommended you and said you'd be a good person to have on my team." Jerry paused, tilting his head. "If, of course, you're interested in what I'm proposing."

"I..." Drew was lost for words. This sounded like exactly the kind of work he wanted to do. "Yes, I'm definitely interested. But I can't think about starting anything new until another bookkeeper is in place here. I won't leave the lodge until then."

"Of course. Since this is a new position I'm proposing, there's no set start date. We can work something out that fits your schedule."

"Would I have to be based in Minnewasta? I'm getting ready to move back to Minneapolis."

"The beauty of working online is that you can do it from anywhere with a good internet connection. We might work together initially, but where you live is up to you."

Drew's mind whirled. The job sounded perfect, but he needed time. "Can you give me a few days to think about your offer? Once the Mistletoe Ball is over, I'll be better able to give it more consideration."

"That's totally fair. Luke told me you were loyal to your family, so I wouldn't expect you to cut and run. Finish your job here and in the meantime, I'll email you more detailed information about the position and the pay you can expect to receive."

They exchanged contact information on their phones and Jerry left. Drew stared after him, still stunned by his offer. Everything was falling in place for him to leave.

Everything except his heart. He had a feeling that no matter where he went, his heart would stay here at the lodge. With Celeste.

ON SATURDAY, CELESTE was grateful she was too busy with preparations for the Mistletoe Ball to think about anything else. The kitchen was a flurry of activity as they prepared traditional Christmas foods such as turkey and dressing and cranberries. Part of the staff worked in the kitchen of the event center while Celeste stayed in the restaurant's kitchen and completed her custard and berry trifle in three beautiful clear glass footed bowls. The dessert table would include, along with the trifle, a Christmas pudding with warm brandy sauce and various Christmas treats like rum balls, gingerbread cookies and mince tarts.

Late in the afternoon, Celeste used a trolley to wheel the desserts to the event center. Lorraine introduced her to Sally and Jennifer, who would be manning the dessert table.

"Jennifer comes to us from Miller's Resort, and she's catered many events. Sally is a new member of our catering staff," Lorraine said. "Today is her first event. Maybe you can fill them in on what you'd like them to do at the dessert table."

"Of course." She shook hands with both women. "I'm glad both of you are here to help us with the Mistletoe Ball."

Sally smiled and nodded but said nothing. Jennifer was more effusive. "Glad to be here. It looks like it's going to be a fun event. Now, what would you like us to do?"

"Your job will be to make sure we have plenty of each kind of dessert on the table. You'll also be serving the Christmas pudding and brandy sauce. It's best served warm, so a steam table will be set up and you can serve guests as they ask for it."

"I noticed you wheeled in a trifle. Are we to serve that as well?" Jennifer asked.

"Yes. There's two more just like it in the fridge in the main kitchen."

They discussed serving sizes for the trifle and the Christmas pudding, and she showed them where to find dishes and utensils in the kitchen. When Jennifer went with another server to set up the steam tray, Sally hung back.

"Could I speak with you for a moment?" she asked.

"Of course. What can I do for you? Are you nervous about working your first event?"

"Well, yes, but that's not what I wanted to talk to you about." Celeste saw her take a deep breath before continuing. "You have a daughter at the school in Minnewasta in the fourth grade, is that right?"

The question startled Celeste. "Yes, that's right. My daughter Hope."

Sally took another deep breath. "I want to let you know that I spoke to my son, really spoke to him. You don't have to worry about him saying things to Hope any more. He knows it's wrong now."

Celeste stared at her. "Saying things? What do you mean?"

Sally's face flushed. "You don't know?"

"No. Tell me what happened."

"Mr. Barnes came to our trailer the other day. He told me that Jacob, my son, had been saying nasty things to your daughter about her hair and her skin."

Her heart dropped into her stomach. "You mean racist things."

"Yes. I'm so sorry. Jacob heard talk like that from his stepfather, my soon to be ex-husband. Mr. Barnes explained to him that it was never right to speak to anyone that way."

"Mr. Barnes? Drew Barnes?"

"Yes. He was firm with Jacob, but kind. He was kind to me, too. He offered me the job here. Since I'd just left my husband, I was in a hard place. He said he was a friend of yours. Didn't he tell you?"

"No." Celeste's mind whirled. Why didn't he tell her what was going on? Why didn't Hope tell her?

The answer came to her instantly. Because neither of them wanted her to worry. They wanted to protect her, especially while her family was in Minnesota.

Sally hung her head. "I'm sorry. I'll understand if you want me to leave."

Celeste reached for her hand. "No, of course not. I'm glad you told me. You were being honest, and I certainly can't fault you for that. Just make sure your son doesn't harass my daughter again."

"He won't. I'll make certain."

"Good." Celeste gave Sally's hand a squeeze before letting go. "Time for us to get to work. Go help Jennifer set up."

Sally nodded and hurried away. Celeste stared after her. Hope must have confided in Drew and he in turn sought out Sally and her son. The bond between Drew and her daughter was even stronger than she imagined.

Drew had gone out of his way to protect Hope, the way a father would. He was a special man, and she loved him with all her heart.

She couldn't let him go.

Chapter Eighteen

DREW'S NERVES WERE on edge all through dinner. He pushed his food around his plate, his stomach tied in too many knots to eat much. He did his best to hide his discomfort, making small talk with his parents, his uncle Cam and Scarlet, as well as Celeste's mother and sister. Hope and Tessa were seated together, wearing pretty party dresses. Their excited giggles made Drew smile.

This night marked the beginning of the end. Whether he took the job with Jerry Fields' company or not, he'd soon be leaving the lodge.

And leaving Celeste. His heart made a painful thump at the thought of not seeing her again.

As plates were cleared away, Scarlet, Cam and Lydia's phones all pinged, indicating an incoming text message. Scarlet reached her phone first, smiling as she read the text. "It's from Ethan. The twins have arrived! A boy and a girl!"

She explained to Nora and Gloria that her sister Harper was married to Cam's brother Ethan. "Ethan says Harper and the babies are doing well, even though the twins came a couple of weeks early. Thank goodness everyone's okay!"

Cam lifted his water glass. "This calls for a toast. To Ethan and Harper and their new family. May they have a happy and healthy first Christmas together."

Drew raised his wine glass along with the rest of the group. "To Ethan and Harper!"

He was happy for them, he truly was. Ethan and Harper had waited a long time to have a family. Their road to love and happiness had been a bumpy one, and they deserved every good thing life had to offer.

But it meant they would soon be coming home with their new family, and they'd want their house back. He'd have to clear out even earlier than he'd thought.

The universe was telling him it was time to leave, whether he wanted to or not.

ONCE DINNER WAS SERVED, the kitchen staff let the temporary crew take over. Maggie wanted the regular kitchen staff to have some fun at the Mistletoe Ball along with their guests. Celeste had invited Carrie, Cheryl and Maggie to change into their party clothes at her apartment. As they ran up the stairs, excitement and anticipation swept over Celeste, something she hadn't felt for a very long time.

But she was also afraid. Was she too late to tell Drew she loved him?

She could hear Maggie and Cheryl laughing in the other bedroom as they got ready. They sounded happy, and Celeste could understand why. Maggie had received a text during dinner telling her that Harper had given birth to her twins and all three were healthy. They had a small celebration in the kitchen at the news.

But the main reason Maggie and Cheryl were so excited was that they both had adoring husbands waiting for them at the ball. Celeste had had that once, too, along with the absolute confidence she was loved above all else.

She wanted that confidence again. That love. But perhaps she'd realized too late how much Drew meant to her.

Carrie stood next to Celeste at the dresser mirror, quietly applying makeup. Celeste put a hand on her shoulder. "You okay, sweetie?"

"Yeah, I'm okay. I just wish..."

She didn't have to finish. Celeste knew she wished Ryan was with her. She put her arm around Carrie's shoulders, her gaze locking with hers in the mirror. "You're going to be okay. We both are."

Carrie gave her a smile. "Yeah, we are."

"Carrie, you know Drew was only trying to look out for you, right? I know what he said to Ryan was wrong but please, try to forgive. It's tearing him apart."

"I don't know if I can forgive him, and I'll probably never forget what he did."

Celeste stared into Carrie's eyes in the mirror. "After my husband died in a car accident, I spent a long time hating the drunk driver who raced through that red light and t-boned Easton's car. I was so consumed with anger that it nearly ate me alive."

"How did you get over it?"

"With a lot of counseling. My therapist encouraged me to forgive because it was hurting me much more than it hurt that driver. She was right. I was bitter and angry, and it affected my relationships with my family and friends. The worst thing was that my anger didn't allow me to be the mother that Hope needed and deserved. For both our sakes, I had to let all that anger go."

"Therapy must have worked. You seem so serene, so in control."

That made Celeste smile. "Lately, I don't feel in control at all."

Carrie turned to look at her. "You're talking about Drew, aren't you? Are you in love with him?"

"Yeah." Celeste blew out a breath. "It's complicated, mostly because I made it that way."

"What do you mean?"

"When I started falling for Drew, so many feelings came rushing back. I was so afraid that if I let myself love him, I'd lose him like I lost Easton. I know it's not rational, but it was there. I made up a lot of excuses to cover my fear, and I hurt him."

"Drew will forgive you." Carrie put her hand on Celeste's shoulder.

"I'm not sure I can forgive myself. But I don't want to let him go, either. I love him, Carrie."

"Then tell him how you feel. Put all your cards on the table."

Celeste put her arms around Carrie and hugged her close. "Thank you."

"For what?"

"For listening. For being so smart and kind."

"Right back at you, Celeste."

Celeste gently brushed the younger woman's hair from her forehead. "Come on. Let's get this party started."

Carrie squeezed her hand. "Absolutely."

DREW WORKED WITH THE catering staff to move tables to the perimeter of the room. When they were finished with the tables, he checked to see if he could help with anything else but was told they had it covered.

He stood on the edge of the dance floor and drummed the fingers of his left hand against his thigh. Nerves coursed through him. Maybe he should leave. Get in his car and drive away. And just keep driving.

He closed his eyes on a sigh. He couldn't do that. His parents would be disappointed if he left abruptly, and he didn't want to cause them any embarrassment. His immature actions had caused them enough distress over the years. He had to at least put in an appearance. Two hours seemed reasonable. He'd stay, make polite conversation, and then get the hell out.

Drew tapped his foot. Two hours couldn't come fast enough.

The band moved into position, ready to play the first song of the evening. The band leader tapped the mic. "Hello, everyone, and Merry Christmas! Welcome to the Solace Lake Lodge Mistletoe Ball!" He paused while people clapped, then spoke into the mic again. "We are the North Woods Band, and we want to see everyone dancing tonight!"

A cheer rose from the crowd as guests filled the dance floor. Just as Luke and Maggie had hoped, there was a festive, joyful vibe in the air.

Drew wished he could feel some joy.

He'd been asked to sit in on the interviews that Luke had lined up next week for the bookkeeping job. He'd move out of the house and into a room at the lodge, as soon as one was available. He'd hang around until a new person was in place. Then he'd go back to his condo in Minneapolis and decide whether to take the job Jerry Fields offered. The only thing he knew for sure was that he couldn't stay at the lodge much longer, not when his heart broke every time he saw Celeste.

He wished he could get excited about the job offer. He'd read the email Jerry sent with details of the job, and it sounded like everything he'd hoped for. But right now, nothing excited him.

"You have a very pensive look on your face."

Startled, Drew turned to his left to see Celeste's mother watching him. He'd noticed Nora Emerson observing him through dinner, as well. He pasted a polite smile on his face. "Just wondering if there's anything else that needs to be done. We want the evening to be a success."

"It's been a wonderful night so far. Everyone is raving about the food. Especially the desserts my daughter created."

Drew gave a genuine smile this time. "Yes, especially the desserts."

"Celeste cares about you very much, but she has a hard time telling you." Nora gave him a rueful smile. "Something she learned from me, I'm afraid. Like mother, like daughter."

Drew didn't know how to respond, so he remained silent.

"All I want for Celeste is for her to be happy. I see now that she's happy here in Minnesota, and I know she's here to stay. She and Hope have made a life here with friends they love. And then there's you. You make Celeste happy."

"Mrs. Emerson, you don't understand—"

"*You* make her happy." Her tone brooked no argument. "You make Hope happy, too. You love that little girl, don't you?"

There was no point arguing with her. "I do. She's a great kid."

"All I'm going to say is don't give up on Celeste. She's worth fighting for."

Drew stared at her. What was she trying to tell him? "Yes, ma'am."

"Have a wonderful evening, Drew."

"You, too, Mrs. Emerson."

As Drew watched her walk back to her table, a spark of hope lit in his heart. Did this mean Celeste felt something for him, too?

"Hi, Drew."

He hadn't noticed Ryan's arrival. Drew shook his outstretched hand. "Ryan! I'm really glad to see you. Carrie is going to be thrilled you're here."

"I hope so." Ryan looked around the room. "Where is she? Is she still in the kitchen?"

"No, Maggie wanted to give the kitchen staff time to enjoy the party. I imagine she's changing her clothes."

"Yeah. Okay." Ryan's jaw was tight with tension and his hands clenched and unclenched on his lap. "Okay."

Drew put his hand on Ryan's shoulder. "Like I said, she's going to be thrilled to see you."

The sound of female laughter rose above the music. Drew and Ryan looked toward the entrance of the event center.

"She's here," Ryan breathed. "My God, she's beautiful."

Carrie stood at the entrance and scanned the crowd. Beside her, Maggie and Cheryl did the same. Drew searched for Celeste, but she wasn't with them. His heart sank.

The moment Carrie saw Ryan, her face broke into a smile. "Ryan!"

She hurried to him and wrapped her arms around his neck. "I'm so glad you came! I've missed you so much."

"I've missed you, too, baby." The husky note in Ryan's voice told Drew he was fighting back tears.

Carrie leaned back to look in his face. "What made you change your mind?"

Ryan glanced up at Drew. "Your brother convinced me to come."

"Thank you, Drew." Tears sparkled in her eyes. "I'm sorry I was so horrible to you."

"I'm sorry, too. I only want you to be happy."

Carrie threw her arms around him and a profound sense of relief eased some of the tension in Drew's gut as he held her. Carrie pulled away to look into his face. "Where are Mom and Dad?"

He pointed toward their table. "Over there."

She put her hand on Ryan's shoulder. "Come on. I'll introduce you to my parents and then we'll talk."

Drew watched them head toward his parents' table. His mother and father both rose as they approached and shook Ryan's hand. Whatever Carrie decided, it was going to be her decision. He trusted her to make a choice that was right for her. He saw her lean over to kiss Ryan. Right now, it looked like her choice was Ryan.

He turned his attention back to the entrance. Maybe Celeste had opted to skip the party. But that made no sense since Hope and her mother and sister were already here. Was she ill? Had something happened to her?

Where was she?

CELESTE'S NERVES JANGLED as she left the ladies room in the foyer and headed toward the entrance of the event center. It had been a long time since she'd worn heels and she wobbled a little as she walked. It had also been a long time since she'd worn a short skirt. She stifled the urge to tug at the hem of the party dress, unaccustomed to showing so much leg.

Would Drew even want to talk to her? She wouldn't blame him if he didn't. She'd sent mixed messages to him from the moment he arrived at the lodge.

But she was finally ready to tell him what was in her heart. She hoped he was willing to listen.

At the entrance, she stopped and scanned the crowd, looking for him. Was he still here or had he decided to leave and avoid her altogether? Her stomach swooped at the thought.

And then she saw him. He was looking directly at her as if he'd been waiting for her. She smiled and his tentative smile in return had her heart leaping in happiness. But he held back, waiting. It was up to her, literally and figuratively, to make the first move.

Her knees wobbled as she made her way through the crowd. She saw no one else, only Drew. He was everything to her. The best man she knew. Those differences she'd been so concerned about meant nothing. Being with Drew was the only thing that mattered.

Finally, she reached him. But now that she had, emotion overwhelmed her and she couldn't think what to say.

Thankfully, Drew spoke first. "When I saw Carrie and the others arrive and you weren't with them, I was afraid you'd decided to stay home."

"I was so nervous I had to stop at the washroom," she confessed. "It's been a long time since I dressed up for a party."

His eyes slowly raked over her, from her heels to her hair. Though he didn't touch her, his scrutiny was a caress to every inch of her body. Celeste shivered in pleasure. "You're worth the wait. You look absolutely beautiful, Celeste."

Drew held out his hand and she reached for it, grasping it tightly. He kept his eyes focused on their joined hands as he spoke. "Your mother...she told me you cared for me, and I shouldn't give up on you." He lifted his gaze to hers. "Is she right?"

"Yes, she's right." She stepped closer. "Drew, I'm so sorry."

Drew's eyes were wary. "What are you sorry about?"

She swallowed hard. She didn't blame him for being cautious. "Sally Mains told me you talked to her about how her son was harassing Hope. Thank you for speaking to them."

He looked away and shook his head. "I only did what needed to be done. I don't want your gratitude, Celeste."

Celeste touched his face. "Well, that's too bad because you have it. What Sally told me, especially the part about you getting her the job here, reminded me how special you are. It made the scales fall from my eyes, and from my heart. I'm sorry for treating you like a friend instead of the most important person in my life."

He turned to look at her once more, surprise etched on his face. But the wariness was still there. "What do you mean?"

"I've spent the last six years building a brick wall around my heart to protect it." She willed herself not to cry. "And then you came along and started blasting away at that wall. I got scared. You made me feel so much, want so much. That's why I lied to you about not wanting to make love with you again."

"You lied?"

"Yes. I'm sorry for hurting you. You've been wonderful to Hope and me, and I treated you so badly." Celeste's voice wobbled but she had to get this all out, to make him understand. "What Sally told me reminded me of what I already knew. You're an amazing, compassionate, loving man, Drew. I don't want you to leave."

She stood toe to toe with him, clutching his hand with both of hers. He stared into her eyes, his guarded expression telling her he wasn't sure he believed her. She couldn't blame him.

"Your mother said Minnesota is your home now." He put his free hand on top of hers. "Is that true? Do you plan to stay?"

"It's true. I'm not going anywhere."

Drew leaned closer, his voice low. "I can't go back to being your friend. I can't pretend anymore. If I was to stay, I'd need more than your friendship."

Celeste tightened her grip on his hands, desperate for him to believe her. "I need more, too. I'm all in, Drew, forever and for always. I want the three of us to be together, to be a family. I love you, Drew Barnes. I want to be with you for the rest of our lives. And whether that's one year or a hundred, I'm never going to stop loving you."

He blinked in surprise. Then a smile of relief and pure joy spread across his beautiful, dear face. "I love you, too."

He pulled her into his arms and kissed her, and Celeste didn't care who saw—his family, her family, their friends. Nothing mattered but being with Drew.

She was finally home.

Epilogue – The following June

DREW LIT THE CANDLES while Hope carefully placed utensils next to the three plates set at the kitchen island. He checked his watch. Five minutes after four. Celeste just finished her shift in the kitchen and would be home soon. He wanted everything to be perfect.

He looked around the apartment. "Is everything ready? Have we forgotten anything?"

Hope clapped her hands in excitement. "Nope. We're good."

She was right. The beef bourguignon that Maggie had prepared was warming in the oven. He'd managed to make a decent tossed salad, and Carrie's beautiful black forest cake, Celeste's favorite dessert, was in the fridge. Carrie had made the cake for him on the weekend when she was in Minnewasta visiting Ryan. She was back in the Twin Cities, attending culinary school in St. Paul. When she finished in a few months, she'd come to work at the lodge as a permanent employee. She'd also marry Ryan when she completed her schooling. Drew was thrilled for them both and was certain they'd have a happy marriage.

The dishes were in place, the candles lit, and the balloons that he and Hope had blown up were decorating the apartment. Everything was ready.

He touched the pocket of his jeans and felt the outline of the ring box. Yes, everything was ready. If all went according to plan tonight, the three of them would soon be moving into his newly purchased house in Minnewasta. Together.

He'd told Celeste he'd get Hope from school and that they'd pick up pizza in town to celebrate her passing her driver's test last week and receiving her license. In reality, he and Hope decorated, cooked, and practiced their lines. He'd even taken time off work, telling Jerry he was unavailable this afternoon. After talking it over with Celeste, he'd accepted the job with Fields Digital Solutions and began working for Jerry Fields mid-January. His job was to follow the money and gather evidence of financial wrong-doing. He found the work challenging and rewarding, especially when they were able to nail a bad guy.

The best thing about his new position was that it had restored his confidence. This was work he was meant to do and he was very, very good at it.

Drew surveyed the room. Nerves danced in his stomach. He had no doubt Celeste loved him, but was she ready for this next move?

Footsteps sounded on the stairs. Hope turned to him, her eyes wide with excitement.

"She's home!" she said in a loud stage whisper.

Celeste opened the door and stepped inside, then stopped abruptly when she saw the decorations and flowers.

"Oh, my goodness!" Celeste's hand went to her throat, and she laughed in delight. "This is beautiful!"

Hope flung herself into her mother's arms. "Congratulations on getting your license, Mama!"

She kissed the top of Hope's head. "Thank you so much, baby girl."

When Hope stepped back, Drew pulled Celeste into his arms and kissed her. "Congratulations, sweetheart."

"This is so lovely, Drew. Thank you."

The love he saw in Celeste's eyes gave him courage. "And it's not over yet. We have a special dinner prepared. But first, Hope and I have something we want to ask you." Drew nodded at Hope as he pulled the ring box from his pocket and got down on one knee.

"Mama, will you marry Drew so the three of us can be a family? And I can have brothers and sisters?"

Hope adlibbed the part about brothers and sisters, but Drew didn't care. He wanted a family as much as Hope did. But as Celeste stared at him in stunned surprise, Drew wondered if he'd miscalculated. They'd talked about a future together and he thought she was ready to take this next step with him. Had he been wrong?

Slowly, a smile spread across her face and tears filled her eyes. "I absolutely want to marry Drew, and I'm so excited for the three of us to be a family. And maybe one or two brothers and sisters. I say yes!"

Relieved, Drew slipped the ring on her finger, then jumped to his feet and wrapped his arms around her. He pulled Hope into their embrace. Happiness and gratitude filled his heart. He had everything he needed right here in his arms.

The End

Want to continue reading in the Love at Solace Lake series? Check out book one in the series, **LIES AND SOLACE.**

Harper Lindquist is determined to make Solace Lake Lodge, the old fishing lodge in Minnesota that she and her sisters inherited from their grandfather, a viable business again. But she needs money to make that happen. The company Ethan James works for invests in the lodge's future and puts up the cash needed to make renovations. As they work together, Ethan and Harper fall in love. But Ethan is keeping a secret that could change everything between them. When Harper learns the truth, will their love story end before it gets a chance to really begin?

Click the QR code to begin reading LIES AND SOLACE!

A Note From Jana

REVIEWS ARE THE LIFE BLOOD for authors. I hope you enjoyed SEEING THINGS, and if you did, I would appreciate you letting other readers know. Please leave a review at the retailer where you purchased the book, on Goodreads, or on your own blog. If you leave a review, I would love to read it! Please email me the link at Jana@JanaRichards.com.

You can stay up to date with me and my upcoming new releases, sales, giveaways and contests by joining my newsletter. You'll receive a FREE ecopy of **HOME TO SOLACE LAKE** as a thank you for signing up. This romantic novella is available only to newsletter subscribers. I'd love to have you on board! Here's the blurb for **HOME TO SOLACE LAKE**:

> After Jerry Fields buried his mother twenty-two years ago, he cut all ties to the small town in Minnesota where he grew up. He swore he'd never return. But when his biological father, a man who never acknowledged him, leaves Jerry his entire estate, curiosity has him returning to Minnewasta. Why did Earl Rogers will him

everything he owned when during his lifetime he didn't give Jerry a minute of his time?

Denise Rogers wants to save the business that her deceased husband loved so much. But when her father-in-law Earl leaves all his property to his illegitimate son, saving the business gets much more complicated. Denise is determined to buy the property from Jerry Fields to keep it from being demolished and turned into condos. She wants to continue to run the business as a marine repair shop, knowing it's what her husband would have wanted. But events throw her plans into disarray and she has to give up on her dream. Until Jerry offers to work with her over the summer to help her buy the property.

Jerry can't stomach the idea of putting his half-brother's widow out of a job and a home, so he decides to stay in Minnewasta to help her. At the end of the summer, Denise will purchase the property from him and they'll go their separate ways. But as they work together, their feelings for each other deepen into love, and they uncover long-held secrets that force Jerry to question everything he thought he knew about his parents. Can Jerry overcome past hurts and fears for a chance at love?

Sign up using the QR code below for Jana's newsletter and receive your FREE copy of **HOME TO SOLACE LAKE!**

Don't miss out!

Visit the website below and you can sign up to receive emails whenever Jana Richards publishes a new book. There's no charge and no obligation.

https://books2read.com/r/B-A-YISD-ETCMH

BOOKS 2 READ

Connecting independent readers to independent writers.

Also by Jana Richards

A Left at the Altar Romance
Her Best Man
There Goes the Groom
Always a Bridesmaid

Love at Solace Lake
Lies and Solace
Secrets and Solace
Truth and Solace
Christmas at Solace Lake

The Victorian Mansion Series
Rescue Me
Take a Chance on Me

Standalone

A Long Way From Eden
Seeing Things

About the Author

When Jana Richards read her first romance novel, she immediately knew two things: she had to commit the stories running through her head to paper, and they had to end with a happily ever after. She also knew she'd found what she was meant to do. Since then she's never met a romance genre she didn't like. She writes contemporary romance, romantic suspense, and historical romance set in World War Two, in lengths ranging from short story to full length novel. Just for fun, she throws in generous helpings of humor, and the occasional dash of the paranormal.

In her life away from writing, Jana is a mother to two grown daughters, grandmother to an amazing granddaughter, and a wife to her husband Warren. She enjoys golf, yoga, movies, concerts, travel and reading, not necessarily in that order. She and her husband live in western Canada with two senior calico cats named Layla and Leelou and an acquarium full of unnamed fish. She loves to hear from readers and can be reached through her website.

Read more at https://www.janarichards.com/.